# A SOLDIER TO THE RESCUE

KAYLIE NEWELL

SPECIAL EDITION

Recycling programs for this product may not exist in your area.

ISBN-13: 978-1-335-47271-7

A Soldier to the Rescue



For questions and comments about the quality of this book, please contact us at CustomerService@Harlequin.com.

Harlequin Enterprises ULC
22 Adelaide St. West, 41st Floor
Toronto, Ontario M5H 4E3, Canada
www.Harlequin.com

HarperCollins Publishers
Macken House, 39/40 Mayor Street Upper,
Dublin 1, D01 C9W8, Ireland
www.HarperCollins.com

**Printed in Lithuania**

1 2 3 4 5 6 7 8 9 10 LIT 28 27 26 25

**"I wasn't sure I was going to make it.**

"I guess I've seen too many hikers get lost around here. So many things can happen, so much can go wrong. It was scary. But when I woke up to see Bonnie...when I saw her..." Her voice cracked.

He leaned down and patted her leg awkwardly. Grady was much better at this kind of thing than he was. He had an excellent bedside manner. Hudson was in the business of finding people. He wasn't so sure what to do with them afterward.

Georgia put her hand over his, and then squeezed his fingers. She was crying openly now, and it was obvious she needed the comfort.

"I know you don't want me to keep thanking you," she said, "but I need you to know how grateful I am to you and Bonnie. You found me, but you were also very kind, and I'll never forget that."

Hudson's face warmed. He wasn't sure if it was because of what she was saying, or the feel of her skin against his. Having a beautiful woman express her thanks like this wasn't exactly the worst thing in the world.

Dear Reader,

I can't tell you how happy I am that you're holding a copy of *A Soldier to the Rescue*! This book is the very first in a brand-new series about three American heroes who are about to embark on the next chapter in their lives.

Retired Army vets and best friends Hudson, Grady and Tad are worried that their best years might be behind them when they arrive in Christmas Bay on a fly-fishing trip to honor one of their fallen friends. But what they'll find instead will be a deep connection to the town, the people, and a sense of home that they've been missing their entire lives. Their most important discovery though, will be love.

I hope that you're as excited as I am to step into this small town by the beach, and let yourself be carried away on the ocean breeze and into a world of romance.

Happy reading!

*Kaylie Newell*

For **Kaylie Newell**, storytelling is in the blood. Growing up the daughter of two writers, she knew eventually she'd want to follow in their footsteps. She's now the proud author of over twenty books, including the RITA® Award finalists *Christmas at the Graff* and *Tanner's Promise*.

Kaylie lives in Southern Oregon with her husband, two daughters, a blind Doberman and two indifferent cats. Visit Kaylie at Facebook.com/kaylienewell.

**Books by Kaylie Newell**

***Montana Mavericks: The Anniversary Gift***

*The Maverick's Marriage Deal*

**Harlequin Special Edition**

***Veterans of Christmas Bay***

*A Soldier to the Rescue*

***Hearts on Main Street***

*Flirting with the Past*
*His Small-Town Catch*
*Her Christmas Flame*

***Sisters of Christmas Bay***

*Their Sweet Coastal Reunion*
*Their All-Star Summer*
*Their Christmas Resolution*

Visit the Author Profile page
at Harlequin.com for more titles.

For our Oregon Crew—Russell and Julie, Jeff and Jill, and Brian and Liz. You've inspired this series, and I love you! Cheers to many more stories to come!

# Prologue

"Don't worry, baby. You're coming, too."

Hudson Cross looked down at his black Lab, Bonnie—a little grayer in the muzzle than she used to be, a little slower getting in and out of bed, but her nose was still as strong as ever. She had several good years left, a lot of time to work, which was a good thing, because he could barely stand the thought of losing her. She was his other half, his partner, his friend. She was also staring a hole right through his head.

He smiled, gave her a pat and stuffed his boxers and socks into his duffel bag. She'd been watching him all morning, following him into the closet, right at his feet as he packed, leaning against his legs as he shaved. She'd been like this ever since they'd come home from Afghanistan—a little clingy, a little neurotic, a little weird. Which was fine by him. He was a little weird, too. He guessed he should give himself some grace in that department. He'd served for twenty-two years. He was retired now, and so was Bonnie, but that didn't mean the memories would ever fade into soft focus, that the trauma would be any less terrible.

But Hudson was really good at pushing those things down where they couldn't hurt so much. There were still nightmares, though. There were still cold sweats out of nowhere. There was the inability to get close to anyone for fear of losing them like he'd lost Jesse. Like he'd lost so many friends over the years.

So, there was that. He was adjusting. He was getting through. And he knew this fly-fishing trip, this one-month getaway with his two remaining best buddies from basic, the one they were taking to honor Jesse's memory, was just what the doctor ordered. Or, at least, that's what Grady said, and he wasn't just a friend, but also an MD. He knew what he was talking about. At least as far as this went.

Hudson sat heavily on the bed and looked out his apartment window to the parking lot below. Definitely nothing to write home about. It was only temporary, though, just a place to be in the interim until he and Bonnie could get into their new search and rescue work. Then he'd decide where they'd land long-term.

His dog jumped up beside him, and he put his arm around her. She was warm, soft, comforting. She put her muzzle in the crook of his neck, like she was asking a question. *What now?* A working dog to her core, she didn't know how to be retired. This new life was confusing for her. Hudson knew exactly how she felt.

He rubbed her soft ears. Just like the Velveteen Rabbit, he thought. His favorite story from when he was a kid. He felt the muscles across his back tense in that now familiar way whenever he thought too much about his life, about the before and after of Jesse. At the very least, he had his health. He had his friends, who were navigating retirement, too. And he had his dog. What more could he ask for?

"Don't worry," he repeated softly. "You're coming, too."

# Chapter One

Georgia Gallagher adjusted her small backpack over her shoulders and looked around. The sun was a little lower in the sky than she would've liked, but she was only going to be out for a couple of hours. Out and back, that's what she remembered Josh, the PE teacher at school, telling her last spring when she'd asked about his favorite hikes. She'd never been on this trail before, but he'd said it was beautiful, if a little remote, and that was okay with her. Remote was the whole point.

Her heart was aching in a way that was hardly bearable, her normally sunny personality cloaked in a fog of grief. She didn't want to see anyone today if she could help it. She didn't want to smile and say hello, and comment on the weather. She just wanted to be alone with her thoughts. With her aching heart. With her precious memories of Sophie, when her baby sister had been healthy and happy, and before the lump in her breast had spread.

Georgia took a deep breath, smelling the pine trees and the sea air, and letting it saturate her lungs and soul. This was what she needed. Nature. Quiet. Healing.

She knew the healing part was going to take time. But if anything was going to do her some good, it was being in the woods where she and Sophie had spent so much time together over the years. They'd camped together as kids, and they'd met up for girls' weekends as adults—Sophie in her tiny Scamp trailer, and Georgia in her tent. They hadn't gone anywhere spectacular, just little campgrounds around Christmas Bay, but those had been fun days. Full of laughter and silliness and long talks and cheap wine. Her sister had been her best friend. And now she was gone, leaving Georgia to navigate this world without her.

The thought, as it always did, filled her with a certain kind of sadness that she couldn't get her arms around. She was still having a hard time accepting the finality of it. And when the tears came, they usually knocked her over with their intensity, making it hard to breathe, or do anything other than wait for them to pass and leave her shaking and hollow in their wake.

She stepped onto the trail, thinking of how Sophie would've admonished her for not telling anyone where she was going. Sophie had always been prepared; they'd joked endlessly about it. She'd been the one with extra sunscreen, with the unscented bug spray, with the air mattress in case anyone's back hurt in the middle of the night. Her sister would probably think Georgia was being careless today, but that was the thing. Lately, her first thought was always, okay, Sophie might not approve, but what's the worst that could happen? Dying didn't scare her nearly as much as it used to, because Sophie had died, and *that* had been the worst thing that could happen.

So here she was, making her way along the trail now with the autumn sun warm on her shoulders. It felt good after the chill of the morning. Winter would be here before she knew it, and so would Thanksgiving, the first one without her sister. She remembered when they were growing up, they'd decorate the house with paper turkeys and popcorn strings. Things had been so good and safe back then. She thought about the fact that she needed to go see her mom when she got home, and make sure she had enough groceries. Her mother was handling Sophie's loss worse than Georgia, and that was saying something. It was scary to see her parents break down. Even though she was twenty-seven, her parents—divorced now, but amicably—had always seemed invincible. Impervious to things that might affect other people's parents. She'd learned the hard way over the last four months that they were in fact, very human and very fragile.

Georgia kept walking, lost in her thoughts. Unaware of how much time had gone by, or the fact that angry-looking clouds had moved slowly over the sun, snuffing out its warmth. Birds and squirrels skittered around her in the bushes, but she barely noticed that, either. She just kept her head down, looking at her hiking boots as she stepped methodically over the trail. Until suddenly, she tripped hard over a small branch. Luckily, she got her balance before eating dirt and possibly breaking her neck, and stood there breathing hard, staring down at the trail. Only it didn't look like a trail anymore, so much as a slightly cleared pathway between the trees.

Frowning, she glanced around. It wasn't just her imagination—the trail that she'd been walking on had petered out to nothing. Either that, or she'd stepped off it accidentally, which was more likely the case. She hadn't been paying attention, after all. She'd been deep in thought, deep in sorrow, and that didn't mesh well with making one's way through the woods.

The first flutter of panic tickled her rib cage as she

turned around and began retracing her steps. She couldn't have gone far off the trail. Or, at least, she *hoped* she hadn't gone far. This was where mud would've been helpful—she would've been able to see her footsteps. As it was, she'd been walking over spongy pine needles and moss, nothing that would leave any evidence that she'd been there at all.

After about fifteen minutes with no luck, and feeling like she was actually moving in a big circle, Georgia forced herself to stop and think for a minute. It wasn't easy—every instinct she had was telling her to break into a run. But she stood there anyway, taking a deep breath, and then another, until her pulse slowed a little.

Overhead, thunder clapped, and she startled. She looked up at the sky, her stomach sinking into her boots. She'd checked the weather app on her phone before leaving her house, and she'd known there was a chance of a storm rolling through this evening. But she'd thought she'd be back in plenty of time before the weather turned. Just like Josh had said—out and back. Only this wasn't turning out to be an out and back at all. It was more like an out and stay, because the chances that she was lost were pretty good at this point. And the temperature was dropping. She was only wearing a sweatshirt and a pair of shorts, not exactly an outfit for a stormy overnight in the woods.

Shivering, more from nerves than anything else, she took her backpack off and unzipped the compartment where she usually kept her phone. If she couldn't find her way back to the trail soon, she was going to have to give up and call the sheriff. Embarrassing, but necessary.

But as she peered inside the pocket and saw nothing

but a pack of gum and her sunglasses inside, the fluttery panic from before grew into something with teeth.

She'd forgotten her phone at home.

And she was lost.

"I'll just remind you, that you're supposed to be on vacation?"

Tad was sprawled out on one of the Airbnb beds, his big frame taking up most of it, as he sipped on his long-neck beer. A local porter of some kind. Something with the word mountain in it, which was fitting. Grady had the other bed across the room and was already snoring. He'd only been retired for a year, but was already used to his afternoon nap. Hudson had the pull-out couch. Bonnie had been curled up by his feet, but she could probably sense his unease, since she'd gotten up a few minutes ago to lean against his legs.

Scooting forward on the couch, he squinted at the TV and rubbed her ears absentmindedly. "I know."

"You *could* just let the sheriff's department handle this," Tad said. "I'm sure they know what they're doing. And probably have more than enough volunteers."

"But they don't have Bonnie."

"No…" Tad sighed. "They don't. And you're going to rectify that, if I know you at all."

"Shut up. He's gonna say something."

Hudson turned the volume up just as a big man in his sixties walked up to the official-looking podium with the US flag on one side and the Oregon state flag on the other.

"Good afternoon," the sheriff said, his voice gruff and gravelly. Not unlike a John Wayne stand-in, Hudson thought somberly. "As you know, Ms. Gallagher has been missing now for just over thirty-six hours. After someone recognized her heading toward Cascade Forest, it's our belief that she went for a hike sometime yesterday afternoon in the southern end, near Cape Longing. We believe there's a good possibility that she got lost, as she's not familiar with the area, but we aren't ruling out foul play at this time. As you know, this mountain range is rugged, so we're working under the assumption that she could also be hurt, so time is of the essence. It also got down to the low forties last night, and we aren't sure how prepared she is for the elements.

"The main purpose of this press conference is to get the word out to the community, and let you know that my office is accepting any and all trained volunteer help that comes our way. We'd appreciate the assistance. Our goal is to get Ms. Gallagher back safe and sound, and the more folks out there, the better. Questions?"

There was an immediate barrage of questions, a cacophony of reporters talking at once, before the sheriff began picking folks one by one.

"Oh, God," Tad said. "The magic words. Outside help."

Hudson gave him a look over his shoulder.

"Smart man," Tad continued, throwing an arm over his eyes. "Putting his ego aside for the job. Good on him."

Hudson nodded, his eyes feeling gritty. They were all exhausted. Their second day of fly-fishing had ended up at a honky-tonk at the edge of town last night, where they'd stayed until the early hours of the morning. Something Hudson found funny. Their asses were usually in bed by ten these days, and it showed. Painfully. It was one of the reasons why Grady was snoring up a storm across the room now.

But they'd wanted to toast to Jesse. And then one drink had turned into two, and so on and so forth. Before they'd known it, they were all drunk and sad, and telling stories that hadn't been told in a very long time. Hudson wasn't sorry. Those stories needed telling.

Bonnie whined at his side, until he rubbed her ears again.

"I think she knows," Tad said.

"I *know* she knows."

"She's got a spooky sixth sense. Some kind of doggy psychic ability or something."

Hudson smiled. "I wouldn't go that far. She's just smart."

"I guess. I'd rather think of her as psychic, though."

Hudson looked back at the TV screen, where there was a picture of the missing hiker. Short brown hair, a pixie cut he thought they were called. Only it was a little shorter than that, almost like it had been shaved recently and was growing out. He immediately thought of Demi Moore in that old movie, *Ghost.* The cut looked good on her. She had small features, big hazel eyes and a nice smile. She looked like a nice person, and Hudson wondered what had happened to her. He wondered if she was hurt, if she'd fallen and broken something. If she was cold and wet and alone.

Instinctively, he was itching to get up and make the phone call. The one that he felt was inevitable. The one to the sheriff's office offering his and Bonnie's help. They were certified, highly trained and more than ready. But Tad was right. This was supposed to be a trip for their mental health. They were supposed to be stepping away from the stress and trauma of their years in the service, and trying to deal with the pain of losing Jesse in a healthier way. That was what they were *supposed* to be doing. But in reality, Hudson knew that change wouldn't come overnight. It would come slowly. He'd only been retired for sixteen months. Tad and Grady even less than that, and learning to live a whole new life on the outside was going to take time. He knew he needed the rest right now. But he also knew he wasn't going to be able to sleep tonight without making that call.

"Hey, man."

He turned to see Tad watching him closely. They'd been friends since basic, along with Jesse and Grady. They'd all bonded the moment they'd met and had stayed close ever since. His friend narrowed his eyes at him now. He could tell exactly what Hudson was thinking.

"Just go," Tad said. "You know you're dying to. The sooner you go, the sooner you can get her home to her family."

Hudson smiled and pushed himself off the couch. Bonnie stood, too, then shook, sending her tags jingling. She was ready to go. She'd been ready this whole time, she'd just been waiting for him to make the first move.

From across the room, Grady snorted loudly, waking himself up. He stared at them for a long second, his blue eyes bloodshot.

"How long was I out?"

"A long time, Gramps," Tad said.

"Where are you going? What are you guys talking about?"

"We've been watching the news," Tad said. "There's a lost hiker and Hudson is going to volunteer with Bonnie."

"Can we help?"

“Just hold down the fort,” Hudson said. “I’ll be in touch. I probably won’t be around to fish tomorrow, but hopefully by Tuesday.”

“There’s no rush,” Tad said. “We’re here for a month. Just find this poor lady, or we’ll have to revoke Bonnie’s badass search and rescue card.”

At the sound of her name, she looked over at Tad and wagged her long black tail.

“Did you hear that?” Tad asked her, slipping into baby talk. He’d been a Green Beret, but he’d ruptured his Achilles tendon a few years ago. He’d been working in cyber security when he’d finally retired.

Bonnie jumped up on the bed and licked his face.

“Gross. Disgusting. Hudson, call your dog.”

But he said this while wrapping her in a bear hug. It was hard to tell where the man ended and the dog began.

“Bonnie, come!”

She wiggled out of Tad’s arms and jumped off the bed.

“Let’s hit it,” he said. He’d already decided he’d call the sheriff from the Tahoe to save time. He could hardly wait to get out there, to give Bonnie the scent and go to work. He’d missed this.

Bonnie sat, and he clicked her worn leather leash on. She waited patiently as he grabbed his jacket and wallet, some dog food and a few collapsible bowls.

He swiped his keys off the end table. “I’ll call you guys when we get out there, give you an update. Wish us luck.”

“You don’t need it,” Grady said. “But good luck anyway.”

Georgia looked up at the star-speckled sky, tiny grains of glittering sand sprinkled over a velvet tablecloth. A celestial special occasion. A table set for the angels.

She giggled at the thought, at the image of a bunch of angels sitting around a dinner table, something that wasn't particularly funny, and wondered briefly if she was losing it. Probably. She'd been out here for a day and a half. She was facing her second night in the woods, and she'd never been colder in her life.

Thank God for the sweatshirt that was soft and oversize. Like a baby blanket for her soul. She'd found a hollowed-out log that had a carpet of thick pine needles around it, and she'd been using that for a shelter. It wasn't warm and it wasn't comfortable by any stretch, but it was better than being out in the elements with nothing at all protecting her. Last night she'd balled herself up for twenty- to thirty-minute periods with her knees tucked up into the sweatshirt like a roly-poly bug, and had used her backpack as a pillow. Then she'd gotten up to move around—running in place, doing jumping jacks, anything to get her blood pumping.

She licked her lips now, blinking through the bluish darkness. She'd finally stopped playing the What If game—what if her phone battery hadn't been low before she'd left home? What if she hadn't put it on the charger at the last minute? Would she even have a signal up here if she'd remembered to grab it when walking out the door? All questions that were sucking the energy from her, and that didn't matter anyway. What mattered was what she *did* have. She was grateful for her Hydro Flask of water, which she'd been nursing—only allowing herself a few sips an hour. She'd also found an old protein bar in her backpack that she'd been nibbling on, so at least her stomach wasn't completely empty, but she was hungrier than she'd ever been. The pangs were like ice picks stabbing through her lower belly, each one sending a jolt of pain straight to her back.

And she was scared. Terrified, actually. She was trying very hard not to think about the fact that she'd seen this very same scenario unfold every year. Lost hikers, many of whom weren't lucky enough to have a happy ending. She was trying to stay positive, focusing on the fact that other than trying to find her way back to the trail that first half hour or so, she'd basically stayed in one spot. She knew that was her best chance at being found sooner rather than later.

But her biggest comfort was the feeling that Sophie was out there, somewhere beyond those glittering stars, keeping her safe. Watching over her. She knew a lot of people would have a hard time believing that—she'd questioned whether or not there was something beyond this life many times herself. But it was a feeling she couldn't deny. As strong and sure as anything she'd ever felt, and she was grateful for the warmth it was giving her now. The hope.

"You're probably pretty mad at me right about now," she whispered. Her jaws ached from her teeth clicking together. Her muscles were cold and stiff. Her head throbbed where there was a sizeable goose egg on her temple—a keepsake from tripping and falling down a small embankment and smacking her head on a rock. "But I can feel you, Soph. Thanks for being here."

Warm tears began streaming down her cheeks. She was surprised she had any left, she'd cried so much over the last few months.

Reaching up, she ran her hand over her short hair. It was soft, almost feathery against her fingertips. She and Sophie had shaved their heads together after this last round of chemo. Georgia's hair was growing back. Sophie's never would.

Tucking her knees into her sweatshirt again, Georgia leaned back against her backpack and stared up at the sky. There was no moon tonight; it was hiding its lovely face. The darkness was all-consuming. So was the sadness. She was cloaked in both, a small, lonely person huddled in the woods on a starry night.

Georgia closed her eyes. Heavy, like her heart.

And slept.

*Stop it, Dodger!* She was dreaming. She was aware of that on some deep, primal level. She was dreaming about her family's little Chihuahua mix who liked to sleep under the covers with her. Who liked to wake her up by licking her chin with his warm little tongue. She laughed and pushed him away, but not very hard because he was so small. She'd end up pushing him right off the bed.

*Georgia!* Sophie's voice. Only it was lower than Sophie's voice. The voice of a man calling her. Low and gravelly. Her dad, maybe? *Georgia!*

She screwed her eyes shut, stubborn in her dream. Wanting to stay there as long as possible. Being called for breakfast by her sister who wasn't her sister, and licked by a dog that had long since crossed over that brightly colored bridge to wait for her on the other side.

*Georgia!*

More licking. More snuffling. Soft, whiskery sniffs against her ear, her jaw, her mouth. In her dream that was fading now, she clamped her lips together, knowing she should be disgusted by dog kisses, but not being able to summon *complete* disgust. She was too happy to be getting them at all.

*Georgia!*

And then, the dream faded away, like the coastal mist, like the clouds burning off on a summer day. She heard herself whimper and opened her eyes a slit to see the grainy sky above, not black anymore, but a bluish, hopeful gray.

Above her was a shadow. Black and moving excitedly. More snuffling. More licking. Footsteps. Heavy and purposeful. The sound of twigs breaking under those feet.

"Good girl, Bonnie. Good, good girl. Georgia? Are you alright? Can you hear me?"

Georgia forced her eyes open wider. The hazy gray light hurt them. But then, everything hurt. Her vision was fuzzy, and for the first time she let herself consider the possibility that she might have a concussion.

"I'm okay… I'm…"

"It's alright, you're safe now. Are you hurt?"

"I fell," she managed. Her voice sounded thick and croaky. "My head."

The man, who was a shadow above her, just like the dog, touched the bump on her temple.

"Ouch," he said. "Looks like you cracked it pretty good. We've got medical folks on the way. They'll be here soon. Are you thirsty?"

She nodded, then winced as she tried to sit up.

"Easy. Just take it slow."

He took her hand in his, and it felt like a bear's paw. Big and warm. She gripped it tight, overwhelmed with gratitude and relief.

"I'm sorry," she said. "I'm so sorry. I forgot my stupid phone, and I didn't tell anyone where… I knew better. I *knew* better."

"It's okay. We're just happy to find you."

She looked over at the black shadow next to her, which was becoming more and more dog-like as her eyes adjusted to the grainy morning light. As if on cue, the shadow dog wiggled her bottom and gave Georgia a lick on the cheek.

"Bonnie, sit. Stay."

The dog did as she was told, but her tail remained in constant motion. *Thwap, thwap, thwap*, against the bed of pine needles.

"Oh, hey," said the male voice, her rescuer. Her angel. "Don't cry. It's okay. You're okay now. You're safe."

She hadn't realized she'd been crying. Sure enough, teardrops were dripping off her chin and onto her collarbone. The neck of her sweatshirt felt soggy in the cold dawn air.

"Here," he said, helping her sit up a little. "I want you to take a few sips, okay?"

He held a bottle of water to her hot, chapped lips, and she took a greedy swallow. The water was cold and clean and heavenly. She took another swallow, which immediately went down the wrong tube, and she coughed.

He set the water down and patted her on the back. "I know it tastes good. But we need to go easy. I promise I'll give you more in a minute."

She could see the wisdom in that as her stomach cramped sharply. Whether from the excitement, or from the introduction of water after so long without a significant amount, or maybe she was getting sick from the elements, who knew. But all of a sudden, the adrenaline from being found was starting to wear off, and she was overwhelmed with emotion. Exhausted from all of it.

"Oh, hey," he said again. This time softer.

And then, she found herself pulled against the solid warmth of his chest. He was wearing a fleece jacket that smelled like fabric softener. It made her belly curl. She was safe. He held her as another wave of emotion washed over her.

Georgia sat there in the pine needles as the sky turned cotton candy pink—her head throbbing, her heart throbbing—and let go like she'd been wanting to ever since losing Sophie. All this time, she'd been afraid that if she sobbed like she really wanted to, if she howled and moaned and gave into her agony, the grief would simply wash her away.

But as this man's arms tightened around her, she knew she wasn't going anywhere. Because he was keeping her anchored.

## *Chapter Two*

Hudson sat in the hospital waiting room with the scent of floor cleaner and black coffee in his nose, not sure what he was waiting for exactly, but knowing he wasn't ready to leave quite yet. He needed to come down off the high of finding Georgia Gallagher alive—dehydrated, traumatized and with a slight concussion, but alive. It was more than he could've hoped for, but he'd known all along that Bonnie would find her. Maybe not in such great shape, but they'd find her. The fact that she *had* been in relatively good shape was exactly why he did this. It was what had motivated him in the army, and it was what was giving him purpose now. Seeing Georgia's parents rush past him with happy tears in their eyes was the biggest reward of all.

But Hudson would be lying if he said he didn't feel some kind of strange tether to this woman whom he'd never met. That he'd probably never lay eyes on again. It had been immediate, the second he took her in his arms and felt her short, downy hair against his neck. As she'd cried, he knew instinctively that her two nights in the woods weren't the only thing that had traumatized her recently. She had more going on, he could sense it, the same way he could sense when Bonnie was about to pick up a scent. He just knew.

His dog lay at his feet now, and he rubbed the back of her neck with his boot. The nurses said she could stay until Grady picked her up, so she wouldn't have to wait in the truck, since she was the hero of the hour.

She sighed, but didn't move. She was beat. He'd just given her a big lunch, complete with her favorite, Goldfish crackers, for dessert. Her vet wouldn't approve, but he wasn't here, so that was that. She'd earned it.

Hudson looked up to see an older man in a forest green uniform crossing the waiting room. His blue eyes were sharp, no-nonsense. His mouth was set in a hard line, but when he locked gazes with Hudson, he broke into a smile. Hudson recognized him from the press conference.

"Hudson Cross?" the sheriff asked, coming to a stop in front of Bonnie, who raised her head and wagged her tail in greeting.

"Yes, sir."

"Sheriff Hicks. It's a pleasure to meet the man of the hour. I take it this is Bonnie?"

At the sound of her name, Bonne stood and shook herself. Then nudged the older man's hand for a pat.

"Yes, sir."

"My sergeant told me where to find you. He said you were career army?"

"Yes, sir. Afghanistan. Bonnie was an accelerant detection dog. Retrained for search and rescue."

"Thank you for your service, son. Do you live in Christmas Bay?"

"No, sir. Only here for a few weeks on vacation. I was happy to help."

"We're grateful to you." The sheriff nodded toward Georgia Gallagher's room across the hall. "She's lucky. Hopefully next time she'll tell someone where she's going."

Hudson knew that had been one of her biggest mistakes, and she was probably going to be judged plenty because of it. Still, he felt defensive of her. He'd seen the look in her eyes that morning, and he wasn't so sure she would've had the bandwidth to think that far ahead.

"You take care of yourself," the sheriff said, giving Bonnie one more scratch behind the ears.

"You, too, Sheriff."

The older man nodded and turned to walk away, his cowboy boots clomping on the freshly waxed floor.

Hudson looked out the window toward the ocean in the distance. The sun was going down; it was almost dusk. He'd only been in Christmas Bay for a few days now, but he liked it. The town was small, charming, but big enough not to be claustrophobic. It was close enough to Portland, just a little over two hours away, that people could easily head to the city for a day or two if they wanted. In Hudson's case, he'd had enough excitement of that kind to last a lifetime. He loved the adrenaline rush of search and rescue, but he didn't want anything to do with the bright lights and fast pace of the city. He wanted to slow down. And this seemed like a nice place to ease off the gas.

He could see the bay from here, could see the boats making their way back from the open ocean to the protection of the harbor—a mother holding out her loving arms. He smiled at the thought. Yeah, he liked Christmas Bay. He liked it a lot.

"Hudson Cross?"

He looked up to see a nurse in pink scrubs standing over him. Bonnie thumped her tail against the floor.

"Ms. Gallagher was asking if you were still here. She'd like to say thank you, if you're comfortable with that." She smiled, obviously hoping he was.

"I'd be happy to. But my dog…"

"It's slow right now, so I think she could come in for a few minutes without anyone making a fuss. We have therapy dogs in all the time."

He nodded, and got up to follow her across the hall with Bonnie at his heels. Her nails clipped on the shining floor. He thought therapy dogs were probably a big hit around here, and that Bonnie would make a good one. She loved nothing more than to snuggle with people who wanted to snuggle back. She'd never met a stranger in her life.

The nurse pushed the door open to room 122 and stuck her head tentatively inside. "Ms. Gallagher? You have a visitor. Two visitors, actually."

Hudson could see a burst of vibrant color beside the bed—blooms of all different kinds of flowers. He smelled them from where he stood, perfumed and sweet. A bouquet of cheerful Mylar balloons shifted and bumped against each other underneath a vent in the ceiling. Georgia Gallagher obviously had a lot of friends and family who were happy about her safe return.

"Oh?" She scooted up in the bed. He couldn't see her face, it was obscured by all the flowers, but he could see that she'd brought her knees up to her chest. The stark white hospital sheets were pulled snug around her.

The nurse turned and nodded at Hudson, a wide smile on her lips. She was clearly enjoying this.

He tugged lightly on Bonnie's leash, but truthfully, she didn't need one at all. When he'd gotten her certified for search and rescue, he'd also made sure she'd passed her Canine Good Citizen test. She was as well behaved in public as she was on the field. A perfect lady.

She walked in with him now, seeming to sense the need for calm energy. Her tail betrayed her excitement, though. It wagged back and forth, brushing against Hudson's legs.

He looked down at the woman in the bed. He thought she'd been pretty before, but he could see now that she was actually stunning. In her late twenties or early thirties, she was pale and had dark circles underneath her eyes, proof of what she'd just been through. Part of her temple and cheekbone had turned a nasty bluish-purple from where she'd fallen and hit her head. Her short hair was a rich mink brown, and her eyes were the color of dark honey.

"I'll just leave you two alone," the nurse said. And before either one of them could say anything, she'd stepped out and pulled the door closed behind her.

Except for the sound of the shifting balloons next to the bed, the room was suddenly quiet, the setting sun casting a champagne pink light over the small space.

"Sit, please," Georgia said.

Bonnie immediately sat, cocking her head.

Georgia laughed and Hudson ruffled his dog's ears. She was a charmer.

"She's so cute," Georgia said. "I can't believe how smart she is."

"Sometimes I think she's smarter than me."

"I had a dog when I was in middle school. His name was Van Buren after the eighth president. He was half basset hound. He could predict the weather."

Hudson lifted his brows.

"He could, I swear. He knew it was going to rain before we did, and he refused to go outside because he was afraid of getting wet. And when he *did* go outside, he'd only pee on the porch. My mom would get so mad. She'd follow him around with a bucket of water and a scrub brush. She called him Urine Van Buren."

Hudson laughed, and Bonnie squirmed, beside herself with wanting to get closer to this new, magical human.

Georgia put her hand out and wiggled her fingers.

"Okay," Hudson said, releasing her.

She immediately went to Georgia, licking her fingers, and then sidling up to the bed for scratches.

"Oh, she's precious," Georgia said. "I can hardly stand it."

"She's a good girl. She loves people, especially kids. They blow her mind. She comes right out of her skin whenever she sees one."

"The sign of the best girl."

"A lot of the dogs in the service are shepherds and Malinois, and they're amazing. But there's something about a Lab. Then again I'm biased, so…"

"Of course you are. You're her dad. You should be biased."

He'd never thought of it that way, but it was fair. He didn't have any human kids. Maybe Bonnie was as close as he'd ever get.

Georgia looked up at him, and her expression fell a

little. Some of the sparkle left her eyes. "I don't know how to thank you, Mr. Cross."

"You can start by calling me Hudson."

"Hudson," she said. "I don't know how to thank you."

"You don't have to. I'm just glad you're okay."

"I was so distracted that day, but I knew better. I should've told someone where I was going. I should've remembered my phone. I should've dressed in layers—"

"But you didn't. You're human. We learn from our mistakes and move on. It's as simple as that."

She frowned. "It's a small town. People don't like to waste the county's resources."

"Anyone who would see it that way has never done much in the outdoors, I can tell you that. You could've done everything by the book, and still got lost. My advice is to try and block out that noise. I'm sure everyone is just happy you're home. And if they're not, they can just pound sand."

She smiled. "Maybe I should make that my first official Facebook post. You know, post rescue."

"Whatever works."

"I wasn't sure I was going to make it. I had to make my peace with it a few times. I guess I've seen too many hikers get lost around here. So many things can happen, so much can go wrong. It was scary. But when I woke up to see Bonnie..." Her voice cracked.

He leaned down and patted her leg awkwardly. Grady was much better at this kind of thing than he was. He had an excellent bedside manner. Hudson was in the business of finding people. He wasn't so sure what to do with them afterward.

Georgia put her hand over his and then squeezed his

fingers. He looked down, taken off guard by the gesture. But she was crying openly now, and it was obvious she needed the comfort.

"I know you don't want me to keep thanking you," she said, "but I need you to know how grateful I am to you and Bonnie. You found me, but you were also very kind in that moment, and I'll never forget that."

Hudson's face warmed. He wasn't sure if it was because of what she was saying or the feel of her skin against his. Having a beautiful woman express her thanks like this wasn't exactly the worst thing in the world. But at the same time, it made him uncomfortable. He knew he'd grown distant in the army, more aloof than he'd been as a young man. It was a way to cope, a way to survive. Guys who felt all the feelings didn't necessarily fare very well in the long run.

After another few seconds, he took his hand away and crossed his arms over his chest.

"I lost my sister recently, and..." Her voice trailed off as she turned to stare out the window. The sun had disappeared into the sparkling ocean in the distance, taking its champagne light with it. The sky was now a swirling violet and orange, and he thought the air outside would be crisp and salty. He found that he couldn't stop looking at her. The sorrow in her eyes was almost palpable. It made sense now, the heaviness that she conveyed. She'd lost her sister. He wondered how, and he thought of Jesse. Of being the one to find her lifeless body in the rubble that day. Something he'd never get over, no matter how many years stretched between that moment and his own last breath. It did something to you, losing someone you loved. It took a piece of you, it left terrible things behind, and sometimes you couldn't bear to look the grief in the face at all. Sometimes it was easiest just to turn away from it. To go on a hike in the woods without telling anyone where you were going. To wear the wrong kinds of clothes and forget for a minute that life was so damn precarious.

He understood this well.

There was a soft knock on the door, and he turned to see the nurse poke her head inside.

"I'm sorry, but the doctor will be in shortly. I hate to rush you…"

"No," he said. "It's alright. Thank you for letting us say hello."

Georgia leaned over to give Bonnie one last pat.

"It was so nice to meet you, Hudson," she said. "I feel like we're bonded now. Does that sound corny?"

He smiled. It didn't sound corny at all.

In fact, he'd just been thinking the same thing.

"Miss Gallagher! Miss Gallagher!"

Georgia looked down at her first graders, all waving their hands from their seats on the carpet, desperate to hear about her two nights in the woods. Nearly all of them had watched the news with their parents, and now they were beside themselves. Their teacher was a celebrity. She'd even made it onto the news in Seattle, before the commercials and after the weekend weather forecast. It was especially exciting, since Seattle was where their former classmate Ruby Davis had moved at the end of last school year. Seattle was where the Space Needle and the big aquarium were. She was famous.

Georgia pressed her index finger to her lips. "Let's

keep it down, kids, alright? I'm not sure Mr. Wallace wants to hear about this from the library."

"He *does* want to hear!"

This, from a particularly wiggly little boy named Grant. He was having trouble keeping his hind end on the carpet. His whole body kept shooting up right along with his hand.

"Grant," she said with a patient smile. "Inside voices."

Georgia had taken a few days off before coming back to school. Her doctor said she needed to recuperate and take it slow, but a couple of days knocking around her house had left her bored and eager to return to the classroom. There was only so much recuperating she could do before wanting to pull her hair out.

Her mom, bless her, was also starting to drive her bananas. She'd been dropping by or calling constantly, and Georgia wasn't sure she could take another baked good, or worried stare, or offer to do the laundry. She was ready to get back to work, even though she was plenty embarrassed. She knew she'd have to face the questions head-on, especially from her students, who were too little to understand she might not be thrilled to talk about it.

"Yes, Sage," she said, pointing to a little girl with pink-framed, coke-bottle glasses.

"Does your head hurt?"

There was a collective *ooohhh* that moved through the room. They were clearly dying to know the answer to this one. Georgia knew they'd be disappointed with a simple, bland *no*, so she made a face.

"The cut oozed a little the first day."

The kids sat up straighter, energized by the word *oozed*.

"It didn't hurt too bad. But there was a big, squishy bump afterward."

*"Eewww."*

Squishy was a good word, too.

"Curtis, you've been waiting so nicely with your bottom on the floor. What's your question?"

"Were you scared?"

The little boy, whose dark mop of dark curls flopped over one eye, leaned forward on the edge of his seat. The other kids grew quiet, and Georgia thought she could quite literally hear a pin drop.

"I was," she said. "It was scary. I thought about my mom and dad, and all my friends, and you guys, and that's what helped me feel better. Looking forward to seeing you all again."

All of a sudden there were two dozen gap-toothed smiles, and an assortment of cute little dimples. Georgia's heart squeezed. She'd been telling the truth—she'd thought about them a lot when she'd been lost. How, if she weren't lucky enough to find her way back or be rescued, they'd struggle with the loss of their teacher.

She pointed to another little girl. "Yes, Clara."

"Miss Gallagher, what was the dog's name that found you?"

"Her name was Bonnie."

"Was she nice?" Clara was having a hard time keeping still, too. Georgia couldn't blame her. The subject had moved from oozing wounds to dogs named Bonnie. It was almost too much to handle.

"Yes, she was very nice. She woke me up by licking my face."

They all said *aww* at the same time, and Georgia's gaze fell on another student with her hand up. Lucy Thorton was having an especially hard time adjusting to first grade. Her parents had just gotten a nasty divorce, and her mother had to walk her into class every day with Lucy clinging to her pant leg. More often than not, there were tears, followed by entire days of not talking. The fact that she had her hand up now had Georgia cautiously hopeful. She'd learned there were ways to get through to even the most shut down kids, but the trick was finding them.

"Lucy, what's your question?"

The little girl, whose fine brown hair was cut into a bob with bangs that skimmed her big blue eyes, bounced gently on the carpet. "Could she come to our Halloween party?" she asked softly.

"Oh, well." Georgia bit the inside of her cheek. "I don't really know if she does things like that." Although, Hudson had said she loved kids. The teacher in Georgia immediately perked up at the idea. She could do a whole lesson plan around search and rescue. Outdoor safety. Even service animals. Her kids would probably be over the moon for it.

"Can you ask?" Lucy asked. "Please?"

The other kids joined in. There was a chorus of begging that made Georgia laugh.

She put her finger to her lips again until they quieted down one by one. When they were all sitting relatively still again, she sighed. It would definitely make a perfect lesson. And Hudson had said he was going to be in town for a few weeks. She'd probably be able to track him down pretty easily. But there was a small voice in the back of her head that was whispering insistently—*be careful with this one...* And why was that? He'd been so nice to her, so gentle and kind. Maybe that was the problem. He was her hero. He was also handsome, sexy, great at his job.

Someone she'd felt drawn to instantly. Still, something about him felt unreachable. Distant, like he was walking through life protecting himself. And that made sense; he'd been in the service for a long time. He'd had wartime experiences that she couldn't understand.

But the simple truth was that she hadn't been able to stop thinking about how it had felt being wrapped in his arms that day. Safe, warm, protected. It would be very easy to fall for someone like that, distant or not, and she wasn't in any place to fall for anyone right now. To open herself up to those kinds of emotions, especially for someone with significant scars. She could get her heart broken if she wasn't careful, and it was already broken enough. Shattered into a thousand little pieces.

If she was smart, she'd keep her distance.

But as her kids looked up at her with their pleading expressions, she knew she wasn't going to be able to deny them. She was most likely going to send them home on their buses and in their parents' minivans and SUVs, and then come back to her room and give in to that perfect lesson plan forming in her head.

The one that had Hudson Cross visiting her classroom with his lovely black Lab, Bonnie.

The one that scared her, if she was being honest.

Maybe even more than being lost in the woods.

# Chapter Three

Hudson stood on the lookout of Cape Longing, the collar of his black fleece pulled high around his neck. The cold October wind whipped fiercely along the cliff, with the blue-gray ocean churning below. The foamy waves thundered against the rocks, sending spray high into the air. Spotted seagulls rode the gusts of wind with their wings outstretched, undaunted by the roller-coaster ride Mother Nature was taking them on. They squawked to each other and dipped and bobbed, making way every now and then for their more glamorous pelican cousins that flew closer to the water, flapping their wings with steady strength and grace.

Hudson took this in with Tad and Grady standing on either side of him. It was one of the most beautiful views he'd ever seen, and he'd been a lot of places, seen a lot of pretty things. The way the mountains stopped at the water so dramatically, as if they were deciding whether or not to take a dip. The way the evergreens stood out against the periwinkle blue sky and the stormy gray ocean. The smell of the sea and the trees and the earth. It was breathtaking, really. He leaned against the railing, staring at the horizon, wondering how it was that he'd survived in the desert so long, without the ocean to center him.

"I could stay here," Tad said, his hands in his pockets. "Seriously."

"Well, nothing's stopping you," Hudson said. "Retired, remember?"

"Damn. You're right. I keep forgetting."

"I don't," Grady said. "I wake up every morning and get to decide whether or not to make the bed."

Hudson smiled. "And then you go ahead and make it anyway."

"Right. That."

"It's wild," Tad said. "Being *retired.* I feel ancient saying that. Remember when thirty was a geezer?"

"I remember when twenty-five was a geezer," Grady said.

"Yeah. And now we're in our early forties and I feel like a high school kid who just graduated. Half the time I don't know what to do with myself."

Hudson knew exactly what he meant. He was still trying to get used to his own freedom after years of adhering to the strictest guidelines and rigid expectations. But that was also what he'd loved about the service. He'd always thrived on structure.

Grady crossed his arms over his chest, his baseball cap pulled low over his eyes. He'd been quiet all afternoon. They'd all been quiet because it was Jesse's birthday. And Jesse was the reason why they were up here, looking at this beautiful view, trying to live each day to the fullest. Cliché, but true.

"I wish she could've seen this," Grady said, his voice thick. "She loved the ocean. I don't think she'd ever been to the West Coast."

"No, I don't think so," Tad said quietly. "California

was on her bucket list, though. She wanted to learn how to surf."

"I remember that." Hudson swallowed hard, thinking of their friend, smiling that smile that was sometimes a little sad, and brushing her blond hair away from her eyes.

Jesse hadn't had much of a relationship with her family. Her mother had struggled with addiction, and she'd never known her dad. She'd been accepted into the army and had formed strong bonds with her friends and fellow soldiers. Even been loved by some of them. And now, three of them were doing their best to carry on without her. Trying to keep her memory alive in their hearts and minds. It was painful, and Hudson felt that most of the time they were clumsy about it, but they were managing somehow.

His phone dinged from his pocket. The sound of a new email coming in. He was in a lot of search and rescue groups, and he didn't like to miss anything, even though most of the emails he got were about training opportunities. He wasn't on social media—he texted, but only the most basic messages, and always without emojis. He thought those were ridiculous. Gmail was his main form of communication, which he realized put him firmly in the dinosaur category in this day and age of social media apps.

He pulled his phone out and swiped the screen open, as Tad and Grady walked over to the edge of the lookout, talking about how long it would take to rappel down the cliffs. Army talk. *Old habits die hard*, Hudson thought dryly.

Opening his email, he stood there staring at it for a second. He recognized the name of the sender right away, and his gut tightened, although he wasn't sure why. Other than locating Georgia Gallagher on the mountain a few days ago, he didn't know her from Adam. There was just that one nice memory of visiting with her in the hospital. She'd had a nice laugh, a sweet way about her. And of course, she'd been beautiful. That hadn't escaped his attention. But there had also been a haunted look in her eyes that he hadn't been able to forget. In fact, he'd thought about her a lot since then, wondering how she was doing, wondering if she'd trust herself to go adventuring again in the future, and hoping she would.

And now, here was an email from her, popping up out of the blue and making him feel weirdly anxious. Not unlike that high school kid that Tad had just been comparing himself to. It wasn't that Hudson didn't have experience with women, but his experience was mostly physical. His emotional connections had been few and far between. He was a career soldier. And career soldiers had complicated lives. If they were lucky enough to have families, their families lived on bases. Their families moved around. Their families sacrificed right alongside them. And Hudson had never met anyone willing to make those kinds of sacrifices for him. Which was fine. He was okay on his own. Or at least, that's what he'd always told himself.

Glancing over at his friends and seeing that they were still talking about their hypothetical rappel down the cliffs, he looked back down at the email and opened it.

*Dear Hudson,*

*I hope you don't mind, but I reached out to Sheriff Hicks to try to find you, and as luck would have it, he had your email address. I'm writing because*

*I'm a teacher—first grade—and I told my kids the story about you and Bonnie finding me, and they're desperate for you both to come for a visit. Specifically, as our Halloween party guests of honor. I know this is a big ask, as you might not do things like this, or you might've already left town, but you never know unless you try. That's what I tell my students, anyway.*

*This visit would coincide with a lesson plan about the men and women of search and rescue, specially trained rescue animals and outdoor safety. I think having you visit our classroom would be somewhat like having Harry Styles visit at this point, as you've been elevated to rock star status.*

*Having said that, please don't feel any pressure to say yes. I haven't told them this is a possibility, so if you can't do it, or simply don't feel comfortable doing it, they won't know the difference.*

*I hope all is well with you. You are, and always will be, my hero.*

*Sincerely, Georgia Gallagher.*

*PS. Give Bonnie a scratch for me.*

Hudson smiled. He'd never been asked to talk to a classroom before, but he was pretty sure Bonnie would end up being the rock star. Which was fine; he was okay giving up the glory. He actually loved the idea of teaching a room full of kids how to be safe in the mountains and near the water. It was so important, as he'd seen too many young people get themselves into trouble. If they could learn how to be prepared and how to respect nature at a young age, there was no telling how many tragedies might be averted.

He typed out a quick reply—no frills, definitely no emojis—letting her know that he was still in town, and he'd be happy to come for a visit.

Then he tucked his phone back in his pocket, picturing her face. Those haunted eyes. And wondered about the sister she'd just lost. What the story was there.

"Hey, Hud," Tad said, walking up to him. "We were talking about barbecue for dinner. There's that place, The Saucy Pig, on the edge of town. What do you think?"

"Sounds good to me."

"Me, too."

"So, what's the consensus on rappelling that cliff? Think you could still do it?"

Tad laughed. "Oh, I *know* you didn't just question my rappelling skills."

"Not your skills. Your geezer knees."

Tad grabbed him in a juvenile headlock and scuffed his knuckles over Hudson's scalp.

"Ass!" Hudson said, twisting away.

Tad ignored that and began walking toward Hudson's big black Tahoe. Bonnie had her head sticking out the driver side window, her entire body wiggling at the sight of them coming back to her.

They both looked over at Grady, watching their friend quietly gaze out over the ocean.

"Think we should tell him we're leaving?" Tad asked.

"No, give him some time." Hudson was prepared to wait all night long if he had to. He wasn't going to pull Grady from the memories he knew his friend was lost in. Memories of Jesse. They all got lost in those from time to time.

As he walked beside Tad in the gusting wind, slower now, and with more intention, he thought again about Georgia Gallagher and the way he hadn't been able to stop thinking about her. He hadn't realized until just now, right that second, but something about her reminded him of Jesse. And he thought it was her magnetism.

And those beautiful eyes.

Georgia followed her mom, slowly pushing the cart down the baking aisle of Cartwright's. Sophie's birthday was coming up, and her mom wanted to bake her favorite cake. German chocolate, a tradition. Only now, it would only be the two of them celebrating.

Georgia watched her pick up a box of cake mix, put it down and then pick up another one, seemingly studying the ingredients, but Georgia knew better. She was lost in her memories, and the tears would probably come soon.

Georgia understood this; she was struggling, too. Every day was a struggle, and she found that she was grasping on to light and comfort wherever she could get it. The fact that Hudson Cross had agreed to come to her classroom to kick off a lesson that she was already very proud of was a big source of light. She'd meant it when she'd said he was her hero.

"What do you think about this one?" her mom asked. Her graying hair was cut into a tidy bob, a dramatic change from the long, silky locks Georgia had grown up with. But she'd needed a change, and her hair was an easy place to start. "It's gluten free."

Leaning her elbows against the old cart, Georgia

gave her a small smile. "But we aren't allergic to gluten, though."

Alice Gallagher watched her oldest daughter for a long second, and then her expression fell. "Oh. Right."

"Whatever you want to make is great, Mom," Georgia said. "It's going to be delicious no matter what."

"Well, Sophie liked the Betty Crocker. So, I guess that's what I'll get."

Georgia wasn't going to argue. She just wished she could take some of her mother's pain away, but knew it was going to be a burden she would bear forever. It would soften some over time, but it would always be woven into the fabric of their lives.

Her mother put one box back, picked up another, and set it gently into the cart, as if she were laying something delicate there instead. "So," she said. "This young man is going to come to your classroom? That's wonderful, honey. What a great experience for the kids."

Georgia's mom was a retired teacher herself, fifth grade, and was Georgia's most treasured sounding board on her career. It made her especially happy when her mom was excited about a particular lesson plan. That was when she knew she was doing something right.

"Yeah," she said. "I think it'll be pretty special. If I can turn this experience into a positive, that's something I can feel good about. It's still so embarrassing, though."

"Georgia, people get lost all the time."

"That's not what Facebook says."

The comments on their local news feed had been particularly ugly last week, something that still made Georgia's cheeks burn. She'd known there was going to be plenty of judgment, and it would eventually die down, but when you were on the receiving end of it, it stung. Plenty.

"Oh, don't get me started on those trolls," her mother bit out. "Janice Evans was one of the loudest ones, squawking about common sense, blah, blah, blah. She seems to have forgotten that her hoodlum son skied out of bounds two years ago and got himself lost overnight. *That* was a waste of county resources. He can't even spell resources, much less appreciate them."

*"Mom."* Georgia tried her best not to laugh, but it wasn't easy. The look on her mother's face combined with the words coming out of her mouth were so out of character, it was comical. She simply had no tolerance for anyone's crap anymore. For someone who'd spent the better part of her life tiptoeing around other people's feelings, it was kind of refreshing.

"It's true," her mom said with a shrug. And there was a twinkle in her deep brown eyes that had been missing for months. But then it was gone again, like a shooting star, leaving just a memory of light behind.

Georgia gave the cart a little shove, and the elderly wheels squeaked in protest. "What else do we need? Eggs? Butter?"

"Both."

They made their way to the end of the aisle, where there was a small line at the checkout. The checker, a teenage boy with a crop of pimples on his forehead, looked like he was struggling to keep up. A woman stood in front of him, holding a fussy toddler and trying to read the cover of the latest *Us Weekly*. Behind her, an elderly man was chatting amiably with a young girl about how candy bars had shrunk over the years— "Just *look* at that

Snickers!"—something the girl seemed to passionately agree with. "Oh, I know. They're like, *tiny*!"

Georgia blinked at the woman bouncing the toddler on her hip, imagining what a wonderful mother Sophie would've made. She'd wanted to get married; she'd wanted a family more than anything. She knew she might not be able to conceive after her cancer treatments and was excited about the possibility of adopting. Georgia swallowed hard. What a lucky little kid that would have been.

Before she could turn back to see where her mother was going, she bumped into a man, almost running his foot over with her cart.

"Oh, my gosh!" she said, looking down to make sure his toes were still attached. "I'm so sorry."

"Georgia?"

Standing in front of her, so close that she had to tilt her head back to see into his face, was Hudson Cross. He looked so different from when she'd seen him last, in dark green fatigues and an official Search and Rescue pullover, that she could only stare at him for a second. Tonight he was wearing khaki slacks and a white collared polo shirt that stretched over his muscular shoulders. He had stubble on his jaw, something that she'd barely registered when she'd seen him in the hospital. She'd never been particularly into facial scruff before, but on him, it looked impossibly sexy.

He smiled down at her, and her heart fluttered.

"Are you okay?" she asked. "Did I get your foot?"

"You didn't. But you looked kind of lost in thought."

"I was. And people watching. You know how that goes."

"I love people watching," he said. "Grocery stores are the best. And airports, those are good, too."

"This is something we have in common."

"That, and a love of dogs. Let's not forget Urine Van Buren."

She laughed. "The porch peeing was his only vice."

"A big one if you ask me. But not a deal breaker."

"Never."

They stood there for a minute, looking at each other. And all of a sudden, there was a charge in the air that Georgia felt—hot on her skin, heavy in her bones. A chemistry that she hadn't felt in a long time.

After a second, Hudson cleared his throat. "Is that your mom over there?"

He nodded toward Georgia's mother, who was reaching over her head for a liter of Diet Coke. She was petite, so she teetered a second before securing it in her hand.

Georgia nodded. "How'd you know?"

"You're both pretty. You look alike."

Her cheeks filled with heat. She was almost thirty, but that compliment coming from this man made her feel like a teenager again.

"Did you get my email?" he asked.

"Oh. Yes, I did. The kids will be so excited."

"Bonnie will be excited, too. I might have to give her a tranquilizer beforehand."

Georgia loved the thought of his big friendly dog losing her marbles over her students. How fun was that going to be? And of course, she'd get to see Hudson again, which wasn't going to be awful.

"Well," he said, putting his hands in his pockets. "I'd better get going. My buddies and I are headed to dinner,

I just came in for some pre-barbecue antacids, because their eyes are a little bigger than their stomachs. I, of course, would never overeat."

She smiled. "If you're headed to The Saucy Pig, you'll need them, too. Overeating there is a rite of passage."

"Noted."

He watched her for another few beats. Long enough for her to warm underneath that gaze again.

"It was good to see you," he finally said.

"It was good to see you, too."

And then, surprising her, he held his hand out. She shook it, and he squeezed her fingers. His skin was warm and rough, electric against hers. Her heart gave up all pretenses and began hammering shamelessly in her chest. Before she could help it, she imagined his big, sexy hands unbuttoning her blouse. Slowly, expertly. For some reason she thought he'd know exactly what he was doing in that department.

And then she looked away, embarrassed by the thought. She guessed she was going to have a hard time maintaining eye contact with him. Sophie would get a good laugh out of this. She'd always given Georgia a hard time about how flustered she got around guys.

"Just let me know when the party is," he said. "And I'll see you then."

"Sounds great. We'll send you an invitation."

"I'm looking forward to it. And I'll tell Bonnie you said hi."

His gaze fell to her mouth for a second. And then he was gone with a nod, presumably toward the antacids that he'd definitely need.

She watched him go. Maybe a little dreamily. And

then saw her mother walking toward her, bringing her back to reality.

"*Who*," her mom asked, "was *that*?"

Georgia grazed her bottom lip with her teeth. "That was Hudson Cross. I almost ran him over with my cart."

"You didn't."

"I did."

"Oh, Georgia."

"His toes are intact. I checked."

"That's good to hear. He's very handsome."

"I know."

"And you're blushing."

Georgia stared at her.

"Sorry," her mom said. "But you are." The twinkle was back. For a minute it felt like old times, when she and Sophie and their mom would all talk and laugh over the silliest things. For a precious moment, Georgia felt comforted by that twinkle in her mom's eyes. Like they might be taking a brief step away from the grief and one toward healing.

And then, as quickly as it had come, it was gone again. And the space that had been full of light a second ago was now filling with tears.

"Oh," her mom said. "I'm sorry. It just happens like this. It comes in waves."

Georgia stepped forward and pulled her into a hug, feeling her own eyes fill with tears, too. It did come in waves. It washed over her like a great wall of water when she least expected it, sweeping her away, flailing and helpless. That's how grief was. It rose up and did what it wanted, when it wanted, leaving swaths of destruction in its wake.

Suddenly, there was a sharp pang of guilt for the feelings she'd had just now, for the attraction and butterflies she'd felt for Hudson. There was guilt for feeling anything for anyone, because happiness of any kind felt like she was moving on, farther and farther away from Sophie. As twisted as it was, the sadness was a comfort. Because that meant she was right there in the trenches. Missing her sister, grieving alongside her parents.

Pulling away from her mom, she brushed the tears from her cheeks. And then looked over in time to see Hudson walking toward the sliding front doors with a small bag in his hand. Tall, broad shouldered, with a sunburn on the back of his neck and a slight tilt to his lips.

When he glanced over, it was as if he might be looking for her. Maybe he'd been planning on waving, on nodding in her direction. Or simply walking out the doors without acknowledging her at all.

But when his gaze met hers, his expression fell, and there was a distinct sympathy in his eyes that she found she couldn't take.

She looked away. She simply couldn't allow herself to feel anything for anyone right now. Even if that person had saved her life. She took a deep breath, and reminded herself that Hudson was going to come to her classroom, but that was it. He and his dog would help teach her students an important lesson. And then she'd never see them again.

It was the safest thing. Sophie wouldn't agree. But then again, Sophie had been the adventurous one. Georgia was the one who protected her heart at all costs.

"Honey?" her mom asked, watching her. "What is it?"

She forced a small smile. "Just thinking of Soph."

# *Chapter Four*

Hudson stood on the edge of the emerald green river, his fly-fishing pole in his hand. It was chilly this morning, but it felt good. Invigorating, after the night in their Airbnb, which was small and a little stuffy.

He rubbed his jaw, looking up at the surrounding mountains that were shrouded in misty clouds. The river was gentle along this stretch, but was roaring down the bend. So much so that he had a hard time hearing Tad and Grady when they shouted to him from several yards away.

At the moment, both his friends were knee-deep in the icy water, their waders keeping them snug and dry, but Hudson hadn't stepped in yet. He was too taken with the beauty surrounding them to start fishing yet.

He took a deep breath, the air smelling damp, like moss and pine. It also smelled salty, since they weren't far from the ocean, though they couldn't see it from where they stood. Colorful aspen wove through the forest of evergreens, their yellow autumn leaves popping against the muted earthy tones of the hemlocks, spruce and Douglas firs. Again, he thought about his time in the desert, and how fundamentally different it was than here. The only thing the landscapes had in common was a shared vastness. A feeling of remoteness that made Hudson feel insignificant.

His phone dinged from his pocket, tugging him away from his thoughts, from the memories of the sand and heat of Afghanistan.

He pulled it out and squinted at the screen.

It was from Sheriff Hicks. A little boy had gone missing from his family's cabin, and they needed his help.

Hudson picked his way through the forest on the southern end of the county. The town where Collin Abernathy had disappeared was really only a town in the technical sense of the word. Three hundred and fifty people. Once upon a time it had been a mining town—practically booming with over a thousand people in the late sixties and early seventies. But the work had eventually dried up, and the only thing left over was the families of the old timers—children and grandchildren who had deep roots here, and still called it home.

Hudson looked around. Dozens of deputies and volunteers were combing the hillside now—some on horseback, some on four-wheelers, most on foot. There were dogs that, like Bonnie, were highly trained and motivated to find the boy whose scent they'd been given. A lot of them worked simply for their favorite toys—old balls or tugs that served as their reward for hours and hours on the trail. In Bonnie's case, it was a little stuffed lamb that she'd had since puppyhood. Or had had versions of since puppyhood. It had disintegrated from exposure and dog saliva no less than a dozen times, and Hudson had had to keep replacing it. But Bonnie didn't care. She loved the damn thing, new or old, original or replacement. When she got it after a long day of work, she knew she'd done a good job. And she wanted to please Hudson to her core.

He'd just let her off her leash and told her to "find it," and she'd bolted into the woods, ignoring the baying and barking of the other dogs, the shouting of the men and women back and forth. The relentless calls of "Collin!" through the thick vegetation and mist that had settled over the small lake to their right. It was that lake that represented the most danger for Collin, a four-year-old who couldn't swim. Of course, the wilderness as a whole could be deadly for such a small child, and every law enforcement officer, every volunteer looking for him now knew it. Time was critical. The sun would be setting soon, and the temperature would be dropping, and the odds of him making it unscathed through a night on his own weren't good.

Bonnie bounded over logs and rocks, cutting through the meadow grass like a knife through butter. She was on the hunt. Sometimes the only thing Hudson could see was her bright red search and rescue harness through the bushes. And then she'd bound out again, her nose no doubt full of all kinds of interesting scents, but only one of them mattered right now.

"Get him, girl," Hudson said under his breath, jogging to keep up with her.

It was getting cold enough that Hudson's fingers were numb. He'd forgotten his gloves in the truck, but he was so focused on his dog that he barely noticed. They'd already cleared two areas south of here, and it wouldn't take long to clear this one, as well. What would take humans hours to search in some cases only took dogs minutes.

And Bonnie was good at this. More than good. In Hudson's opinion, she was the best.

He jumped over a downed tree, following her through the brush, farther away from the rest of the search party. His heart hammered in his chest. It was an adrenaline rush, being out here with his dog. But at the end of the day, there was only one reason why he did it. Only one reason why he'd done it in the army. To save lives. He just hoped this would be another happy ending. Sometimes it wasn't. Jesse hadn't had a happy ending. Neither had so many of his friends over the years.

He pushed that quick, painful thought to the back of his mind, determined to keep it there until he and Bonnie had done their jobs. He couldn't be distracted out here, he couldn't have his thoughts wandering, or he might miss something that could mean life or death. And all of a sudden, he wasn't thinking of Jesse, or the army, or even Collin Abernathy anymore. He was only thinking of keeping Bonnie in his sights as she plunged even deeper into the woods. Making sure he was aware of where he stepped, so he didn't break an ankle or his neck.

And then, she disappeared. Like an apparition, she vanished into the shadowy brush and didn't pop back out again.

He slowed, watching the spot where he'd seen her last. His pulse tapped in his neck, reminding him of what was at stake here. This was just a baby they were looking for. Nothing more than a baby.

Swallowing hard, he waited. And a moment later, Bonnie started barking. She'd been trained in victim loyalty—she was supposed to stay with the person she'd found and bark to alert Hudson. It was the sweetest sound in the world. And one that always made his hair stand on end.

He ran toward his dog, his hand on the radio at his hip. Hoping against hope that Collin was conscious, that he was uninjured. That he would be able to be placed directly into his mother's arms, and not into the gurney of a Life Flight. All thoughts that bounced across Hudson's frontal lobe as he tore his way through the mountain brush, the sharp twigs tearing at his clothes.

Finally, he broke through the brush and into a small clearing. Only big enough for a dog and a tiny child.

Trying to catch his breath, he looked down at the little boy. Curled into Bonnie's side, holding tufts of her fur in his hands.

Hudson sank to his knees and looked him over. No blood that he could see, no broken bones. Collin had the biggest green eyes he thought he'd ever seen. He was scared. His face was dirty and tear-streaked. But he looked healthy. He looked okay.

"Collin? I'm Hudson. This is Bonnie. We're so happy to see you, buddy."

After a few seconds, the boy shifted and sat up in the damp leaves where he'd made a little bed. "Where's my mommy?"

"I'm going to get her for you. She's pretty worried. I'll need to carry you out, it's a little bit of a hike, and we're the only ones out this far. Is it okay if I pick you up?"

"Can the doggy come, too?"

Hudson smiled. He turned to his dog, his very best girl, and rubbed her silky ears. Then reached into his pack for her lamb.

She immediately began to wiggle.

This was why they did what they did.

"Have you been watching the news?"

Georgia looked up from the pile of papers she'd been grading to see Thomas Paisley standing in the doorway with his hands on his hips. He was a new teacher, and this was only his second year at Christmas Bay Elementary, but he was a born educator. The kids loved him, his fellow teachers loved him, but Georgia loved him the most. She was his mentor, but they were also best friends. He was watching her now with a mischievous look on his face.

"I have no idea what you're talking about," she said, forcing herself to look back down at her papers.

"Girl, you know *exactly* what I'm talking about."

Thomas sauntered up to her desk and tapped it with one neatly trimmed nail.

"I'm busy," she said.

"Right."

"I am."

"Not too busy to have been watching the news."

She sighed and looked back up at him. Then reached up to adjust her glasses. "Okay. I saw the news."

"This guy is too good to be true. Like, what's wrong with him? There has to be something wrong."

"No, he's pretty perfect. I mean, if you're asking me."

Thomas smiled. "Oh, I'm asking you, alright."

"He's here temporarily. Visiting. Volunteering his time with the sheriff's office. He's not staying."

"So? That doesn't mean you can't reach out to him."

"I did. I asked him to our Halloween party, remember?"

Thomas rolled his eyes dramatically. "Come *on,* Georgia. I'm not talking about a first-grade party." He looked behind him to make sure they were still alone, then turned back to her. "I'm talking about *shagging* the man," he whispered.

This time she did laugh.

"Seriously, though," he said, his expression growing somber. "You need this. Why don't you go on a few dates? Get back out there?"

She shook her head. "He's too good-looking. Like he should be in a beer commercial or something. He's probably got a girlfriend."

"But no ring?"

"No ring. It doesn't matter, though. I'm not in the market to have my heart broken by a man who's just passing through."

Thomas leaned down and touched her shoulder. "He'd be crazy to break your heart, honey."

She gazed up at him for a long, meaningful moment. Her eyes stung with tears, but she held them back. "Thank you. And I love you for saying that."

"I sense a *but* coming."

"*But,*" she said, "I'm just not up to it."

He gave her a small smile. "Okay. I hear you, and I'll stop pushing. But if you decide you are up for it, you know where I am. I'd love to help you pick a first date outfit."

She chuckled as she watched him walk away.

And then she was alone again, just her and the ever-present stack of papers to grade. She put her red crayon down and looked out the window, where a crowd of paper skeletons were taped, doing their boneyard dance. Raindrops made their way down the glass. It was blustery outside, chilly. She thought about Collin Abernathy, and how Bonnie and Hudson had found him before he'd had to spend the night in the woods. In the rain and cold. It was hard to think of a little boy going through what she'd gone through when she'd gotten lost, but it would've been infinitely worse for Collin. Infinitely scarier.

She licked her lips absentmindedly. Thomas had asked if she'd watched the news, and she'd said she had. But the truth was, she hadn't just been watching it—she'd been glued to it. From the minute word had gotten out that Collin had been missing, she'd been watching, refreshing the local news' Facebook page every half an hour. She'd been thinking about him constantly, and wondering if Hudson would be helping in the search effort. Turns out, he had and then some.

Putting her chin in her hand, she thought about Bonnie. About what a good, sweet girl she was. And about Hudson, and what wonderful work he did with search and rescue. She'd told Thomas that she wasn't going to contact him, and that was true. At least for the most part. But she wondered if sending a little care package to Bonnie would count.

Just to let them both know how much they were appreciated.

"Damn," Tad said, taking a pull on his longneck beer. "If I'd known how many women you'd land being with search and rescue, I would've gone into it a long time ago."

Hudson smiled and took a pull on his own beer. They'd found themselves back at the honky-tonk on the edge of town. It was turning out to be a favorite bar of theirs to grab a beer after fishing. It was a comfortable place to relax and listen to music. And they had killer nachos, which, as far as Hudson was concerned, was reason enough to come.

"That's not why I do it," he said, watching Grady at the pool table, currently sucking pretty hard. He'd always been terrible at pool but kept coming back to it again and again, as if somehow thinking he'd improve overnight. He needed to stick to medicine.

"But you can't deny the women part."

No, he couldn't. Since the subject of that comment was currently batting her lovely baby blues at him from across the room now.

"She's pretty," he said. "But I'm not—"

Tad held up a hand. "You're not interested, I know."

"I'm just past the whole hookup thing. I don't have the energy for it anymore."

"I don't think that's why you're not over there getting her number right now, man. I think it has to do with someone else."

At that, Hudson looked over at his friend. The music was thumping, the lights down so low that Tad's face was cast in a bluish shadow. The neon beer signs buzzed behind him, as the bartender leaned over and wiped down the bar a few feet away. Her tight orange-and-black-plaid shirt gaped open—he assumed that was a nod to Halloween coming up—and exposed her ample cleavage. Christmas Bay was not without its share of attractive women. But Tad was right, as usual. Hudson was only thinking of one at the moment.

"Can you blame me?" he asked.

"Nope. No blame here. She seems sweet. And sending that stuff for Bonnie was thoughtful. But watch out, dude. We're leaving next month, remember?"

"What do you mean?"

"Just that long distance isn't your thing."

Hudson had had a grand total of three serious relationships over the years, and all of them had been long-distance. And all three had failed miserably. His exes had told him that he was emotionally unavailable. They'd said he had an inability to commit. And they'd been right. But Tad was wrong in thinking that long-distance relationships didn't suit him. They actually suited him just fine, because they were safe. When he was thousands of miles away, everything could be a hypothetical. *What if we took the next step? What if we got married? What about a family?* It was only when he found himself in the same town with someone that things got complicated. Those hypotheticals turned into questions that he couldn't run away from anymore, and he'd seen too many relationships, too many families broken apart by the simple by-product of living to be able to face any questions head on. Even when you thought things were safe—accidents happened, sickness happened, war happened. He'd seen it all, those casualties of living.

He felt a tap on the shoulder and turned to see that the woman from across the bar had made her way over without him even noticing. He'd been too busy thinking of his train wreck of a personal life.

Tad cleared his throat. "I think I'll go try and teach Grady how to play pool. At least enough to stop embarrassing himself."

With a polite nod at the woman, he stepped away and

left Hudson alone with her. Hudson watched him walk off, making a mental note to kill him later.

"I kept waiting for you to come over," she said.

He smiled and took a drink of his beer to avoid answering.

She leaned against the bar, looking undeterred. "Strong silent type, huh?"

"Just tired, I guess."

"I'm Bree, by the way."

Her eyes sparkled, but a dull headache was beginning to throb at his temples. He remembered when he was younger and went out with his buddies. This was just the kind of interaction they'd hoped for when they'd stepped inside a bar, pulsing with pent-up sexual energy. He'd gone home with his fair share of girls back then. It was the uniform, the job they were attracted to. They didn't know him as a person, but that hadn't bothered him so much because it was just a night with a pretty woman that he was most interested in. Now, it felt different. Disrespectful. And like he was trying to be someone he wasn't. He wasn't that kid anymore. He wished he could feel as unattached as he'd been in his twenties, because it had been easier that way. This wasn't so easy. This feeling of loneliness.

The thumping music overhead changed to something slower and sexier. An older country song that he recognized but didn't know the name of. Bree immediately smiled and put her hand on his arm.

"Dance with me? I love this song."

Setting his beer down, he took her hand, leading her toward the dance floor, weaving in between people as they went. It was almost midnight and the place was hopping now. But all he could think about was his bed back at the Airbnb, and how Bonnie would jump up and put her head on his knees. How he'd sleep fitfully tonight because they'd found Collin Abernathy. They'd done their job. But beyond that deep satisfaction was an emptiness that was always with him now. Since losing Jesse. He was simply tired. He just wanted to sleep.

Instead, he turned to the woman beside him and brought her close. He put his arm around the small of her back and held her hand in his. The lights flashed across her face as she looked up at him, and he began taking her around the dance floor. He'd learned how to two-step when he was stationed in Texas. It was the only dance he knew.

"My God, you are one good-looking man," she said, pressing herself against him. She was soft, her curves reminding him of past loves, past regrets. And then, inexplicably, he thought of Georgia Gallagher, and how she'd felt in his arms.

He didn't answer Bree. Instead, he turned her in a circle and then pulled her next to him again. She laughed, her teeth straight and white in the dim light of the bar. She had a nice smile.

He had a brief thought of pushing his guilty conscience aside and going home with her if she wanted him to. Of spending the night pressed against her naked body and taking all the comfort she was willing to give.

"The paper said you were in the army," she said. "My older brother was in the army. He was killed in Somalia. I was little when it happened. I don't remember him very well."

She said it matter-of-factly, but there was a melancholy

look in her eyes that spoke volumes. He understood little sisters and brothers not getting to know their siblings. Of babies being born after their fathers had been killed. Of little kids growing up without a mom or dad, and having to connect with them through stories and pictures, and brief articles about their passing that were sandwiched somewhere between the stock market and sports. He understood this very well, and all of a sudden, the thought of going home with her just made him sad. The last thing she needed was a night with a man who was emotionally unavailable. His exes were absolutely right.

The song that he couldn't remember the name of came to an end, and another one took its place. "The Monster Mash." He wouldn't have been able to dance to that one anyway.

He held on to Bree's hand for a few seconds, and she smiled up at him. She didn't have to say what she wanted, he already knew. He leaned down to give her a kiss on the cheek. She smelled like perfume and whisky.

And then he glanced over to see Tad and Grady watching him. They seemed ready to leave, too.

"Can I buy you a drink?" she asked. Looking sweet and hopeful.

Somewhere deep down, he longed for something more, but he wouldn't have been able to say what it was. He simply didn't know.

"I think it's time to call it a night," he said. "Thank you for the dance."

# Chapter Five

Georgia stopped in front of her classroom and turned to see her kids in a line behind her. Buzzing with excited energy, despite the fact that they'd just had gym and had been running and jumping for the better part of an hour.

Today was their Halloween party, and they'd been counting down all month long. Georgia was looking forward to it, too, but that had everything to do with the fact that Hudson was going to make an appearance. She hadn't seen him since the day in Cartwright's when she'd almost run his foot over with her cart. But they'd been emailing back and forth. She'd sent Bonnie a gift basket full of treats and toys, and he'd thanked her for that. And then they'd corresponded over the next week or so about nothing in particular. It was like neither one of them had wanted to cut their communication off completely with an, *Okay, then, I'll see you at the party!* Instead, they'd talked a little about her job, and his, and how he was liking Christmas Bay so far. Surface level conversation, but to her it had felt significant. Of course, she knew she could be reading into that. He was a nice guy. He didn't seem like the type to leave an email hanging.

So, here she was. Dressed up all in black with a feathery kitty tail pinned to her jeans, and whiskers and a nose drawn on her face, and looking forward to seeing this man much more than she probably should be. Since she'd told Thomas she wasn't interested in someone who was just passing through, she'd been trying to convince herself of that very same thing since the shopping cart incident.

"Miss Gallagher, Andy pinched me!"

"I did not."

"Shut up. You did, too."

"You shut up!"

Georgia put her hands on her hips. "Madeline, Andrew, we don't tell each other to shut up. And we don't pinch. We keep our hands to ourselves."

It was hard trying to sound authoritative when you were wearing cat ears. But her kids knew her well, and they immediately responded to the steely tone of her voice. They quieted down, and Madeline's hand shot up in the air.

"Yes, Madeline. Thank you for raising your hand."

"When is the party again?"

"As soon as we get settled. Mr. Hudson will be here soon."

Several kids squealed.

Georgia held a finger to her lips until they quieted down again.

"I forgot my lunch. Can I call my mom?"

This, from Lucy, who was standing at the back of the line, looking sad, as usual. Finding an excuse to call her mom was a daily ritual. If not hourly. She was having such a hard time. Her mother had called Georgia to report that Eddie Thorton had come to get his things this weekend, and they'd had a huge fight that Lucy had walked in on. So, she was especially sensitive today.

"Honey, your mom is at work. You can have hot lunch. How does that sound?"

Quick tears filled the little girl's eyes, and Georgia's heart squeezed. She walked over and pulled her into a hug.

"Boys and girls, go ahead and go inside, and sit at your desks. I think we'll play Heads Up, Seven Up until the party."

That did it. An afternoon playing their favorite game *and* having a party was almost too much excitement to take.

Georgia laughed as they bounded inside the classroom, not insisting that they walk in a single file line like she usually did. They'd been extraordinarily good up until this point, and attempting to control them too much was like trying to hold back the tide.

Lucy walked quietly next to her, leaning into her side. The worst of her tears seemed to have passed, thank goodness, but as far as her students went, she was Georgia's biggest worry this year. There were always a couple of kids who struggled in every class. Whether it was with acting out, or being shy and withdrawn, they needed her extra help, her extra attention to thrive in school. It was hard because sometimes they didn't do well, no matter how much she tried to reach them. But most of the time, she saw great strides by the end of the year. It was her favorite part of teaching, getting to see kids grow and learn despite the obstacles standing in their way.

She leaned down to the little girl who was holding her hand so tightly. "Lucy, go sit down, okay? Are you excited for the party?"

She nodded.

"What are you most excited for?"

She looked up at Georgia, her blue eyes impossibly big. Then she chewed on her chapped bottom lip. “I’m excited to see Bonnie,” she said softly.

“I’m sure Bonnie’s excited, too.”

Georgia caught a movement at the corner of her eye, and she turned to see Hudson standing in the hallway, off to the side so the rest of the kids couldn’t see. Her belly tightened. Bonnie was sitting next to him, perfectly polite, wagging her tail as she stared longingly at Lucy. She was wearing a pair of purple sequined bat wings that caught the light. Her eyes were liquid caramel, her fur as black and shiny as onyx.

Hudson looked down at Lucy with a warm smile, and she immediately smiled back. But that probably had more to do with Bonnie than anything else.

“Is it okay if Bonnie says hello?” Hudson asked. “She’s dying to.”

Lucy looked up at Georgia questioningly.

“Of course.”

With the smallest touch from Hudson, the dog came over to the little girl and sat at her feet, tail sweeping the floor, in constant motion.

Georgia wasn’t sure if Lucy had a dog at home, but she must’ve been at least somewhat familiar with them because she seemed immediately at ease, her body language softening.

She let Bonnie sniff her, and Hudson caught Georgia’s eye. That was good. Someone had taught her that.

Once Bonnie had sniffed her hand, then licked it for good measure, Lucy sank to her little knees. She put her hands into the dog’s scruff and let her lick her cheek. Even though it was obvious that Bonnie was beside herself with doggy joy, she stayed calm and gentle, conscious of not knocking Lucy over or overwhelming her in any way.

Lucy grinned. "Good girl," she cooed. "Good dog, Bonnie. You're such a good girl."

Georgia took this in, her heart close to bursting. It was obvious there was a connection here. And maybe Bonnie was just that kind of dog—Georgia suspected that she was. Still, what was happening between child and animal was undeniable. An unspoken warmth, a mutual love was passing between them, and it was the first time Georgia had ever witnessed anything like it.

She caught Hudson's gaze and mouthed, *Thank you.* He smiled back, two deep dimples cutting into each scruffy cheek.

*"It's Bonnie!"*

And just like that, the peaceful moment popped like a birthday balloon. The rest of the kids had spotted the dog in the hallway, and pandemonium ensued.

"Oh, my gosh, she's so cute!"

"I want to see!"

"Tristan, you just stepped on my big *toe*!"

Hudson's eyes widened. "Uh-oh. Sorry. What did I do?"

Georgia laughed. "You didn't do anything. This is my life. Just one second…"

Ushering Lucy into the classroom, she held a finger to her lips, and the kids immediately hushed. There was too much on the line. They knew the sooner they calmed down, the sooner they were going to get their hands on Bonnie.

"Boys and girls, I want you to meet our special visitors. Do you remember what their names are?"

"Mr. Hudson and Bonnie!" the class said in unison.

"Very good. I—"

Before she could say anything else, about ten little arms shot into the air.

She turned to Hudson. "We'll have to get the questions out of the way first," she said under her breath, "or they might explode."

"Oh, I get it. Fire away."

"Class, Mr. Hudson can answer your questions, but we're going to have one question per student, okay? And then he's going to tell us a little bit about search and rescue, and how Bonnie finds people who are lost. We want you all to stay safe when you go camping, or go for hikes in the woods. Are you ready?"

They wiggled in their seats.

"Tristan, what's your question?" she asked the little boy with the unruly shock of red hair.

"Is she a bat for Halloween?"

"She is," Hudson said. "It was between that and angel wings, but she was too chubby for those. They didn't fit."

They all giggled.

Georgia smiled and pointed to a little girl. "Heather?"

"How old is she?"

"She's almost nine," Hudson said. "She has some gray hair now, but she used to be jet-black."

"Ooohhh," they all said in unison. Some of them leaning forward over their desks to see if they could glimpse the gray hair in question.

"Michael," Georgia said, pointing to a little boy on the edge of his seat.

"How does she find people in the woods? How did she find Miss Gallagher?"

“That’s a really good question,” Hudson said. “When someone gets lost, we give her something of theirs to sniff, so she has their scent. Like a shirt or jacket. Then, she goes to work. She can look for people much faster than humans can. Dogs have very strong noses. They smell about ten thousand times better than people do.”

Michael’s brown eyes were wide, the freckles scattered across his cheeks reminding Georgia of spilled brown sugar.

She pointed to a little girl in the back who was waving her hand impatiently.

“Yes. Peggy.”

“Can she do any tricks?”

“She actually can. She knows how to speak and how to play dead.”

“Can we see?”

The entire class squirmed at the prospect of getting to see this for themselves.

Hudson looked at Georgia. He wasn’t going to do anything without her approval. Having such a strong, capable man looking to her for permission made her toes curl.

She nodded. “Sure. Go for it.”

“Bonnie,” he said. “Play dead!”

She immediately dropped to the carpet and rolled over on her back, her four paws in the air. The class erupted in belly laughs, and Georgia grinned at Hudson, utterly charmed.

He was enjoying this, she could tell. Which only added to the butterflies that were brushing against her rib cage.

“Bonnie,” he said again. “Alive!”

She jumped up with a bark and wagged her tail. The kids clapped, and a curious teacher who was passing by in the hallway paused to see what all the commotion was about.

"Okay, kids," Georgia said, looking at her watch. "Can you thank Mr. Hudson for answering your questions?"

"Thank you, Mr. Hudson!" they said in unison.

"After he tells you about his job, he and Bonnie are going to stay for a little while, and you're welcome to pet her, but one at a time, and very gently, okay?"

They nodded eagerly from their seats. Lucy gazed at Bonnie with a small smile on her lips. She'd been the very first one to pet the dog that all the other kids were going nuts over, and clearly that was a secret she was coveting. The look of contentment on her face was so different than what Georgia was used to seeing, that she just gazed at her for a second. She hadn't even asked again about calling her mother, which was a fairly big deal.

Hudson stepped close. "What is it?" he asked quietly.

"Nothing. I just think you made their day. Maybe their entire month. Are you sure you don't mind staying for a bit?"

He looked down at her, and she swallowed hard. He was so handsome.

"I'm sure," he said. "I'm just happy to be here."

Georgia watched her last student climb onto the bus with a wave. It had been a long day, and her feet were hurting, her back a little sore from bending over desks all afternoon, but she was in an undeniably sunny mood. Even the low clouds overhead, which threatened rain soon, couldn't dampen her spirits. And she knew exactly why.

As if on cue, Thomas walked over with a knowing

smile. "So," he said. "Tell me about the party. How'd it go? But judging by the look on your face, I can already tell."

"Stop! I don't have a look."

"Oh, honey. Yes, you do."

Georgia laughed, crossing her arms over her chest as the wind picked up. Normally she'd have to pull her hair back in weather like this, put it in a ponytail to keep it from turning into a rat's nest. But with it so short, she didn't have to worry about things like that anymore. She wondered if she ever would've had a pixie if it hadn't been for Sophie. Probably not. Her hair had always been part of her identity. Sad, but true. Long and dark, she'd shared that characteristic with her sister. But when they'd decided to buzz it off together when Sophie's had started falling out, she hadn't thought twice about it. Leave it to cancer to teach someone that hair is just hair.

Thomas nudged her in the side. "I think it might be time to ask this guy out. What do you think?"

"Just passing through, remember? You're too much of a romantic. I could think of fifty reasons why it wouldn't work."

"And I can think of fifty why it would."

"Thomas, you're a bad influence."

"And that's why you love me."

"I do love you."

"It would do you some good, you know. Getting out, getting to know someone new."

She sighed, chewing her cheek for a second. He had a point. She knew she'd curled into herself since Sophie's passing. She'd taken care of her for a long time before she'd died. And then that hole had been filled with grief-with missing her, with worrying for her parents, and how they were handling it. The only time she got out lately, other than her hike from hell, was to go to work. Thomas was right, it would probably do her some good.

"It's been fun flirting with him," she said. "It's been fun having daydreams about him…"

"You're having daydreams about him?"

"You saw him today."

"Good point."

She gave him a small smile. "But realistically, I'm just not ready to go there. Even if he wasn't just passing through."

Thomas considered that, the wind buffeting his strawberry blond hair. He put his hands in his pockets and watched Georgia for a long minute.

"What?" she asked.

"Nothing. It's just that I wonder what Sophie would have to say about that."

Georgia looked down at her boots. Thomas wasn't going to sugarcoat anything. He was bringing out the big guns by asking that question. By forcing her to look at this through her sister's eyes. It was Thomas who'd come over in those early days and gotten her out of bed. Had helped her get dressed and get something to eat, even when she'd insisted that she wasn't hungry. He was such a good friend. And that meant he was tough when he had to be.

"You know what she'd say," he said quietly. "Don't you?"

She didn't answer that. Instead, she gazed out over the school's soccer field to the ocean beyond. She could see the choppy, white-capped swells from where she stood.

Suddenly, she missed her sister with an ache that made

it hard to breathe. She'd been conscious of the grieving process these last few months, but she'd just recently noticed glimpses of healing. Of smiling and laughing, and being happy for moments at a time. As she'd watched the buses pulling away this afternoon, with thoughts of Hudson in her head, she'd been happy. There was no doubt about that. But then there was the guilt that went along with being happy. Thomas had hit a nerve with asking what Sophie would think of all of this. All she wanted was to sit down with her sister and talk about it.

Seeming to know exactly what she was thinking, he stepped close and pulled her into a hug. He smelled good. Like coffee and fabric softener.

"Hey, you," he said. "I'm sorry."

"It's okay."

"It really isn't. That was stupid of me. I just want you to be happy, and sometimes I don't think before I say stuff, and I'm always getting onto the kids about that same thing. I should know how to take my own advice by now."

Georgia smiled against his shirt. "It's that no-filter thing that keeps me so entertained, Tommy. And you were right. Sophie would want me to put myself out there more. She was fearless when it came to men. She was fearless when it came to everything."

"You've got that same blood running through your veins, kiddo."

"Actually, before she got sick, I was learning to sew some wild oats. I was learning to let my hair down a little."

"I could totally see that about you."

"That I have wild oats?"

"Oh, for sure. It's always the quiet ones."

She laughed. "So…you think I should call him."

"I think you should follow your heart. Wherever that might lead."

"That's very romance novel of you."

"Thank you."

She pulled away and brushed her bangs out of her eyes. A few drops of rain hit her face, and she looked up at the dark clouds hustling across the sky. "I think we're in for some weather."

"It's Friday night," Thomas said. "You want to grab a drink? I'm buying."

She shivered in the cool breeze. "In that case, yes."

"You should call her," Grady said.

He frowned at the cut on Hudson's shin. It had finally stopped bleeding, but a colorful-looking bruise was now blooming around the outer edges. This was what happened when you tried fly-fishing in the wind and rain and slipped on what must've been the sharpest damn rock on the Oregon coast.

Hudson leaned over and narrowed his eyes at it. "Gross."

"You're current on your tetanus, right?"

"Yeah, I cut my hand on a dog food can last spring. I got one then."

"You don't need any stitches. But you'll need to keep it clean. River water is full of bacteria."

"Thanks, doc."

"That'll be fifteen hundred dollars, please."

"Piss off."

Grady laughed and walked over to the window of the

Airbnb, looking out to where the wind was whipping the bright yellow Scotch broom back and forth.

"Seriously, though," he said. "You should call her."

Hudson stuck the bandage back in place and rolled his pant leg back down. He glanced over at Bonnie, who was dreaming in her dog bed. She whimpered and her paws twitched. Probably chasing a squirrel up a dream tree.

He got up from the couch and walked over to where his friend stood looking out the window. The ocean churned in the distance. It had turned out to be a bad day for fishing, even though their motto in the beginning of fall had been Rain or Shine. Turned out that three middle-aged guys who were mediocre fishermen at best didn't last long in inclement weather.

"Call her," Hudson said. "As in to ask her out?"

"Yeah."

"I didn't know you..."

Grady turned to him and smiled. "You didn't know I could tell? I could tell the second you got back from seeing her in the hospital that day. It's kind of obvious."

Grady's expression grew somber as he looked back out the window again. Hudson watched him, knowing something was wrong, but not having any clue what it was. Grady was one of his best friends, more like a brother than anything else, but they weren't in the habit of having deep talks. Their friendship was mostly based on shared experiences. They'd bonded deeply over what they'd been through, what they'd witnessed during their time in the army. And of course, over the loss of Jesse. But talking was not their strong suit. Up until now, anyway.

Hudson stood there with his hands in his pockets, waiting for Grady to say something. To tell him what was going on. He'd been more withdrawn lately than he and Tad had ever seen him before.

"Don't wait," Grady said quietly. "Don't make the same mistake I did."

"What do you mean?"

"With Jesse."

Hudson and Tad had always known Grady had a thing for Jesse, but they'd seen it as more of a crush. Nothing serious.

But something in the way that Grady was standing, the way he was staring out at the ocean, gave Hudson pause. He watched his friend, suddenly seeing him through a different lens. For the first time, he considered the possibility that Grady was grieving more than just a friend.

"Hey," he said. "What's going on?"

Grady rubbed his jaw. Then looked over at Hudson. There was no mistaking the misery in his eyes, the sadness there.

"We had a thing," he said. "Jesse and I. You didn't know that, did you?"

Hudson's stomach dropped. Not unlike that feeling of being on a carnival ride that fell right out from underneath you.

"No, I didn't."

He thought he'd known most things there were to know about Jesse, but he'd been wrong. It made him sad to think she and Grady had kept this a secret. But of course, they would've. If it had gotten out, it would've introduced all kinds of complications into their relationship, and their friendships with Hudson and Tad. Not to mention their working relationships with their fellow soldiers and superiors.

"How long?" he asked.

"Long enough to fall in love with her."

Hudson grit his teeth. Felt them jam together almost painfully. He remembered a day when he'd walked into a tent to find Jesse and Grady sitting close. Closer than friends would probably sit, but the possibility that they might be more than that just hadn't occurred to him. Now, the puzzle pieces were beginning to slide into place.

"I'm sorry I didn't tell you," Grady said. "We didn't know how. And we really weren't sure if it was going to last anyway. We didn't want to make things weird with you guys. We didn't…"

His voice grew hoarse and then trailed off.

"You don't have to be sorry, Grady. You didn't have to tell us a damn thing."

"But you loved her, too."

"Not like that."

Grady swallowed visibly and ran a hand through his hair. His watch glinted in the late afternoon sun that had broken briefly through the clouds. It was sunny and rainy at the same time. Hudson thought he'd heard somewhere that that was good luck. Or maybe it was bad luck. He couldn't remember.

"Maybe if I'd told her more, maybe if I'd been more…"

"Stop. You can't do that to yourself. And there's nothing you could've done. It was just a random bomb. An awful, horrible day. It could've been anyone."

Grady looked over at him, and his eyes were bloodshot now. A little glassy.

"She was pregnant, Hud."

Hudson stared at him. The world suddenly slowed on its axis. It was barely turning anymore, as the words began to seep into his consciousness. *Pregnant?* It was too sad, too cruel to accept.

"Are you sure?"

"She told me the day before. We didn't really have time to process. It would've changed the trajectory of her career, that's for sure. We would've had to decide what we were to each other, how we fit into each other's lives. We didn't have time to decide any of that, or to even let it sink in."

Grady paused, his jaw muscles bunching. He hadn't shaved that morning, and Hudson couldn't remember the last time he'd seen his friend with scruff. He was always so put together. That was what a lifetime in the service did to you. Hudson was still getting used to the fact that he could sleep in, let alone grow a beard if he wanted to.

He stood there next to his friend, wanting to say something to comfort him, but he was having a hard time with the shock of it himself, with all of it. Knowing that Jesse had been carrying a baby, Grady's baby, was almost too much to bear.

Grady cleared his throat. "Anyway, I don't know why I said anything now. Except that if I could go back and do it again, I wouldn't leave anything unsaid or undone."

Hudson nodded and stared out at the ocean, his mind churning right along with the water. He put his hand on his friend's shoulder, and held it there for a long minute before taking it away again. He wondered if Tad knew about this, and guessed he didn't. He would've said something, if he'd known what the hell to say.

Discovering the weight that Grady had been carrying all this time made it hard to breathe. It was all Hudson could do not to cry for his friend, but he hadn't cried since he'd been a little boy. Not even when Jesse was killed.

He wondered if there was something fundamentally wrong with that. Or something fundamentally wrong with *him*. Pushing his emotions down had been the only way to get through a life of war and service and conflict. It had been a way to survive, a way to reach the other side as a relatively whole person. But the problem with pushing those emotions down was that he didn't know how to feel them now. When his world was safer, when it couldn't hurt him nearly so easily anymore, it was the emotion that he was truly afraid of.

So, he didn't say anything like he really wanted to. He just stood there in quiet solidarity with his friend, hoping he knew how much he meant to him. How much he cared. And thinking about what Grady had said about leaving nothing unsaid and undone. Was that just for people you loved? Or did it extend to people you could love if given the chance?

He thought about his afternoon at the elementary school, and the pretty teacher who'd left him feeling upside down, inside out.

But it didn't really matter how she'd left him.

He was just passing through.

# *Chapter Six*

"Please, Mrs. Thorton. Sit down."

Georgia ushered Lucy's mother to a chair in the back of the classroom and then pulled one up opposite her. She'd been crying, that was obvious.

"I'm sorry," the other woman said, holding a tissue to her nose. "I know this is your grading period, that's what the receptionist said. But I needed to talk to you, and I didn't want to wait for a call back."

"No, I'm glad you came by. I'm never too busy to talk. I hope everything's okay?"

Grace Thorton looked far away for a second. Then her watery gaze came back to Georgia. Unsettled, jumpy. She was most definitely not okay.

"I don't know what to do about Lucy. She's having so much trouble at home. Her dad and I tried getting back together, and that…" She swallowed visibly. "That didn't go very well."

Georgia reached out and touched her knee. It was hard to know how to help in situations like these, but the first step was being a good listener. Offering information on resources if Grace asked for it, and hopefully she would. Georgia's first priority was her student, and making sure her home life wasn't dangerous. So far, she hadn't seen any indication that it was. So far, it just seemed profoundly unhappy.

"I'm sorry," Georgia said quietly. "Lucy is such a bright girl. She's so sweet and sensitive. I know this must be very hard for you both."

"The hardest thing is watching her struggle. She has nightmares almost every night. And lately she's been wetting the bed."

Georgia frowned, her heart aching for the little girl that she'd grown so fond of over the last few months. She'd known Lucy was struggling; she could clearly see that in class. But it was worse than she'd guessed.

"Have you thought about taking her to a counselor?" Georgia asked. "I can give you the numbers of a few good ones."

"Our insurance doesn't cover that. I checked."

"Well, the school has a wonderful counselor. She's not here full-time, but we can have Lucy meet with her the next time she's here? Talking about it would probably help. She could get some tools to help manage her anxiety."

Grace chewed her bottom lip. "But wouldn't the other kids know she was talking to her? I don't want them to think she's got problems."

Inside, Georgia screamed. The stigma around therapy was real. Over the years she'd watched so many kids suffer because they didn't have access to someone professional to talk to.

"The other kids wouldn't know unless she said something. But even if they did know, I think the benefit to Lucy would far outweigh the potential negatives."

The other woman seemed to consider this. "Okay," she said wearily.

Georgia nodded. Then thought of how Lucy seemed to come out of her shell at the Halloween party. How she'd seemed lighter, happier that afternoon than she had all year.

"Mrs. Thorton," she said. "Do you have a dog at home?"

"No. My mother had a little dog that would visit sometimes, but she moved in with my sister last summer. They live in Astoria."

"Was Lucy close to your mom?"

"She loved her. She spent a lot of time over at her place."

"And she liked the dog?"

"She was crazy about him. Why?"

Georgia smiled. The warmest, sweetest idea taking hold.

"I think I know someone who might be able to help," she said. "And she happens to be crazy about Lucy, too."

The morning of Halloween dawned foggy and cold. The chilly sea air seeped into Georgia's bones, staying there no matter how high she cranked the heat in her little house.

She sat now in a corner booth at Gran's Diner, wrapped in a fuzzy gray cardigan and holding a hot cup of coffee in her hands. Her stomach was in knots. Mostly because she was about to see Hudson Cross again, and this time it wasn't going to be in her classroom with twenty first graders tugging at her sleeve. Today, they were going to sit down and talk face-to-face. And yeah, that had everything to do with Lucy, and the seed that had planted itself in Georgia's brain the day Grace Thorton had come in. But she'd still be seeing him again, and that was enough to make her pull out her compact from her purse and check her reflection.

For the life of her, she couldn't understand why she cared so much. It didn't matter how she looked. There was no future with Hudson. There wasn't even a present with him. The problem was, she'd developed a good old-fashioned crush, and it didn't matter how much she reasoned with herself, how much she reminded herself that she wasn't ready to be feeling this way, or even how much she said it out loud to Thomas. She felt it just the same.

She looked over when the door to the diner opened, bringing with it a cold blast of salty air, but it was just an elderly couple walking through. She smiled at the gentleman, who held the door open for his wife as she shuffled along, much slower than he was.

Georgia watched as they as sat at a table at the far end of the diner, with eyes only for each other. She used to be much more of a romantic before Sophie got sick. Believing in happily-ever-afters and love that lasted a lifetime. It wasn't that she didn't still believe in those things, but she was much more hesitant to open her heart to the possibility.

Even so, she put her chin in her hand and gazed at the couple, feeling her heart flutter a little. She wondered what their story was. Wondered what had happened to them over the years, and knowing that it couldn't have been all sunshine and roses. Nobody's life was. But here they were, together at the end, looking very much in love. It was enough to make the backs of her eyes sting as she thought of her sister, and all the things that would never be. But for the first time, there was a tiny spark of light, where before there had been only darkness. Georgia could live for her sister. If she was lucky, she could experience the things that Sophie hadn't been able to.

The thought filled her with a brief warmth, just as the door opened again. And this time it was Hudson walking through. She stared at him, her breath catching in her throat. He was the kind of man—tall and imposing, broad shouldered and square jawed—that stopped traffic. Well, traffic that happened to include anyone with an active libido.

He looked around the diner, and then his gaze caught hers. He'd been in the sun lately, had a little bit of a burn across his nose. The effect was dazzling, and Georgia had to remember to blink.

"Good morning," he said, walking up to the booth. Then sliding in across from her.

"Good morning. I ordered you some coffee. I wasn't sure how you like it, but I asked for some cream and sugar just in case."

"The coffee in the army was pretty much black sludge, so I'm not used to anything fancy. But it would probably taste better that way."

She laughed. "I wouldn't know. I just recently learned to drink it."

His eyes widened. "You just recently *learned* to drink coffee?"

"Yup."

"I'm sorry, but what the hell did you do before that?"

"Stayed tired."

He nodded at the cup in her hands. "So, how do you drink it now?"

"Five sugars and one creamer."

He smiled. "Five sugars..."

"I like sweet things."

He watched her for a long moment, his gaze darkening slightly. "So do I."

Her cheeks warmed. She could get used to this subtle flirting. The way his eyes twinkled when he looked at her. The way he was sitting—leaning forward with his elbows on the table. As if he was trying to get closer to her. She could get used to all of it.

The server came over and set Hudson's coffee down. She wore little pumpkin earrings that dangled cheerfully next to her face. "Are you two ready to order?"

"Oh," Georgia said. She'd almost forgotten they were in a public place, much less somewhere to eat. "We might need a minute?"

Hudson nodded, and then they were alone again. The diner buzzed with the comforting sounds of people talking and laughing, of utensils scraping against plates. It was familiar to Georgia. This had been one of her and Sophie's favorite places to grab breakfast on Saturday mornings. Sometimes their mom would join them, and they'd sit by the window facing the ocean, talking about work and friends and life in general. Those had been good times. Simpler times.

"What's good here?" Hudson asked, picking up his menu.

"Everything's good."

"Everything, huh?"

She nodded.

"Well, then. I might have to pig out."

"Now you're speaking my love language. I was trying to decide between pancakes and biscuits and gravy."

"Oh, my God," he said. "Biscuits and gravy. My grandma made the best biscuits and gravy I've ever had in my life. Ever."

She smiled. She'd never known her grandparents; they'd died before she was born.

"Were you close with your grandmother?"

He glanced up at her. Then frowned. "Very."

"I'm sorry… Is that a painful subject?"

"Not at all. I just realized nobody has ever asked me that before. Which is weird, because she was such a big part of my life before she passed."

"I wonder why nobody's asked."

"Probably because I'm not usually the most approachable guy in the world. And I've never talked about her to anyone before. Which is also weird. Seems like you have the magic touch."

"Hardly. I'm just curious about people. Curious about you."

At that, he leaned back in the booth. "Curious about me, huh?"

"Yes."

"What do you want to know?"

"Where do I start?"

One corner of his mouth tilted. "Wow. You *are* curious."

"Told you."

"Well, I'm curious about you, too."

"I'm pretty much an open book," she said. "What you see is what you get."

"I doubt that. Everyone has a story."

"I like that. Makes me sound intriguing."

"That's exactly what you are."

He was definitely flirting. Which could get dangerous.

Taking a sip of her coffee, she tried to get her bearings. Reminded herself why she'd wanted to meet him here in the first place. She could ask him about himself all day long, and that didn't change the fact that he didn't live in Christmas Bay. That he was leaving at some point soon. That behind those sparkling eyes, there was a mysterious depth that would take a lot longer than a talk over morning coffee to explore. And that scared her a little, if she was being honest.

"I guess I should tell you what this is all about," she said.

He watched her. His gaze intent.

"Do you remember my student from the other day?" she asked. "The shy one who met Bonnie in the hallway?"

"I do. Lucy. She was adorable."

"She really is. She's also struggling. Her parents are getting a divorce, and her mom came to talk to me the other day. I had an idea. It might be a long shot, and I don't know what your schedule is like, but—"

"She was better after she got to spend some time with Bonnie," he said.

It wasn't a question. It was a statement—like he wasn't surprised at all by this outcome.

"Yes," Georgia said. "In fact, I can't remember when I've seen her this relaxed. She has so much anxiety, and when she was with Bonnie, it just seemed to melt away. I know it's not a cure-all, but I was hoping…"

"I'd love to help. Anything I can do, count me in."

Georgia gazed at him over the table. She hadn't thought he could get any sexier, but he just had.

"This is wonderful," she said. "Seriously. I think a few more visits to the classroom would be amazing for her. She's going to be seeing the school counselor, and I feel like visits from Bonnie might really complement that."

"We're going to be in town until Thanksgiving. So anytime. All we're doing is fishing, and we can do that anytime."

She watched him closely. She knew just enough about him to want to know more. He was here with his two best friends, but she didn't know anything about them, except that they all seemed exceptionally close. She wondered where he lived, what his time in the army had been like. All things she was dying to ask.

"What?"

"Nothing," she said. "Okay… It's just that you're kind of a mystery to me."

"So, you think I'm interesting."

"I think you're very interesting."

He took a sip of his coffee, then put it down again.

"What do you want to know?" he asked.

She laughed softly. "You can take the girl out of the small town, but I guess you can't take the small town out of the girl. Everyone around here knows everything about everyone else. Mostly, at least. But that doesn't mean I have to know everything about you. You're free to tell me to pound sand."

"I would never."

He said it with that teasing look in his eyes that she found so attractive, so magnetic. But she wasn't fooling herself into thinking that he was suddenly going to be open and vulnerable where she was concerned. Hudson Cross *was* mysterious, and that was probably because he'd spent years being very careful who he let in, and who he didn't.

She picked up her menu again and made a show of looking more interested than she actually was in the breakfast selections. "So, what looks good?"

He reached out and touched her hand, and she glanced up again.

"Not so fast," he said. "What do you want to know?"

Her heart tapped against her rib cage. She was finding it hard not to lose her train of thought when she looked at him.

"Anything?" she asked.

"Anything."

She sat back in the booth. His gaze dropped to her mouth for a second. Just briefly, but long enough to confirm there was definitely chemistry between them.

"Why are you here, Hudson?" she asked quietly. "It seems like it might have to do with something more than just fishing."

His mouth tilted. But the warmth in his eyes cooled a little at that. She wondered then if she should've taken him up on the offer to ask him anything. If she should've just stopped while she was ahead.

"I'm sorry," she said. "It's none of my business…"

"No, it's okay. If it seems like I'm hesitant to talk about it, I am. But that doesn't mean I don't want to talk about it. I just haven't ever. Not really. And that probably sounds strange to you, and I guess it is strange. Not to have anyone in my life that I talk to about the heavy stuff. I have close friends, and they're here with me on this trip, actually. But it's different talking, *really* talking about the painful things."

It was more than she was expecting him to tell her. And he still hadn't disclosed anything. But what he'd said had come from a place that was very deep, she could tell. Very deep, and very tender.

She nodded. "I understand that. I have good friends, too. The best, but it's hard opening up, no matter how much you love someone."

They sat there, the sounds of the diner still humming around them. But it felt different somehow, like it was only the two of them now. Georgia chewed the inside of her cheek, quiet. If he was going to say anything else, she wanted him to offer it, and not offer it because she'd asked. Or worse, because she'd pushed.

He took another sip of coffee, then put his cup down, staring at it and looking far away for a second.

"Active-duty service is very hard," he finally said, his voice low. "You go in so young and so full of piss and vinegar. And so many of your friends are the same way. You grow up together, you get so close. And you all think alike. You just assume you're all going to serve, and retire, then get old and die in your sleep. And of course, not everyone is that lucky. Life really packs a punch. I've had to learn a lot of things through losing those people. And the lessons change you. Every single one."

Georgia sat there, hanging on the words. Gazing at him through a different lens. The lens of common ground.

"I lost someone special," he continued. "We all lost someone special, my buddies and I. She was one of our best friends, and we decided to take a trip every year to remember her. So, here we are."

It made sense now. And even though Georgia could've guessed that he was dealing with trauma like this, there was a validation in the explanation.

"I thought I recognized that look on your face," she said.

"What look?"

"Grief."

His expression was still guarded, but there was something in it that said he wasn't going to shut down. To shut her out, like she expected he might.

"It's that noticeable, huh?"

"It's a club that nobody wants to belong to," she said. "I'm so sorry about your friend."

He ran his thumb along the lip of his coffee cup. He had nice hands. Strong and thick, with long, blocky fingers. She studied them for a minute, before finding his gaze again.

"She was killed in a checkpoint explosion," he said. "Bonnie and I weren't on duty that day, and I can't let go of the feeling that Bonnie might've found that bomb. It's a losing game, of course. That 'what if' shit. But I can't seem to help it. I dream about it. I have nightmares about it. I think about it all the time."

Georgia's stomach turned at that. She understood not being able to let it go. Sophie had found her lump six months before she actually went in to have it checked. She'd told Georgia about it, and she couldn't forgive herself for not dragging Sophie to the doctor right away. She should've done it by her hair if she had to. But she hadn't, and now she lived with that guilt, along with everything else.

"What was her name?" she asked softly. "Your friend."

"Jesse."

It was a nice name. Georgia wondered if it had been short for Jessica. She'd had a friend named Jessica when she was little. She'd cut all her hair off at her fifth birthday party, and her mother had screamed so loud, the neighbors had come running.

"What about you?" he asked. "You said you lost your sister."

Someone dropped a plate in the kitchen, and she startled at the sound. It jerked her back to the present.

"I did," she said. "Her name was Sophie. She was a couple years younger than me. She had breast cancer. She was amazing. You would've liked her. Everyone liked Sophie."

"I'm sure I would've. If she was anything like you, I'm sure I would've liked her a lot."

She smiled, but there was a lump in her throat now. The same one that ambushed her at the most awkward moments. Sophie would've thought it was funny, the fact that Georgia sobbed at the drop of a hat these days. She'd never been much of a crier before. Sophie had been the one who cried during phone commercials and sappy movies, and had always given Georgia a hard time about not tearing up herself. *Do you have a heart of stone, or what?* She could hear her sister's voice, and then her laughter, ringing like a distant bell.

"When did she pass?" Hudson asked. He was watching her closely, leaning forward, elbows on the table. Invested in her, invested in her story.

"At the beginning of July. Coming up on four months now."

Hudson nodded. "You're in the thick of it, then. The hardest part."

"I guess I am. Sometimes I wonder if it'll get any easier. And then I think that I don't want it to get easier, because the pain makes me feel close to her. I feel guilty when I have days when it's not as sharp. How messed up is that?"

"It's normal. It's the cycle of emotion. People can tell you all day long what to expect, but the truth is, you can never understand what it's like until you've been through it yourself. So, yeah. It's a club, just like you said."

"How long ago was Jesse killed?"

"Almost two years ago. Someone told me once that the grieving process takes between six months to a year for most people. Which is ridiculous, giving it a timeline like that. But I found myself thinking about it a lot in the beginning. Counting down the months, like I'd feel better when that amount of time had passed."

He looked down at his coffee again. It was clear that he'd cared deeply for her. And was still struggling with her passing, with that monumental loss. The guilt was evident on his face and in his body language. He was sitting stiffer than before, more rigid.

"Tell me about your friends that you're here with," she asked, wanting to shift the conversation to something lighter.

"Grady is a doctor, and Tad is a computer geek. We've been friends since basic. They're good guys, the best."

"And you're on this trip together. That's really nice, Hudson. I can't think of a lovelier way to remember Jesse. What made you decide on Christmas Bay?"

"We saw a viral YouTube video about the fishing here.

Some guy from Scotland was going on and on about it. We looked it up online and booked a few days later."

"How are you liking it so far?" she asked.

"The fishing is great. But it's more than that. It's the time together that's been good for us. We've always been close, but now we're bonding over Jesse, and that's different. Something you can't explain to people."

"I understand."

"You would. You lost a sibling. Loss is loss. People will try and put a label on it if you let them, but it's important not to put something like this in a box."

She felt that to her bones. "You're absolutely right."

They watched each other for a long moment. Georgia could feel her heart beating in the hollow of her throat.

"So," he said. "Tell me about your parents. I saw them at the hospital. Are they still together? Do they live in Christmas Bay?"

"They're divorced, and my dad lives in Springfield now. He's seeing a much younger woman, so that's been interesting. He and Sophie weren't estranged exactly, but there was tension between them because of it. My mom was still coming to terms with the divorce when Sophie got sick. It's this whole thing. They haven't been able to lean on each other very well. I'm kind of in the middle, trying to help them both, without upsetting either one of them. Anyway…yeah…" She sighed. "We all have a lot of unresolved feelings. Sophie used to be my sounding board. I miss that so much. Do you have any siblings?"

He nodded. "I have a half sister, but she's much older. She lives in the Midwest, so I was never close to her. I'd like to be, though. Someday. My mom was kind of a hot mess, and my dad was in and out of my life. My childhood was rough, and other than my grandmother, I had no nobody to look up to, no examples of a healthy relationship. That's why the army was such a good fit. Offered stability and structure, and gave me role models, which I was in desperate need of. I was pretty close to becoming a high school dropout with a drug problem when my grandma died. And then a recruiter found me."

"So," she said. "The army was your family."

"It was my life, for a long time. It's a hard adjustment being out of that environment. But I've got my friends. I've got my dog."

"And she's the best dog."

"She really is."

He smiled, and it was warm and sexy. Actually, everything about this man was sexy.

She took a sip of her coffee, suddenly feeling shy. Like he might be able to read her mind if she wasn't careful.

"Honey! What are you doing here?"

Georgia looked up to see her mother walking over. Windblown, pink-cheeked, her eyebrows raised in genuine surprise. She wore a black sweater with a jack-o'-lantern embroidered on the front. She'd been shopping at the Methodist church holiday bazaar, and it showed.

"Oh… Mom. Hi. Uh, Hudson and I were just having coffee." She nodded toward Hudson, bracing herself. Her mother had an embarrassing tendency to say the most out-of-pocket things. Especially when it came to guys she liked.

He stood. And towered over her five-foot-two mother, who stared up at him with her mouth literally hanging open.

"So, *this* is Hudson," she said, sounding a little breathless. "We never got to thank you at the hospital. But I've heard all about you from Georgia. Honestly, she's just gone on and on."

He looked over at Georgia, and her face caught fire.

"Mom, really," she said. "I just said that he came to our class party."

"If you say so, honey. Also, you did *not* mention how handsome he was."

*"Mom."*

"It's okay," Hudson said. "I can live with handsome."

Her mother grinned, clearly charmed.

Georgia looked around, hoping to see one of her mom's girlfriends who would usher her away. "Who are you here with?"

"Julie. Are you trying to get rid of me?"

"Why would I be trying to get rid of you?" So, it showed.

"You always used to do that when you were on dates. You never wanted your dad or me to say *anything.*"

"I'm not on a date."

"Is this a date, Hudson?" Her mother looked up at Hudson with her hands on her hips. "I'd like to know, because Georgia never tells me anything."

*"Mother."*

Hudson rubbed the back of his neck. "Uh…"

"Don't answer that," Georgia said.

"You can tell me."

"Mom, what's gotten into you?"

"Nothing! I'm just interested in your love life."

Georgia stared at her. Ever since Sophie's passing, she'd been subdued and sad, and so far from her normal self that sometimes Georgia didn't recognize her anymore. So, even though this was embarrassing, it was also light-years better than the sad interactions they'd had over the last few months.

Hudson looked down at his boots, and it was obvious that he was trying not to laugh.

Georgia gave him a look. He shrugged.

"I just want to thank you for finding my baby that day," her mom said. "I don't know what I'd do if anything ever happened to her."

"It was my pleasure. Your daughter is very special."

"She is. She and her sister have been the light of my life. Well," she said, taking a deep breath and fanning her face. "I'd better stop or I'll just start crying, and poor Georgia has had enough of that to last a lifetime."

Georgia gave her a small smile. It was the hardest thing, watching her mother struggle like this. And watching her dad, who'd always been a beacon of strength for their family, change and age over these last four months. She wished that her parents still had each other, but that ship had sailed.

"Oh, it looks like Julie snagged our favorite spot," Georgia's mom said with a wave to her friend. "Georgia, did you know we've been coming here a few times a week?"

"I didn't. That's great, Mom."

"We're taking a yoga class together, and we have breakfast afterward to put the calories right back on."

Georgia laughed. "Naturally."

"No yoga today, though. Just breakfast..." She looked from Georgia to Hudson, and then back again, and a surprisingly comfortable silence settled over the three of them.

"Well," she finally said. "It was so nice to meet you, Hudson. I was just teasing about the date thing. Mostly." She winked. "Have a good morning, you two."

And then she was headed across the diner to Julie, who was waiting in a bright purple rain jacket and a matching knit hat. Georgia watched them, happy that her mom was getting out with her friends. It was a healthy step.

Hudson slid back into the booth.

"I'm so sorry about that," Georgia said. "But honestly, it's nice to see some of her sass come back. She hasn't been this feisty in a while."

"Don't be sorry. She's great."

"She wants me married off, in case you couldn't tell. Sophie wanted kids. She was planning on adopting before she passed. My mom was so excited to be a nana. She would've been a good one."

"Do you think you'll have kids?"

"I'd love kids. Someday, hopefully."

He nodded.

"How about you?" she asked. "Do you see a family in your future?"

"I've never let myself think that far ahead. My life has never been right for a family, for settling down. And now I feel like I might be past the age for it."

"Never! Picasso had kids into his eighties. Not that you're anywhere close to eighty. Or that I'm advocating for eighty-year-old first-time dads, but you know."

He chuckled. "I'll keep that in mind."

"Seriously, though. You should."

"To be honest… I'd be terrified of messing it up. What do I know about marriage? About fatherhood?"

"You'd learn as you go. You're a good person, you'd be a great dad."

His expression was suddenly dark, and she could tell that this probably wasn't the first time he'd been asked that question. She could see the look of hesitation in his eyes when she'd mentioned kids. It was hard for her to think of him doubting himself like this, but she'd also been a teacher long enough to know that a messed-up home life could have deep and lasting effects. Sometimes lifelong effects. Those doubts had been planted when he was a child, and his time in the service, surrounded by friends who'd had similar experiences, had only magnified them.

Georgia frowned and looked out the window. The wind had picked up since they'd been inside and gusted against the glass, rattling it.

"I bet the waves are pretty big right now," Hudson said.

"You should come back for the king tides. It's incredible."

She looked back at him. His eyes were so blue, they reminded her of the water at the edge of the rocks along the cape. Blue green. So clear that you could see all the way to the bottom.

"So," he said. "It's Halloween. Do you have a lot of trick-or-treaters in your neighborhood?"

"I'm not sure. I'm never home on Halloween."

"Why not?"

"We have a carnival at school every year," she continued. "It's kind of a big deal. The PTA goes all out. The teachers dress up and bake things for prizes. I actually love it. It's my favorite holiday."

"Huh. I pegged you as more of a Christmas girl."

"I love Christmas, too. That's my second favorite."

"This carnival," he said. "Can anyone come?"

"Of course."

"Would you mind if I stopped by?"

Her heart fluttered in her chest. Her kids would be thrilled to see him tonight. And they weren't the only ones.

"I'd be lying if I said I didn't want to see you in that cat costume again," he continued.

She smiled slowly. "If you come, you'll have to dress up, too."

"Um…"

"Yup. House rules."

"Is that a challenge?"

She'd never been much for challenges. She'd always taken the safer choices when they'd been presented to her. Hudson Cross was not a safe choice.

But here she was. Holding his gaze. Confident in her attraction for him, even if she knew it wasn't a good idea, and that it most certainly wouldn't go anywhere. Where could it go?

Still, she knew this was a challenge she was going to accept in more ways than one. The only question was who would win in the end.

# *Chapter Seven*

"You look ridiculous."

Tad stood in the middle of the room with his arms crossed over his broad chest. He looked Hudson up and down and then shook his head again.

"I have to meet this girl," he continued. "Anyone who could get you to do this, I have to meet."

Hudson laughed. "The kids should like it."

"Are you kidding? They're going to lose their minds."

This, from Grady, who held up his phone and took a picture.

"Delete that," Hudson said.

"Yeah, I don't think so."

Hudson looked down at his costume and was pretty damn proud of himself, actually. He'd looked online for some ideas, and then had gone to several stores to execute his masterpiece. Black gloves for paws. A black headband and some floppy pieces of black felt for the ears. And of course, a long black tail. He was Bonnie.

His dog contemplated him from her bed across the room. She yawned, then put her head back on her paws. She was unimpressed.

"Want to know what I think?" Tad asked.

"No," Hudson said.

"I think that deep down you've always wanted to dress up like this. I think deep down you are a large child walking around in a man suit."

"I think you're full of it."

Grady tucked his phone back into his pocket. He had his glasses on tonight since he'd lost a contact earlier in the day. It was at the bottom of the river. Or in some fish's belly by now. He looked like a doctor right then. Good-looking, polished. Out of all of them, he'd been most Jesse's type. Hudson couldn't understand why he hadn't guessed at their relationship before. Hindsight was always twenty-twenty.

"So, what are we supposed to do for Halloween?" Grady asked. "Sit around and look at each other?"

"Come to the carnival," Hudson said. "Say hi."

"I'm not dressing up." This from Tad, who still had his arms crossed over his chest. He was the grumpy old man in the group.

"You can go as a dumbass," Grady said. "No costume needed."

"Very funny."

"Boys, boys," Hudson said. "Am I going to have to separate you?"

"Let's go to the movies," Tad said. "There's something old playing. *Poltergeist*, I think."

"I don't like horror movies," Grady said.

"You don't have to *like* them. It's Halloween."

"I guess. Popcorn for dinner?"

"I'm in."

"Good," Hudson said. "I won't have to find a sitter."

"Hilarious," Grady said. "You're the one dressed up like your dog."

"Yes, but he's also the one who's probably going to get to second base tonight," Tad said. "So, there's that."

"No bases," Hudson said. "We're just friends."

Tad rolled his eyes. "Come on."

"He's right," Grady said. "I've never seen you like this." He eyed Hudson's dog ears. "Literally."

A gust of wind blew against the Airbnb's windows. The ocean beyond the beach was churning, the waves slamming against the rocks in a flurry of dramatic foam and spray. Every now and then the lighthouse horn would call through the early Halloween evening, warning any fishing boats that were just now coming in. But most of them hadn't even gone out, the weather was too nasty, too dangerous. It gave Hudson the chills, thinking about being out on that dark water tonight.

"I'm not saying I *don't* like her," he said, picking up his wallet and tucking it in his back pocket. "But I've got baggage. She's got baggage. And I don't even live here."

"Sounds like you've given it some thought," Tad said.

"Who wouldn't? She's beautiful. Smart, sweet…"

"The list goes on and on," Grady said.

"Yeah, that."

"Remember what I told you the other day. Don't be an idiot."

"Too late," Tad said.

Hudson smiled and threw his friend a look.

"I'm serious," Grady said.

They all grew quiet—the only sounds were the ticking of the clock above the fireplace and the muted roar of the waves outside. Hudson knew Grady was very serious. He suddenly pictured Jesse in her fatigues, her blond hair pulled into a bun. And a bolt of pain, as strong as if someone had physically inflicted it, tore through his chest.

He reached over to grab his keys from the coffee table. Wondering if this was a mistake. Wondering if he'd eventually have to weather the storm he was creating for himself by seeing Georgia tonight.

"So, we shouldn't wait up?" Tad asked dryly.

"I won't be late," Hudson answered. "Just friends, remember?"

Even as he said it, he knew that was probably stretching it. Since he never wanted to get naked with his friends.

Georgia stood in front of her carnival booth with "Werewolves of London" thumping in her ears. She was surrounded by about twenty goldfish in individual little bowls. Whoever tossed a quarter that landed in a bowl got to keep it. She remembered having a similar game at her own elementary school carnival when she was a kid, but back then, nobody really cared who the goldfish went home with, or if they'd be good fish parents. Times had changed, thankfully, and Georgia was using this booth as a chance to teach her kids about living things and responsibility, and she was also making sure that moms and dads were on board, since they were going to be the ones feeding said fish and cleaning their bowls. Well, them and Georgia, since she usually ended up with the classroom critters that her families couldn't keep anymore.

She watched a steady stream of kids skipping by in their little costumes—witches, goblins, bunnies, a box of M&M's, even a bottle of Elmer's glue.

"Miss Gallagher!"

She turned to see one of her kids in a *Blue's Clues* costume and smiled.

"Hi, Tristan. Happy Halloween."

"Thanks," he said, brushing his thick red hair out of his eyes. "I went trick-or-treating and got lots of candy."

"Oh boy. That sounds fun."

"How do you play this game?"

"You just toss a quarter toward the bowls, and if it goes in, you get to keep a fish."

"Ooooh, cool!"

"But you have to ask your mom or dad first. Make sure it's okay."

"Okay, I'll be right back."

She watched him run off. She should've told him to walk. But she had to admit, he looked pretty cute with his blue polka-dot ears flapping behind him.

She looked at her watch. Then scolded herself for looking. Ever since Hudson had mentioned coming tonight, she'd been on pins and needles. She didn't know why; it wasn't like they were going to start making out in front of the goldfish booth, but all she could think about was him. Which was a big change, since before meeting him, all she'd been able to think about was Sophie. And there was the guilt again.

"Meeeoww."

She looked up to see Thomas standing there, giving her a teasing smile.

"Looking good, Miss Gallagher," he said. "Hoping to see someone special tonight?"

Georgia reached up and adjusted one of her kitty ears. "Does it show?"

"No, you always look fabulous. But you *are* a little

flushed. Of course, that might be because it's a thousand degrees in here."

"Right?"

"I thought they were going to get the AC fixed before the school year started."

"Cheaper just to open the doors."

"When there's not a monsoon outside."

"Yes, that."

Thomas hadn't exactly pulled out all the stops in the costume department—he was just wearing a witch hat and a black Christmas Bay Elementary sweatshirt, but Georgia still thought he looked adorable. Thomas always looked adorable—but then again, she was biased.

He pushed his hat toward the back of his head. He was wearing glasses tonight, so he was also giving off a Harry Potter vibe.

"How long do we have to be here, again?" he asked, fanning himself.

"We just got here!"

"I know, but I have a martini with my name on it at home. It's been a long week, girl."

"Oh, I know. I'm dead on my feet."

"You mean your paws."

"Those, too."

Thomas glanced over her shoulder. "Don't look now, but your Prince Charming just walked through the door."

Georgia's eyes widened. "He did?"

"He absolutely did. And Georgia… Oh, my God. He's dressed up."

"He is not."

"He is."

Georgia couldn't stand it. She turned around, not car-ing that Hudson might catch her looking, or recognize what must be the hopeful, slightly dreamy look on her face.

And then she saw him. And her heart just about popped.

"Thomas…"

"I know. I *know.*"

"I told him he had to dress up, but I was just kidding."

"Well, he took you seriously."

"Or he's just trying to make me swoon."

"Is that what you're going to do? This is worse than I thought."

She laughed but couldn't take her eyes off Hudson, who was standing in the middle of the gym, looking around. Obviously looking for her. And then his gaze locked with hers, and she really was afraid she would swoon.

"He's so…" she said under her breath.

Thomas elbowed her in the ribs. "Are you going to go say hi, or are you just gonna stand there staring at him like I look at my first cup of coffee in the morning?"

She glanced at the booth behind her. She'd completely forgotten she was in charge of it.

"Don't worry," Thomas said, reading her mind. "I'll take over here. Go."

She gave him a quick hug. "I'll be back in a few."

"Don't you dare. Go do musical chairs, there are legit full-size cakes for prizes. Have your palms read, Madam Kathy is in the breezeway. Aka Trey's mom with the eighties perm. She's great, told me I have a long lifeline. And dry skin."

"Aren't you using that lotion I gave you for your birthday?"

Thomas took her by the shoulders and turned her

around, facing her toward Hudson and the rest of the room full of ghosts and goblins.

"Go," he said.

He gave her a playful little shove, and then she was weaving her way through kids and parents and grandparents, toward the man who was grinning at her now. In a dog costume, that he'd obviously put together at the last minute, making her heart flutter like a teenager's.

"Happy Halloween," he said as she walked up to him.

"Happy Halloween. You take your challenges seriously."

"Hell yes, I do. Might as well know that about me from the get-go."

"Is there anything else I should know?"

"Like the fact that I can't take my eyes off you?"

Had he actually just said that? She was starting to fall for this guy, there was no doubt about it. And then what? She reminded herself that it wasn't too late to get a handle on this. She could slow it down anytime she wanted. Which would be the smartest thing. The safest thing.

From somewhere in the farthest corner of her mind, she heard Sophie whisper softly, *You've been safe your whole life, Georgia. Why not be risky for once?*

Hudson gazed down at her, making her entire body hum. If he could make her feel this way without even touching her, she wondered what he could do with his hands.

"So," he said. "What now?"

"Well, I thought we could do musical chairs. Cakes for prizes. Tommy says they're pretty amazing."

"Tommy?"

"My best friend. He teaches here, too."

"Ahh, well, that sounds like a plan."

"Mr. Hudson!" They both looked over in time to see one of Georgia's students, a little girl in a pirate costume, launch herself at Hudson. She squeezed him around the middle, nearly knocking him off balance.

He laughed. "Hey, there."

"Are you a dog?"

"I'm Bonnie. Remember her?"

"Oh, how cute! Is she here? Can I see her?"

"She's actually at home tonight."

*Home.* Georgia wondered how she'd be feeling if he really did live here. If he weren't going to be leaving soon. Would she be more confident in the feelings she was starting to have? Or maybe it would be scarier, because if he wasn't leaving, there would be nothing standing in their way. Not technically, at least.

Heather, the little pirate, gave Georgia a hug, too. "Bye, Miss Gallagher!"

Before they could say anything else, she was running off, presumably toward her friends, or another carnival game, or another hug.

"You're a celebrity around here," Georgia said.

"Nah. Bonnie's the celebrity. I'm just the spokesman."

It was more than that. Much more. He radiated a mixture of warmth and charisma that the kids immediately picked up on. Whether he knew it or not, he was a natural with them.

"Well, should we get our cake walk on?" she asked. "And I hear there's an amazing, slightly novice palm reader outside, if you're into knowing your future."

"Lead the way, Kitty Soft Paws."

"Come on," she said.

And held out her hand.

* * *

Hudson walked close enough to Georgia that every now and then their shoulders would touch. The storm had blown itself mostly out to sea, and there was a brilliant half-moon hanging above them. The stars had come out, twinkling against the ebony sky like precious stones.

After musical chairs, where Hudson had won a cherry pie that he'd put in his truck ten minutes ago, and the palm reading session, where he'd been told that true love was in his near future, they'd decided to take a walk on the elementary school track. The carnival was still hopping, with "Li'l Red Riding Hood" thumping from inside the gym.

He'd taken his ears and tail off a while ago, but Georgia was still in her cat costume. Complete with a fitted black turtleneck and skinny jeans (with a tail attached, of course). The jeans were what had his throat dry as he looked over at her now. She was gorgeous, but he was pretty sure she wouldn't think so. There was an air of humility about her that he found completely irresistible in someone so beautiful.

"Well," he said. "I have to say, Christmas Bay Elementary really knows how to throw a party."

"Right? I'm kind of surprised. Every year, we outdo ourselves. It's fun. The kids love it."

"Seems like the teachers love it, too. And the parents."

They continued walking, with the sound of the waves slamming against the beach in the distance. Hudson took a deep breath, letting the salty air saturate his lungs.

"Damn, I could get used to this."

Georgia looked over, her thumbs tucked in her belt loops. "Christmas Bay?"

He nodded. "Not just the town, all of it. The people, the lifestyle. Being near the ocean. It's kind of amazing."

"I know. I didn't always feel that way, though. When you grow up in such a small town, there's this phase of wanting to leave. Of thinking the grass is going to be greener on the other side of the fence."

"Have you ever left?"

"For college. I went to Idaho State. And it was great, it was an adventure, but when I graduated, all I could think about was coming home. I love it here. And I missed the water."

"I can see why you would."

"Where did you grow up?"

Talking about himself had never been very comfortable. Mostly because he didn't feel like there was much to say that would interest anyone. Nobody wanted to hear a sob story about a crappy childhood, and how he'd never been anywhere or done anything worthwhile until he'd enlisted in the service.

But tonight, for the second time that day, he found himself wanting to tell her.

"Chicago," he said. "Not in a great part of town. Nothing I'd ever miss or want to go back to."

"Where do you live now?" she asked.

"Colorado. Outside of Denver."

"Colorado is lovely. I went there once for a cheerleading competition in high school."

"You were a cheerleader?"

She nodded proudly. "I could even do the splits. I seriously can't believe I never tore anything. Or landed on my head."

He smiled. "I'm sure you were very good."

"I was alright. But I loved the friendships I made. That was the fun part."

They kept walking, the air cool on Hudson's bare arms. He probably should've grabbed a jacket from the truck, but the gym had been so stuffy, the blustery breeze felt nice.

"So, why Colorado?" she asked.

"No reason, except that it's centrally located. You can get to just about anywhere from the Denver airport."

"I was expecting something more romantic."

"Sorry. I'm a world-class rock climber, and that's my home base."

She laughed. "So…you really are unattached. Just going where the wind takes you?"

"I don't know," he said. "Maybe that's how it is. But it's kind of sad thinking of a life like that."

"You've got your friends."

"But no family. No…"

He let his voice trail off. Now he was getting into unfamiliar territory. What had he been about to say? No wife, no kids?

"Do you ever think about those things?" she asked, looking straight ahead. The question was intimate, the moment quiet and tender. The truth was, he'd been thinking about them more often lately. Since losing Jesse. Since finding out she was pregnant, and Grady had been so close to having a family of his own. And then it was gone—they were gone—in a ball of fire and a curtain of smoke.

"I do," he said. "I didn't used to. But I do now."

She slowed, crossing her arms over her chest. Shivering a little underneath the moonlight.

"Are you cold?" he asked.

"A little."

"Come here."

She looked up at him.

"I won't bite," he said. "Much."

After a second, she stepped close. "Should I be afraid?"

"Depends on what you're afraid of."

"You."

"I'm a teddy bear."

He reached out and pulled her against his chest. Then rubbed her back in gentle circles.

"Have to get the blood flowing," he continued. "Heated up."

"It's already pretty warm."

"Oh, yeah? Why do I like the sound of that?"

She tilted her head back and looked him in the eyes. She wore an open, vulnerable expression that reminded him of the first time he'd seen her, lost in the woods. She was still grieving, he reminded himself, and it probably wouldn't take much to take advantage of that now. But was that who he wanted to be? The guy who saw a crack in her armor, and just walked right on through?

"Thank you for coming tonight," she said. "The kids loved seeing you again."

Her eyes were wide and dark. Lovely. Drawing him in. Before he could think better of it, he reached up and cupped her cheek in his hand. Knowing very well that he shouldn't, knowing that he was leaving. It felt like he was opening a door that was supposed to stay locked. For both their sakes.

She closed her eyes as he rubbed his thumb underneath

her lashes. Then opened them again to gaze up at him, her lips parted slightly.

"Hudson…"

"I know. I know it's not a good idea…"

"That's not what I was going to say."

He wanted to kiss her more than he'd wanted anything in a long time. Her skin felt like cool silk underneath his fingertips, and her body was soft and supple against his stomach and thighs. He wanted to slide his hands down her hips, but there were so many reasons why he shouldn't.

"There's a great spot on the beach," she said. "It's not far from here. It's beautiful. Now that the weather's cleared, we could build a fire and watch the ocean. Have you ever done that before?"

It was such a simple question, such a simple thing. Because he'd been so many places, and done so many things. But he'd never done that.

He shook his head. "No."

"What do you think?"

He watched her, feeling the connection between them deepen. There was something there other than just attraction. A common thread bound them together, a thread woven through pain and tears and sleepless nights. Standing there with an arm around her waist, it was more evident than ever how alike they really were. Except he wasn't the sticking kind.

"I'd like that," he said.

She had no idea what she was getting herself into. And he hated himself for it.

# Chapter Eight

Georgia sat on the giant, gnarled piece of driftwood, washed up on the beach during some long-forgotten storm, and looked up at the sparks that rose into the night like stars.

Hudson sat beside her, getting up every now and then to poke the fire with a stick and throw more kindling on. It had been years since she'd done this. Since she and Sophie had been in high school, when all the kids had come out here on Friday and Saturday nights. These days it was quieter, abandoned for the college parties in Eugene and even Portland, where high school students would go for the weekend. Things were different now, faster paced and more exciting, and a midnight fire on the beach didn't appeal to as many kids as when she was in school.

She wrapped her cardigan snug around her shoulders, breathing in the campfire smell. She'd have it in her hair and clothes when they left, but she didn't care. It reminded her of happier times, which was exactly why she'd wanted to share it with Hudson.

He leaned forward now, elbows on his knees, his sweatshirt stretched tight across his muscular shoulders. She thought he was going to kiss her tonight when they'd been walking on the track. She'd been hoping he would.

But she'd still been wearing her cat ears, had the whiskers drawn on her cheeks, and she felt ridiculous. She wanted to change into something else, to wash her face and dab a little perfume behind her ears first.

And now, here she was. Waiting for him to touch her again, but afraid that she might've missed her window. Maybe he'd had time to think about it. She definitely had, and was more confident than ever that it would probably be a mistake. But that didn't change the fact that she wanted it. She wanted him.

When he'd pulled her against his chest earlier, she'd been able to feel his heartbeat against her cheek, and something had changed for her then. She recognized the attraction she felt as something that wasn't going to be controlled. Or denied. At least not easily. At least not if she was going to keep finding herself in his general vicinity. And that wasn't even a question, because she'd made sure that she would be. He was going to be coming to her classroom to work with Lucy. He was going to be bringing Bonnie. He was going to be front and center for the next few weeks, and whatever she was feeling for him definitely wasn't going anywhere.

So, here she sat. Underneath the dark, Halloween sky, next to a man who scared her, quite frankly. But not enough to listen to her own instincts. The ones that were trying to keep her heart in one piece.

He sat beside her, quiet, staring at the fire. At the sparks rising into the chilly air with the ocean waves crashing beyond the beach. She wondered what was going through that head of his. It seemed like he was a little lost, and that made her sad. She wanted to scoot closer, to put her arm around him and feel his body heat again.

But something about him right then intimidated her. He was so darkly handsome, so incredibly masculine that his sex appeal was almost off the charts.

He turned to look at her. "What?"

She didn't say anything—she didn't trust herself to.

"Has anyone told you lately how pretty you are?" he asked.

She looked into the fire. She'd been around long enough to recognize a line when she heard it. And it was working.

"Hey," he said.

"Yeah?"

"You don't believe me, do you?"

Reaching over, he took her hand. Then raised it to his lips and kissed her knuckles. His mouth was warm, the scruff on his jaw tickling her skin in the most erotic way.

"You are beautiful, Georgia," he said, his voice lower this time. Laced with meaning.

This time she looked into his eyes. They were so dark, she could hardly tell they were blue anymore. She was losing herself, and that was a very scary thing. What in the world was she getting herself into?

Before she could properly worry about the answer, he leaned close. She could smell his scent—fabric softener, soap. It mingled with the smoky scent of the fire, of the salt in the air and water. It made her dizzy with longing.

He reached up and touched her chin with his thumb, tilting her head gently to the side. She felt her lips part slightly, instinctively. Felt her back arch with the need to be closer.

And then his mouth was on hers, moving over hers in a way that coaxed a soft moan from her throat. Without letting herself think about it, she put her arms around his neck, twisting her body so that her breasts pushed against his chest. She was embarrassed by how much she wanted him, by how much it must show. But he only reacted hungrily, deepening his kiss, cupping the back of her head in his hand.

Beyond them, the waves crashed. They matched the frantic beating of Georgia's heart. The strength of her desire.

She tilted her head, and he broke the kiss to trace her jawline with his tongue. It was warm and wet, flicking over her skin until he came to her earlobe. He exhaled softly next to it, and she shivered, trembling all over.

"Hudson," she breathed. She didn't know what she wanted to say, couldn't verbalize what she was feeling. But his name escaped her lips anyway, as if uttering it would quench this hunger.

He pulled away a little—enough to look down into her face. He was breathing hard, and it gave her a little thrill knowing she was doing that to him. Knowing she could affect him this way. She wasn't the only one drowning in this. He was, too.

"I wasn't prepared for this," he said. "I wasn't prepared for you."

He looked over at the fire, and the muscles in his jaw bunched. It was stubbly; he probably had a five-o'clock shadow at ten in the morning.

"I'm not sure this is fair to you," he said.

The words weren't a surprise. She knew the reality of their situation. He was leaving. There were so many things in the way, it was hard to pick just one that stood out. Even so, her heart sank. She'd known one of them would have to address it pretty soon, but she would've been happy to live in denial just a while longer.

"I'm a big girl," she said. "I know what I'm doing."

"But you don't know who you're doing it with. I'm a bad bet, Georgia. And I like you enough to ask you to trust me on that."

"Do you rob banks? Are you going to murder me in my sleep?"

He gave her a small smile. "I wouldn't go that far."

"Then I can handle it." Even as she said it, she wasn't sure she could. Because she knew exactly what he was talking about. It was her heart he was most concerned with. And if she was smart, she'd be concerned, too.

She reached up and put her hand on the back of his neck. Ran her thumb lightly over his tanned skin, let her fingertips play over the short hair brushing his collar.

"Maybe we should just enjoy it while it lasts," she said quietly, the flames popping and crackling next to them. Warming her face, even as the breeze blew against it. Buffeting the fire and making it dance.

"You mean enjoy each other while it lasts."

"That, too." She smiled. She was kidding, but not really. She wasn't used to being bold. She was used to letting men make the first move. But her time with Hudson was short, and something about that was making her want to throw all caution to the wind. Did that mean a one-night stand? She wasn't sure. But she didn't want it to end here. Not even close.

He got up, surprising her. Taking his warmth with him. She watched him take a few steps in the sand and turn to the ocean, his hands in his pockets. The breeze blew through his hair, and the shadows from the fire danced across his face.

"Are you happy, Georgia?" he asked.

It was such a straightforward question, so out of the blue, that she sat there for a minute, thinking about it.

"It depends on the day," she said. "Before Sophie died, I would've said yes, for the most part. But loss changes you. I know you understand that."

He nodded.

"Are you happy?" she asked.

He waited a beat. Then two. The fire continued crackling, but with less intensity now. The coals glowed bright orange, but the flames were getting smaller, growing weary of the effort.

"I'm empty," he finally said.

He turned and looked down at her, and she glimpsed a brief expression on his face—one of torment and agony. And then it was gone. He was composed again. He'd put his mask back on.

She got up, wrapping her cardigan around her shoulders at the sudden chill moving through her. She didn't know what to say, or if there was anything she *could* say. She simply wanted to be close to him and offer the comfort of her body.

When she took his hand, she felt the tension in his fingers. He was stiff and unyielding.

"You can talk to me, Hudson."

He smiled, but there was no warmth in it. Only a distant pain.

"I was just sitting there," he said. "Sitting next to you, and I realized how good it would feel to stay in one place for longer than a few months. For longer than a deployment."

Her bangs blew into her eyes, and she pushed them away, hoping he wouldn't stop there. That he would trust her enough to go on.

"I'm doing the search and rescue," he said. "And that's good. I'm helping people, and that's important to me. But at the same time, I know I'm chasing something that I'm never going to find."

"What's that?"

"Jesse," he said quietly.

Her throat ached at that.

"But it's not just her," he continued. "It's friends, acquaintances. Even guys I never liked or knew that well. Everyone who ever died over there. I'm trying to find them all in those lost people."

It was almost too sad to bear, too profound to process. The wind blew against her face, through her hair. It was like a lover, whose touch had grown cold.

"I don't know why I'm telling you this," he said. "I'm here, I'm alive, so poor me, right?"

"Please don't say that. I'm so glad you made it out of there. I'm so glad you're here with me."

"But am I? It feels like there will always be a piece of me that's missing."

"That's true," she said. "Just like there will always be a piece of me that's missing. But we have to find a way to go on, to get through it, right? There's no getting over it, but we can get through it."

Someone had told her that once, and it had encompassed exactly how she felt about loss. About healing. About moving forward when a part of you would always want to hang back and languish. It was a daily process, finding the strength and courage to get through the pain.

He nodded. "You're right."

"But?"

"I don't want to hurt you, Georgia."

"So, don't."

She knew it wasn't that simple. She knew what he was wrestling with was significant, and even though she understood loss because she was wrestling with it herself, his situation, his trauma was very different. She didn't want to be hurt, either. It made perfect sense to walk away from this man while the walking was good. But she knew that he was probably going to have to be the one to do it, because she was already in too deep. She'd realized that the second his lips had touched hers.

He was quiet. His jaw working in that now familiar way. He hadn't answered her, he hadn't responded with anything at all, which was enough to send a tremor through her heart. It was no surprise. Like the lighthouse beacon on the other side of the jetty, she could see the warning a mile away.

He put his arm around her, and even his instant warmth couldn't ease her mind.

"Come on," he said. "It's getting late. Let's get you home."

"That's it, folks," Sheriff Hicks said. "Let's get him home."

The large circle of search and rescue volunteers began to disperse—going to their vehicles to get backpacks, supplies and radios, and whatever else they might need for the day. Half a dozen dogs yipped excitedly at the tension in the air, waiting for the cue from their handlers that it was time to get to work.

Hudson held snugly on to Bonnie's leash, wanting to give everyone time to scatter before giving her the scent. An elderly man with Alzheimer's had wandered away from his family's cabin on the edge of the river, and time wasn't on their side. An autumn storm was blowing in, bringing with it plenty of wind and rain. The river was already high, its normally placid currents on this stretch now bordering on dangerous, and his wife was beside herself. Mother Nature could be unpredictable enough for a young, healthy person, but someone who was in a weakened state, mentally and physically, was incredibly vulnerable to her wrath.

Reaching down, he rubbed Bonnie's velvety ears, watching as the deputies on horseback began disappearing into the thick woods, the evergreens and shrubs swallowing them whole.

"It's good to have you back."

Hudson felt a hearty slap on his shoulder and turned to see the sheriff standing there. Tall and imposing in his cowboy boots and dark green uniform.

"It's good to be back," Hudson said. "I appreciate you keeping me in mind."

"You're one of the best we've got out here. And I don't say that lightly."

"Thanks, Sheriff."

"We weren't sure how long you were going to be in town. I feel like Mr. Gardener might've lucked out that you're still here. I hope so, at least."

"I hope so, too."

"He's a nice man. He was a history teacher at Christmas Bay High for thirty-five years. His grandson plays football with my nephew. Everyone knows everyone here."

"I've noticed."

The older man smiled, pushing his Stetson up on his forehead. "Small towns are like that. Not much privacy, but we make up for it in a sense of community and home. We care about each other."

"I've noticed that, too."

The sheriff nodded, squinting in the face of the early afternoon sun and looking out toward the river. "I'll be sorry to see you go. My deputies like you. Hell, everyone likes you."

Hudson ran his hand over Bonnie's sleek head. She leaned into his leg, ready to go, but being very good, very patient, as always. Even though he usually tried to tune out what other people thought, it was nice to hear that he was liked. It was nice to feel like he belonged here, even if it was temporary, as always. The sheriff was right, there was a sense of community in Christmas Bay that was undeniable. He'd seen similarities in some of the small villages in Afghanistan, where family and a sense of home was everything. People were people, no matter where in the world they lived.

"Just keep it in mind," the sheriff said. "In case you want to come back. Or in case you want to stay."

Before Hudson could answer, the older man was walking away. Busy with his deputies, with the job at hand.

Hudson watched him go. In case he wanted to stay? He was just vacationing here. But maybe the look on his face was evident, or the way he carried himself. Or the way he talked to people, like he'd been hungry for this kind of belonging for a long time.

He looked up at the sky, at the angry clouds gathering near the horizon, and thought of the elderly man lost and wandering right that minute. He thought about what he'd said to Georgia the night before, about looking for what was missing in his life and never finding it. But that didn't mean he was going to stop searching.

And suddenly, all other thoughts were pushed to the back of his mind, as he pulled one of Mr. Gardener's T-shirts from his jacket pocket and lowered it to Bonnie's nose.

"Let's get to work, baby."

Hudson picked his way over the forest floor, over the plethora of rocks and gnarled, exposed roots.

Bonnie ran up ahead, laser focused on the work at hand. Her nose was lowered to the carpet of pine needles, catching scents that Hudson could only guess at, as her tail waved frantically in the air.

The sounds of the search party surrounded them. Other volunteers calling to each other and to Mr. Gardener through the mountain stillness. Horses nickering through the trees. The radio crackling on Hudson's hip, with coordinates and updates and sheriff department chatter. It was already a little after six, and the sun had dipped her golden head behind the towering mountain peak to his right. On the other side of that was the Pacific Ocean, its waters undoubtedly sparkling with the changing light of the autumn evening.

Hudson stopped and peeled off his backpack. "Bonnie, come!"

She froze up ahead and turned back to face him, her tongue lolling out of her mouth. But she didn't move.

"Bonnie!"

He frowned. It wasn't like her not to listen to a command. She always listened, always did as she was told. Her job depended on it.

Still, she didn't move. Just kept staring at him and wagging her tail. She hadn't alerted on anything, but it was clear that she didn't want to stop working, she didn't want to be pulled off the trail, even for a drink of water.

Normally Hudson would force the matter—she had to obey him in order to keep her safe. But a funny feeling was tickling his nerve endings. His partnership with his dog, the deep bond they'd formed, was based on trust. She trusted him explicitly. And he trusted her. She was a highly intelligent animal, and she seemed to have a sixth sense where searches were concerned. She'd had it with bombs. And now she had it with people. Right then she was telling him she needed a little more time.

Gritting his teeth, he put his backpack back on. "Fifteen minutes," he told her. "That's it. Then a break, got it?"

Cocking her head, she watched him.

"Okay, hop to it," he said, waving her on. "Don't make me look bad."

With a yip, she turned and put her nose back to the forest floor. Right as thunder rumbled ominously in the distance.

Hudson looked up, hoping the rain would hold off as long as possible. Hating the thought of Mr. Gardener out here, wet, cold and confused. The temperature was going to drop tonight, and with the wind chill, that would make things a hell of a lot more complicated.

He let his gaze fall back to his dog. But she was nowhere in sight.

He stopped and listened. Straining to hear her tags jingling, the rustle of her paws in the brush. The feeling he'd had a minute ago began to manifest itself physically, until his heartbeat was skipping over his rib cage like a stone.

Thunder rumbled again, setting his teeth on edge.

And then she barked.

He broke into a run—through the trees and brush, over the rocks and tree stumps, toward the sound of her alerting him to a find.

He broke through a clearing, and then came to a jarring stop. Breathing heavily, his heart hammering in his chest, he looked across the meadow to see his dog in an elderly man's lap.

Bonnie was licking his face frantically. He had a thin arm thrown over her back. There was blood on his long-sleeve button-down shirt—it looked like it was coming from a gash on his cheek. But otherwise, he seemed alert and healthy.

"Mr. Gardener?" Hudson lowered himself to the ground in front of him and pulled Bonnie's lamb from his pocket. She took it eagerly but made no attempt to vacate her spot on his lap. "I'm Hudson Cross. We've been looking for you. How are you feeling?"

His bushy white eyebrows knitted together. "I don't know what's happening."

The words pierced Hudson's heart. "I know, it's a little scary, right? You're in the woods, you just got lost. But

I'm here to help you get back home. Lillian is going to be really happy to see you."

At the mention of his wife, Mr. Gardener's faded blue eyes brightened. "Lillian?"

"Yes, we're going to get you back safe and sound." Hudson looked him over quickly, touching the edges of the wound on his cheek and making sure there were no broken bones. "Sheriff Hicks says you were a history teacher, is that right? History was my favorite subject in high school."

"You were one of my students?"

"No, I grew up in Illinois. A long way from here. But I've heard some great things about you. That you were a really good teacher."

The elderly man smiled, the skin around his eyes delicate as paper. "I took my kids to Washington, DC, one summer. They saved all year. Washed cars and things like that. I was so proud of them."

Hudson cued his radio and let the search party know that Mr. Gardener had been found, and that he was okay. He was coming home.

Then he turned back to him and smiled. "And I'm sure they were proud of you. I don't think any of my teachers knew my name, let alone cared enough to take me on a trip across the country. That must've been something else."

"Oh, your teachers should've known your name. Every kid is special, every one of them."

Hudson wondered what his life would've been like if he'd had a teacher like this as an impressionable teenager. If he'd had a father figure in someone other than drill sergeants. He wondered if he would've been softer around the edges now, as a middle-aged man. There was no way to know, of course, but the thought skittered across his mind anyway.

Mr. Gardener frowned, the brief sparkle in his eyes dimming now. Replaced by a look of fear, of being lost in the caverns of his own mind. "Who did you say you were again?"

"I'm Hudson. It's nice to meet you."

"It's nice to meet you, too, son. I'm not sure where I am..."

Hudson took his hand in both of his.

"Don't worry," he said. "I've got you."

# *Chapter Nine*

The only thing Georgia had ever really liked about November was Thanksgiving. Because of the pie, of course, and the fact that it was that much closer to Christmas. This morning, as she looked out of her classroom window at the gray and the fog, she made a conscious effort to enjoy the day, and every day leading up to the end of the month. To see them as a gift—which was exactly what they were.

Since losing Sophie, she'd come to think of a lot of things this way. Mondays, rainy weekends—the list went on and on. On it were things that she used to jokingly complain about, but were now no longer so terrible. And no longer so funny. Life was short. Shorter than she'd ever realized before, and she appreciated every minute of it now. Even the gray minutes. Even the rainy ones.

Her kids had gone home half an hour ago, leaving her classroom empty and quiet for the first time since that morning. She put her chin in her hand, staring out the window, knowing she should be taking advantage of this time to work out her lesson plan for the week, but not being able to concentrate on much other than this sudden wave of gratitude that had washed over her. Leaving her warm and calm, which was a feeling that she hadn't enjoyed for a long time. And why was that? The profound changes she'd experienced since Sophie's passing was one. Hudson Cross was the other.

If anyone had asked right then, Georgia wouldn't have been able to say that she was happy, necessarily. At least not in the traditional sense of the word. But she felt… peaceful. Like happiness might eventually follow. Someday. And that was a very powerful revelation for someone who'd been trying to find their way through the darkness for so long. She could see light up ahead.

She looked down at her grade book, open to today's date. The slots next to Lucy's name were empty. She hadn't been in class most of last week, and again today. Georgia chewed the inside of her cheek. Grace had called to let the school know that Lucy hadn't been feeling well, but there was something about her prolonged absence that was gnawing at Georgia's belly.

Taking a deep breath, she reached for her cell. It wouldn't hurt to give her mother a call, just to check and make sure she was alright.

She dialed and waited for an answer. And right before she thought it would go to voicemail, Grace picked up.

"Hello?"

"Mrs. Thorton, this is Georgia Gallagher. I just wanted to see how Lucy was feeling. Several kids have been out with the flu, and it's a bad one."

There was a significant pause on the other end of the line. "Yes, I know. My friend had it last week. But that's not why Lucy has missed school."

Georgia frowned. "Oh?"

"I actually thought about calling you, but I wasn't sure

if I should. You've been so helpful, but I know there's only so much you can do."

Georgia switched the phone to her other ear. "Don't ever hesitate to call. I'm always here. What's going on?"

"This is hard for me… But I had to call the police on my ex-husband last week."

Georgia's stomach sank. She waited, her breathing shallow. Poor little Lucy. She was such a sensitive little soul. This was probably devastating for her.

"It was pretty scary," Grace said. "And Lucy has completely shut down. The counseling was helping before. At least, I think it was. But she's having such a hard time. She's sucking her thumb again, and she hasn't done that since she was a toddler. I'm kind of lost, Miss Gallagher."

Grace paused, and Georgia could hear her start to cry. Softly, as if she was trying to hide it.

"I'm so sorry," Georgia said. "I can't imagine how hard this must be for you both. Do you have family support? Support from friends?"

"I have great friends. But the rest of our family isn't here. Honestly, I've thought about moving to Astoria, where my mom and sister are. I just haven't wanted to pull Lucy out of school. She loves it here so much. I'm just not sure how safe it is for us in Christmas Bay anymore."

"You have to do what's right for you," Georgia said. "And kids adjust quickly, I can tell you that. She'd settle in, as long as she's got you. And other family members in her life would probably work wonders."

"If I can hold off until the end of the year, that would give me time to save more money to move. And it would make more sense for Lucy to start at a new school after summer vacation. But I've got to figure out how to help her with this anxiety. It's awful, just awful."

Georgia swallowed hard. "It sounds like it. Listen, I'm here. Just tell me what I can do."

"Well, you'd mentioned comfort visits from Bonnie, that search and rescue dog? Lucy has been talking about her for weeks."

"Absolutely. In fact, I just spoke with her handler the other day, and we're working on getting some times set up when she can come to the classroom."

"That's the thing," Grace said. "I'm not sure I can get Lucy back to school right now. Even with that as an incentive."

Georgia stared out the window again. The mist was clinging to the glass, making it look like a dreamscape outside. It was like she'd just woken up and her eyes were trying to adjust to the world around her.

"What if Bonnie came to you?" she asked.

"I mean…that would be amazing. But would it even be possible?"

Georgia didn't know Hudson that well yet, but the man she did know was incredibly warm. He wanted to help people.

"I can't say for sure," she said. "But let me reach out to her owner and ask. Can I call you this evening? Will you be home?"

"I'll be here," Grace said. "How can I thank you for this?"

Georgia's heart swelled with love for her student. For this family, that was struggling to keep their heads above water. She understood the struggle part, even though their struggles were very different. Drowning was drowning.

"Having Lucy back at school will be all the thanks I need," she said. "I'll talk to you this evening, Grace."

Hudson looked over at Georgia in the passenger's seat and smiled. Bonnie had her head hanging over the backrest, her chin on Georgia's shoulder. The dog was leaning into her like they were long-lost friends. Bonnie loved everyone, but there was a connection between her and Georgia that he couldn't deny.

Georgia stroked Bonnie's ears and said something soft under her breath that Hudson couldn't hear.

He looked back at the road and adjusted his seat belt over his shoulder. "I think it's safe to say that she likes you."

"She's the best girl. Aren't you the best girl?"

Bonnie answered with a quick swipe of her tongue.

"I can't guarantee where that mouth has been," Hudson said.

Georgia laughed. "I can guess well enough."

"You should see Tad. She gives him full on dog kisses. On the lips. It's disgusting."

"Urine Van Buren used to give the best kisses. Until my mom convinced me that I was going to end up with some weird dog disease if I kept letting him do it. That was the end of that."

"If anyone were going to end up with a weird dog disease, it would be Tad, and so far he's still kicking. But I'll keep you updated."

"Thanks so much. I'll be sure to report back to my mother." She scratched Bonnie behind the ears. "I really appreciate you doing this, Hudson. I know Grace was hesitant to ask. She's a nice person. It breaks my heart that they're having such a hard time."

Hudson rubbed his thumbs over the leather steering wheel. "I'm glad she asked. This is Bonnie's jam. She's got this way with people."

They continued making their way down a narrow mountain road as the sky overhead began changing colors with the setting sun. The mist had cleared away, leaving the air cool and crisp. Now the evening loomed—dusk beginning to wrap her arms around the small, coastal town. A few stars were visible in the darkening sky, pale pinpricks in the fabric of the heavens.

Georgia looked out the window as they turned onto a narrow dirt road. "I guess I didn't realize they lived so far out."

It was exactly what Hudson had been thinking, too—it was remote. They'd only passed one car in the last few minutes, the driver a somber looking character wearing a cowboy hat and a deep scowl. He guessed all the neighbors probably knew one another and were suspicious of anyone else on the edge of their properties.

"It should be right up here on the left," she said, looking at her GPS. "That long driveway through the trees. Good grief, I don't even think the buses come out this far. Grace must have to drive Lucy into town every day."

"That's a haul. Especially when there's weather."

*Or*, he thought, *when there's a violent ex-husband in the picture.*

Georgia had told him about Lucy's dad going to jail. He'd apparently assaulted her mom, which was enough to keep him behind bars for a while. But what about when he got out? What would he do then? The fact that the nearest houses weren't near at all made it an even more unsettling situation. Georgia had said Grace was planning on leaving town. He hoped this guy wouldn't make that hard for her.

Hudson slowed for some deep potholes in the dirt road, thinking again how hard it would be getting in and out of here when there was rain or snow. The highway leading into town could be bad enough, but the side roads that weren't paved would be hard to navigate.

After a minute, a small A-frame house with a sagging roof came into view. There were a couple of rusted-out cars in the driveway, where weeds and brambles had begun to grow tall, reaching up with their spindly arms for the cracked windows and side mirrors. Hudson looked around at the towering evergreens surrounding the house. They would block most of the sun during the day, and he imagined that night would be dark and foreboding out here without moonlight.

Up on the rickety porch, there were flowerpots full of colorful blooms, and a rocking chair that seemed inviting, despite the rest of the property's gloominess. Evidence that Grace Thorton had probably been trying to keep a nice home for her family.

Imagining this made Hudson's gut tighten. Made his heart squeeze uncomfortably in his chest. He'd encountered a lot of poverty overseas. He'd seen things that he hadn't been able to shake for days, weeks, months. Even now, some of those things would come back to haunt him when he was least prepared for it. In his dreams most of all, where he'd wake with a start and a lead weight in his stomach.

Like so often happened in his civilian life, something

about this house brought it all back. The small glimmer of hopefulness on the porch, the way the flowers were leaning toward the light between the clouds. But most of all, the ominous feeling that hung over the place. Despite what Grace might have been trying to do, it did not seem like a happy place. In fact, he immediately felt the need to look into his rearview mirror to make sure nobody was behind them. A habit, leftover from his time in the service. He didn't like to have his back turned to anything.

Georgia exhaled softly. "Lucy's an only child. It must get lonely out here all by herself."

Hudson pulled up to the front porch and cut the engine. They were immediately enveloped in the heavy quiet of the woods.

Unbuckling her seat belt, Georgia looked around.

"You okay?" Hudson asked.

"I'm good. It's just a little creepy."

They climbed out just as the front door opened. Grace Thorton stood there, wearing a heavy sweater and a pair of faded jeans.

"Hey, there," she said. "I hope the drive out wasn't too bad. It can get a little hairy when the sun goes down."

Smiling over his shoulder, Hudson clipped the leash to Bonnie's collar. "It wasn't bad."

"Grace," Georgia said, "this is Hudson Cross. And Bonnie."

"I can't tell you how much I appreciate you both coming all the way out here. I'm just so thankful."

As Hudson climbed the steps, he could see that she was wearing a lot of makeup. She turned her head so they couldn't see the side of her face, then moved her hair in front of her cheek.

"I'm just glad you called," Georgia said.

Bonnie tugged on her leash, eager to get at this new human. To sniff and lick her, and maybe get some scritches in the process.

Grace bent to pet her. "Hi, there, Bonnie. How are you?"

Bonnie wagged her butt. Barely holding still long enough for Grace to pet her at all.

"I think she likes you," Hudson said.

"She's beautiful." She straightened again. "I have to apologize for the house. Some things got broken last week, and I haven't had a chance to get them fixed."

"Don't worry about that," Georgia said. "We're just happy to get to see you and Lucy."

Grace opened the door, and they followed her inside.

Hudson looked around, his gaze settling on a broken window across the room. A sign that violence lived here—but mostly it was evident in the way that Grace held herself. Like she was afraid—afraid of people. Afraid of life.

"I told Lucy you were coming, but she still wouldn't come out of her room," she said. "She's made a little cubby in her closet. I've been trying to be patient—that's what the therapist said to do—but I'm worried."

"Of course you are," Georgia said. "But she's going to be okay. You're doing the right thing with therapy. That's exactly what she needs right now. That, and her mom."

"I just have all this guilt that I let it go on for as long as I did. But I was so scared that…"

She didn't finish. Hudson could only imagine what she'd been about to say.

Feeling a dull anger at her ex-husband build in his

chest, he leaned down and unclicked Bonnie's leash. "Is it okay if she goes and finds her?"

"Please," Grace said. "She'll love that."

Hudson watched Bonnie trot down the hallway, her tail waving back and forth like a flag. She disappeared into one of the bedrooms, and a second later, they heard soft, little girl giggling.

"Bingo," Hudson said.

"Can we go say hi?" Georgia asked.

"Of course." The other woman looked relaxed for the first time since they got there. "I'll put some coffee on."

Georgia walked down the hallway and Hudson followed. The house was small, but nicely kept. Sparsely furnished with cozy, mismatched pieces, and family pictures on the walls. He tried not to think of the chaos behind those smiles, the pain behind the glass.

When they got to Lucy's room, he looked around. There was a pink princess bed pushed up against the wall and a little bookcase next to it that was stuffed with worn and tattered paperbacks. There were a few stuffed animals strewn on the floor, a couple of Barbie dolls, but that was it. Hudson wondered what she played with, hoping it wasn't on a phone or iPad all the time. Maybe she spent a lot of time outside.

When he was about four or five, he remembered having an imaginary friend named Peter who kept him company when he was lonely, which was a lot. He didn't know much about kids—maybe Lucy was too old for imaginary friends. Or maybe she didn't get lonely at all. He hoped she didn't, but it was hard thinking of her in this house, with parents who were fighting, with nobody to turn to for comfort. Not even a pet. He'd been there. He understood how it felt.

He looked down at where she'd made a little fort in the closet. Bonnie had crawled inside with her, and she had her small arms draped around the dog's neck, had her face pressed into her fur.

Georgia sank to one knee and reached out to pet Bonnie, but only had eyes for Lucy. She was obviously a good teacher. But she was an even better person, and he didn't think he would've been able to look away from her right then if he'd tried.

"You know," she said, "Mr. Hudson is going to be bringing Bonnie into our classroom for visits. Did your mom tell you that?"

Lucy nodded.

"I'd sure hate for you to miss that," Georgia continued. "It wouldn't be the same without you."

The little girl seemed to think about that. "Will you tell Kiersten I said hi?"

"I sure will. She misses you. I know she'll be so happy when you come back to school. And so will I."

That got a little smile. "What about Toby?"

"Oh boy. Toby misses you, too. He has no idea who to play handball with at recess."

"I miss recess."

"It's pretty fun, right?"

Hudson stood there quietly, watching them talk and trying to blend in as much as possible. Something was happening between them—a foundation of trust being built.

The hardwood floor creaked behind him, and he turned to see Grace standing there in the shadows of the hallway, watching, too. Silent tears were streaming down her face. She looked over at him and smiled. Other than what Georgia had told him about Lucy's situation, he could only guess at the rest. But this seemed like progress, and any kind of progress was good.

Georgia reached out and tucked a silky lock of Lucy's hair behind her ear.

The little girl looked up and fixed Hudson with a pleading look. "Can I take Bonnie outside to play fetch, Mr. Hudson?"

"She loves fetch," he said. "Any old stick will do. Or a tennis ball, if you've got one."

"I think we have a couple on the porch," Grace said. "You can take her outside, but don't go far. Stay inside the property fence, okay?"

"Okay, Mama. Come on, Bonnie. Wanna play ball?"

Bonnie licked Lucy's face and gave an excited yip. Hudson wasn't sure if she actually knew what she was excited for, but she'd figured out that she was going somewhere with this small human, and that was reason enough to be happy.

Lucy crawled out of the closet, and Bonnie followed her. Then shook, her tags jingling.

"Let's go, Bonnie. Let's go, girl."

And then they were headed outside, little girl and black Lab, looking like the very best of friends.

"Well," Grace said. "Let's celebrate with a cup of coffee. And I think there's some cheesecake in the freezer."

Georgia sat on the edge of the couch, sipping her mocha. Grace Thorton could make a mean cup of coffee, and the warm mug felt good in Georgia's hands. The temperature had dropped outside when the sun had set, and Lucy had come inside a few minutes ago to put a jacket on. Bonnie's tongue was lolling out of her mouth, her tail in constant, happy motion. It seemed like she was having the time of her life, but the best part was that Lucy was engaging. She was active, and even working up an appetite. Grace said she'd only been picking at her meals for days, but when her mom had mentioned pizza tonight, her eyes had lit up.

All good things. All wonderful things, actually. But what was making Georgia's heart beat a little heavier now was how close Hudson was sitting. His thigh brushing against hers and creating a warm friction between them.

Licking the mocha from her lips, she snuck a look at him. He was listening intently as Grace told them about the possibility of moving to Astoria. He was so handsome that her mouth went dry, making her grateful that she had something to drink. That she had something to do other than gawk at him and lose her bearings.

She let her gaze shift to Lucy's mother again, who'd relaxed enough by now that she'd forgotten to keep her curtain of hair carefully positioned next to her face. There was clearly a bruise there, covered by thick makeup, blooming dark and sore looking across her cheekbone.

Georgia looked quickly away, not wanting it to be obvious that she'd noticed, but feeling a rush of compassion for this woman who'd had such a hard road.

"Have you ever been to Astoria?" Grace asked, setting her mug on the coffee table. "It's adorable. It's where they filmed *The Goonies*."

"Oh, man," Hudson said. "Best movie ever."

"I've never seen it," Georgia said.

Grace's eyes grew wide, and Hudson turned to stare at her.

"What?" she asked.

"You've never seen *The Goonies*?"

She shook her head.

"And see, I thought we were headed toward a serious relationship, but now I'll have to rethink that."

Her cheeks warmed. He was just kidding, but the words lit a fire in her belly anyway. A relationship with Hudson Cross. The thought was enough to make her knees go weak. She hadn't let herself go there. She hadn't even daydreamed about it, for fear of getting her heart pulverized.

But here he was. Joking about it over coffee. Giving her a teasing wink and making her forget herself for a second.

Clearing her throat, she smiled at Grace. "I think it's wonderful that you want to go live where your family is."

"I'm just so excited. My sister and I are best friends. Lucy has never met her because Eddie refused to go up there, or let her come here. I think he felt threatened by how close we are."

"Did she know what was happening between you two?" Georgia asked.

"I never told her. I just lived with it so long, that I was starting to think it was normal, the abuse. My sister would have seen right through him, so I guess he had good reason to keep us apart."

Georgia knew that Sophie would have been the same way. She'd been a mother bear. Fiercely protective of her friends and family.

"My sister was my best friend, too," Georgia said.

"Was?"

"She passed in the summer. Cancer."

Hudson watched her. She could feel the comforting weight of his gaze, and all of a sudden, she wanted to lean into him. To feel his warmth and solidness, like the night they'd kissed.

"Oh no," Grace said. "I'm so sorry."

"Me, too." Hudson's voice was rougher, quieter.

She nodded. What could she say? Nothing that she hadn't replied with a hundred times before. For some reason, this time, she just wanted to sit with those words. Just let them be. *I'm sorry...* She was sorry, too.

"If Sophie were alive," Georgia said, forcing some evenness into her voice that she didn't feel. "I'd go where she was, too. You're doing the right thing, making this move. I'm just so happy for you and Lucy. You deserve this, Grace, you really do."

The other woman licked her lips and looked down at her hands for a second. She was clearly moved. She'd mentioned friends, but Georgia wondered how alone she really was out here. If she had someone she could turn to, someone she could trust. But it sounded like she had that in her mom and sister, and pretty soon, they'd be together again. Grace would have her best friend, and Lucy would have an aunt and grandmother who would no doubt adore her. There was strength in numbers.

"Mom!" Lucy called from outside. "Uncle Brian is here!"

Grace immediately stiffened.

From outside, Bonnie started barking. Not the playful yips from before, but deeper, throatier barks, tinged with urgency. Georgia stiffened, too.

Hudson stood and walked over to the window in a few long strides.

"He heard," Grace said under her breath. Almost like she was talking to herself. Her face had gone deathly pale. "How could he know? Nobody knows."

"What is it?" Georgia asked.

Before Grace could answer, Hudson headed out the front door.

Georgia got up and followed. When she stepped onto the porch, she saw a tall man in the shadows who was holding on to Lucy's hand. A dirty truck with big tires idled in the driveway. The little girl looked scared. Her eyes were wide, her bottom lip trembling in the headlights.

"Lucy," Grace said, stepping onto the porch beside Georgia. "Come here, please."

"Who's this?" the man asked, looking at Hudson suspiciously.

Hudson held Bonnie's collar. The dog had stopped barking, but her hackles were standing straight up, forming a stiff ridge from her shoulders to her tail. She let out a low, rumbling growl.

"Lucy," Grace said again. "Come to Mama."

The man didn't make any move to let her go.

"Are you gonna introduce us, Gracie?" the man asked.

Grace moved past Georgia and down the porch steps. "This is Lucy's teacher and her friend. Not that it's any of your business, Brian. Let her go."

The other man seemed to be deciding whether or not that was true, before he finally let go of Lucy's hand. She ran to her mother through the darkness, clearly shaken.

Georgia watched this with a growing sense of anger. All the progress that they'd made with Lucy tonight might be completely undone by this jackass.

"I know you're not thinking about leaving with Eddie's kid," he said. "I heard that, and I knew it wasn't true. I know you wouldn't do something like that."

Grace bent down and picked Lucy up, then climbed the steps again. Quickly moving next to Georgia. *Strength in numbers...*

"I'm not talking to you about this," Grace said. "Please leave."

"Is that any way to treat family?"

"Eddie and I are divorced. You're not my family anymore."

"Gracie..."

"She asked you to leave," Hudson said.

The other man turned, and his expression went from condescending to icy. "Stay out of this, brother."

"Brian," Grace said, "please."

His gaze shifted to Georgia, and he looked her up and down, obviously trying to make her uncomfortable.

Hudson stepped between them, blocking his view. It wasn't hard to do; he was tall. And thick through the shoulders. A detail the other man had probably noted. It was clear that if he wanted a fight, he'd have his hands full with Hudson.

Being a teacher and dealing with difficult parents on the regular, Georgia knew a thing or two about deescalating a situation. She could tell that Hudson didn't want to provoke this guy, but he wasn't in the mood to let him stay, either. It was a delicate balancing act that was enough to set her teeth on edge. To make her palms sweat, despite the chilly wind buffeting her short hair.

"Lucy," Grace said. "Go inside, okay?"

"But Mama—"

"Inside, honey."

The little girl did as she was told, looking at her uncle over her shoulder as she went.

When she closed the door behind her, Hudson took an audible breath.

"Lucy's been a having a hard time and wanted to see the dog," Hudson said. "No big deal. But this is scaring her. I'm sure you don't want her to be scared…"

The other man narrowed his eyes, as if that was a trick question.

"You don't want that, do you?" Hudson pressed.

"No…"

"I bet Grace would be open to talking over the phone?"

Grace nodded.

"What do you say?" Hudson asked.

"I guess. I'll call you, Gracie."

"Fine," she said coolly.

Georgia watched as he stood there for a long minute. Then he turned to climb into his idling truck. The tension in the mountain air was almost palpable as he put the truck in Reverse, the tires kicking up chunks of mud.

And then it was rumbling back down the dirt road and leaving the three of them staring after it.

"He's always been a jerk," Grace said under her breath. "He just wants to intimidate me."

"Do you think he's dangerous?" Georgia asked.

"I don't think so. Eddie's the dangerous one."

Hudson leaned down and gave Bonnie a pat. "Do you have anyone you can stay with in town? Just in case? You're pretty isolated out here."

"I hope it doesn't come to that. Lucy has been so upset

as it is, I'd hate to take her away from her familiar environment."

Georgia watched the truck's taillights disappear through the fog that was coming in off the ocean. The woods surrounding them seemed extra quiet now, extra still, and more than a little creepy. She shivered, unable to help it.

Hudson caught her gaze, and they looked at each other for a long minute. She'd had no idea when they came out here how involved this situation with Lucy was. How deep it really went. She wondered what might've happened if they hadn't been here when Grace's brother-in-law had shown up. If Hudson hadn't blocked his way from coming up onto the porch.

Ever since he'd found her lost in the woods that day, Georgia had felt undeniably safe with him. She'd attributed that to the search and rescue thing, but it was becoming more and more apparent that everyone probably felt that way in his presence. He was just that kind of man.

And her heart, completely unchecked now, began to pound.

# *Chapter Ten*

"Can you pull over for a second?"

Hudson turned to look at Georgia in the shadowy cab of his Tahoe and frowned. She'd been quiet since leaving the little house in the woods, seeming to be deep in thought. But to be fair, so had he. He hadn't been able to stop going over and over what had happened in the driveway. It had given him a bad feeling, all of it, and he'd grown pensive on the drive back to Christmas Bay.

He turned his blinker on now, easing the truck over to a pullout on the side of the mountain road. They hadn't passed a single car in about a mile, making it feel farther away from town than ever. Making that uneasy feeling in his stomach even more pronounced.

Putting the SUV into Park, he turned to Georgia. He watched her crack her window and take a deep breath of the damp air.

"Sorry," she said after a few seconds. "I was feeling a little dizzy. Like I might need to get out. I think I'm alright now, just unsettled."

"I hear you."

She looked over at him, her hazel eyes dark, her skin powder white in the moonless night.

"You were pretty great tonight," she said quietly. "I was impressed."

"Nah. He was all bark and no bite. At least I hope he's no bite."

"Grace seems to think so. But I didn't like the look on his face. Or how he was holding on to Lucy. It gave me the chills."

"Me, too."

She chewed the inside of her cheek, and his gaze dropped to her lips. It always seemed to end up there, on her mouth. She was so tempting. And that was starting to scare the hell out of him. Just where did he expect this to go? Where was she expecting it to go?

"Thank you for coming out here tonight," she said. "It was so nice of you."

"I was happy to. And so was Bonnie. I think she may be a therapy dog in the making."

"I think you've both got a second retirement career in your future."

"Retirement career," he said. "Is that an actual thing?"

"I don't know, but it fits."

"I'm not sure I know how to actually retire at this point. Neither do Tad or Grady. I'm in good company, at least."

"It's got to be strange, coming from a place as regimented as the army."

"It is, but I'm liking it. I like Christmas Bay."

She watched him through the dim light of the cab. "I meant the job must be strange. The search and rescue stuff compared to the bomb squad."

"Right…"

"But you like Christmas Bay?"

He thought about that. He'd just told her that he liked

it. But it was actually more than that. He felt comfortable here. He felt at home here. He wondered how much of that had to do with the town, and how much of it had to do with Georgia. Either way, he wasn't looking forward to the thought of leaving.

"I do," he said.

"I'm glad. But I'm going to miss you when you go."

He probably never should've kissed her, and he'd known that in the beginning. But he'd done it anyway, and her heart wasn't the only one on the line now. His was, too.

He gazed out the window over her shoulder, into the darkness of the forest beyond the truck. For the first time in his life, he longed for words that eluded him. He wished he could just tell her how he felt, but at the same time, he wasn't sure. Was he starting to fall for someone he'd just met?

"Sorry," she said. "I know we're just supposed to be enjoying this while it lasts. Sometimes it's hard not to look into the future, though."

He reached over to run his knuckles across her cheekbone. She was so pretty that his chest tightened.

"When do you think you'll be leaving?" she asked.

"We were planning on staying a couple more weeks."

"My mom and I are going to do a small turkey," she said. "I think my dad might be going on a trip. Thanksgiving was always one of Sophie's favorite holidays, so I think it'll be easier for him that way. But we're going to be celebrating. That's important to us. And I just thought..." She shrugged. "That you and Tad and Grady might want to come over to our place for dinner. If you're still here."

The invitation, extended so casually, was the first one he'd ever gotten for Thanksgiving. Ever. He'd been deployed half his life, and holidays had come to be just like any other day.

But the way Georgia was looking at him now, so warm and sweet, was like someone massaging life into his heart. And he immediately wanted to recoil from that. Because if he accepted that feeling, if he opened himself up to it, it could be taken away again.

He leaned back, quiet. It was like he'd shuttered right there in front of her. It was stupid, really. She hadn't asked him to marry her, for God's sake. But she was someone he could get serious about, and then what? That was the million-dollar question.

She was hurt now, he could tell. But instead of looking away or changing the subject, she lifted her chin a little.

"Are you going to tell me what you're thinking?" she asked.

"I'm not thinking anything." That was a lie, but it was the best he could do under the circumstances.

"I can handle you leaving," she said. "But I want you to be honest with me while you're here. I need you to talk to me, Hudson, or I'm going to feel like you don't care enough to talk to me."

He grit his teeth. She had him there. She wasn't pulling any punches, she wasn't going to sugarcoat it, and he realized then that he'd expected her to just let him get away with keeping her at a safe distance. Everyone else had. It was what he did; it was how he got along. Other than his close group of friends, he functioned by not functioning. At least not well. But Georgia Gallagher wasn't having it.

"I know you might not even be here by Thanksgiving," she continued. "So it might be a moot point anyway. But I guess I want to know if you'd come to dinner if you *were* here."

"Does it matter?"

She seemed to think about that. The wind outside buffeted the truck, and the evergreens surrounding them swayed, their canopies so thick and expansive that they blocked out the night sky overhead. He could smell the faint scent of her perfume, and it was making his head swim.

"I've been trying to be the kind of woman who can do something like this without any strings attached," she said. "But I'm not sure that's who I am."

He watched her. "Who are you, Georgia?" He thought he already knew. She was the kind of person who, when she allowed herself to love, loved deeply. But he wanted to hear her say it. He wanted her to tell him how she felt, which wasn't fair because he hadn't gone there himself.

She licked her lips, and they glistened in the soft lights of the dashboard. Her lashes were dark smudges under her eyes as she looked down, keeping her gaze from meeting his.

"I fall too hard," she said. "I wear my heart on my sleeve. I think I've been more guarded since Sophie died, more afraid of feeling. But Lucy has been bringing up all kinds of emotions for me, and the fact that I'm feeling anything at all is a good thing. It's like a limb that's fallen asleep, and you have to shake it to get the blood flowing again. And since I met you, my whole body has been tingling."

And then she looked up, locked gazes with his. The expression on her face was like a baseball bat to his chest.

"So," she continued. "I can't just pretend this doesn't mean something to me, because it does. And even if you're leaving, even if we don't see each other again, I need to know that it means something to you, too."

It was a simple request. She just wanted validation. She just wanted him to say what she needed to hear. Hudson had never had a problem blowing some smoke when he'd needed to before. He wasn't a liar, but he could pile on the charm when the moment called for it.

But the thing with this moment was that he had no clever reply up his sleeve. Nothing that would put her at ease that *wasn't* a lie. Which left him with the truth. And if he admitted to her what he'd been afraid of admitting to himself, then what would happen?

She waited, the low idling of the Tahoe the only sound between them. He ran a hand through his hair, feeling his heart knock in his chest. He couldn't believe how hard this was. Which told him exactly how he felt about Georgia.

"If I wasn't leaving," he said, his voice rough, "I'd have a hard time not loving you."

And there it was. What she'd needed to hear. And what he'd been so afraid to say, and even more afraid to feel.

She reached over and took his hand. Squeezed it gently.

"Thank you," she said.

"For what?"

"For saying that. Because when you leave, I'm going to hold on to it."

He knew that the deeper they got, the bigger the odds were that she'd never hear from him again. And that made him feel like a broken man.

"I think this might be what healing feels like," she continued. "To be able to say the hard things, and do things that scare you, and let people in." She shrugged. "Or maybe that's just wishful thinking. All I know is how I feel. And it's been lighter since I met you."

*Lighter.* It was a word he could get used to. He felt the same way. Exactly the same way. The idea that he might be healing some since Jesse's death, since retiring from the service, had never occurred to him until now. But to be fair, he hadn't let himself go there, either. Every time painful thoughts entered his head, he pushed them right back out again. And Jesse was usually one of the most painful thoughts that his mind could muster.

He reached up again and cupped her cheek in his hand. Leaned toward her slowly. Knowing this was exactly why he'd taken her home the night of the bonfire on the beach, instead of kissing her again like he'd wanted to. Because touching her was a wild card. Kissing her was a game of roulette that could be the end of him. Or the beginning of something else.

Those thoughts, those facts, didn't matter so much right then. Not like they had that night. Because right now, he was fairly lost in the depth of her eyes. Of her scent, which reminded him of those little pink wildflowers on the side of the road in Colorado. The ones that were the color of a new sunburn on fair skin.

And then his lips were on hers, moving over hers. And her arms were around his neck, in a way that said she didn't want to let him go. Tonight, or two weeks from now. He could feel it in the way she kissed him back.

He'd only been in love a handful of times, and each of those experiences had ended badly. Not because they couldn't have worked, but because he hadn't known how to make them work. Worse, he hadn't wanted to. But this felt different.

He didn't want to leave Georgia, either.

Which meant he was in deep, deep trouble.

Georgia looked at her watch, then put her chin in her hand, listening to her mother talk about her day while unpacking the groceries.

It was cold and windy outside, the weather rolling in off the ocean severe enough for surf advisories that afternoon. But she'd promised Thomas she'd go on a hike with him, and he was holding her to it. Even if they blew away in the process. His words, not hers. For her part, she had no interest in blowing anywhere.

She had about twenty minutes before she had to meet him at the trailhead, but her mom seemed to be enjoying the conversation, and Georgia didn't have the heart to remind her that she had to be leaving soon. This was the first time in the last few months that she'd seen her mother so relaxed. Not necessarily cheerful, but at least not so sad, and that was a very good thing.

"I think I might ask Julie over for Thanksgiving," her mom said, putting the coffee creamer into the cabinet. "Her kids will all be traveling this year, and she has nowhere to be. Is that okay with you?"

"Of course. It's your house. You don't have to ask me."

"But it's our holiday."

Georgia smiled. "It is our holiday." She thought of how much she and Sophie used to love getting up early to watch the Macy's Thanksgiving Day Parade when they'd been in high school. They'd gotten hot chocolates from Starbucks, always with extra whipped cream, and had curled up together on the couch with their cat, Potato. A random memory.

"Honey?" her mom said.

"Hmm?"

"Are you okay?"

"Just thinking. Remembering Soph."

Her mom nodded and opened the fridge door to put a quart of milk in, but she was moving slower now. As if she was making her way through her own memories. Maybe thick and sweet like warm honey. Georgia hoped the images she might be conjuring up were good ones. Ones from before the cancer, before everything had changed for their family.

Closing the fridge door again, her mom looked over. "Did you ask Hudson if he and his friends could come? I sure would love a full house on Thanksgiving."

Georgia would love that, too. But if how he'd acted the other night was any indication, he wasn't planning on sticking around. No matter how much she wanted him to. But she'd known going into this that what they had was finite.

"I asked," she said. "But I don't think he's going to be here. He'll be leaving soon."

Her mom frowned, the lines around her pretty mouth deepening. "Oh, I'm sorry, honey. How are you feeling about that?"

"Truthfully?"

"Truthfully."

"Kind of heartbroken."

Her mom walked around the kitchen island and pulled her into a hug. She smelled like Georgia's childhood. Like drugstore perfumes, and lotions with coconut in them.

Georgia lay her head on her shoulder, feeling like a kid again. She let herself sit there for a moment, in her mother's arms, breathing in her comforting scent. And then, after a minute, she leaned away and ran her hand through her hair, smoothing it. Trying to compose herself.

"I don't think I've ever seen you like this," her mother said.

"I'm not sure how it happened so fast. One minute I was fine. The next..."

She didn't know what it was that she wanted to say exactly, but it was sobering. This feeling of falling, of being so out of control when it came to Hudson.

"That's how it happened with your father," her mom continued. "Like a lightning bolt out of a clear blue sky."

Georgia sat back on the stool and tucked her hands in her lap. She thought about the stories of when her parents had met, when they'd dated and fallen in love. Their relationship hadn't lasted, but it had been intense and deep for a lot of years. They'd tried hard to stay together, for their kids, for each other, but they were simply better apart. Even so, Georgia knew her mom missed her dad terribly. He was still her best friend, but now that he had someone else, she wasn't sure where she fit into his life anymore.

"I used to think it wasn't possible to develop feelings this fast," Georgia said. "But when it happens to you, it's kind of humbling."

"That's a good way to put it."

Georgia reached for her purse. But before she could sling it over her shoulder, her mom put a hand out to stop her.

"Now, wait just a minute," she said.

"What?"

"You're not going without telling me what you're planning on doing about this young man, are you?"

"He's leaving, Mom."

"He might be leaving, but that doesn't have to be the end of it."

Georgia's cheeks warmed.

"Try and make it work, honey."

"It's not that easy. I'm not sure he wants to make it work."

"What does your gut say?"

Georgia pulled in a deep breath and let it out slowly. Her mom had raised Sophie and her to trust their instincts. *That's why you've got them!* she'd say when they were little. And she'd been right. Most of the time, at least. But in matters of the heart, those instincts could be a little murky. At the moment, they were telling her to protect herself. And they were also telling her not to let this one go. What was she supposed to do with *that*?

She leaned forward and gave her mom a quick peck on the cheek. "I've gotta go. Thomas is waiting."

Her mother looked out the window incredulously. "You're hiking in *this*?"

"It's just a little wind."

"You're avoiding the question."

"Not avoiding it. I just don't know the answer."

"Georgia Anne. Look at me."

"Uh-oh. The middle name."

"You bet your butt. This is what Sophie would've told you. And she's not here, so I'm telling you…"

Georgia looked her in the eyes. There was a fire in their deep brown depths that she'd missed.

"I know you don't trust this kind of thing easily," she said. "But promise me you'll at least give it your best shot?"

Georgia wasn't sure what that meant exactly. Throw herself on the hood of Hudson's SUV as he was driving out of town? What her mom had in mind was undoubtedly more subtle, but the thought of him leaving was enough to make her want to do just that. The intensity of that feeling, of that longing, unsettled her. Her mother was absolutely right—she didn't trust it.

"Promise me, honey," her mom continued. "Tell him how you feel. Show him how you feel. Don't let him just disappear without a fight."

Georgia swallowed hard. "You're right. Sophie would've said the same thing."

Her mother gave her a quick hug and then patted her thigh. "Okay. You can leave now. Tell Thomas I said hello."

"I will."

She put her purse over her shoulder. And when she walked out the front door into the grumpy coastal weather, she thought about what her mom wanted her to do. She wanted her to hold on tight to her happiness, to this new feeling that she'd found.

Holding on was the easy part. The trick was knowing when to let go.

Georgia made her way along the narrow, winding trail with the wind snatching at her hoodie. She was following Thomas as he climbed toward the Cape Longing lookout that was about ten minutes away now, but it was going to be a race to see if they would beat the rain.

She wanted to be enjoying this. Taking in the gorgeous, blustery scenery. Smelling the impending rain in the plump, low-lying clouds. Spending time with her best friend outdoors, where she really loved to be. But the truth was, this storm, and the hike itself, were bringing back the trauma of getting lost a few weeks ago. She hadn't really thought getting back out in Mother Nature would be so difficult. A hurdle for sure, but she didn't think the feelings another hike would stir up would be so scary.

Or maybe she just hadn't dealt with them yet. Since meeting Hudson, since falling for Hudson, it felt like she'd been living in some kind of alternate universe. One that was giving her a false sense of security. One that was allowing her to forget about the scary stuff for longer periods of time. Of course, those things were still with her. Some of them would always be with her.

Slowing, she forced a deep breath. Then put her hand on her chest, where she could feel her heart hammering out a panicky rhythm. She'd never had a panic attack. At least, she didn't think she'd ever had one. But Sophie had had a few, and what she was feeling now felt dangerously close to how her sister had described them. She thought about the other night, when she'd had to ask Hudson to pull over. It was possible that one had been knocking at the door then.

"Thomas, I think I might need to stop for a minute," she said.

Her friend turned, then came back to her in a few quick steps. "What's wrong?"

"I'm not sure," she said, leaning against a large rock on the side of the trail. "Being out here after getting lost… I think I overestimated my strength a little."

"Here, sit down. There's no hurry. We can turn around now if you want to."

Georgia settled herself on the rock, feeling its sharp

edges bite into her bottom. But she didn't care. Just being off her feet was helping. Or maybe that was Thomas's warm, comforting presence. He'd started rubbing her back, looking down at her from underneath his orange knit cap. Her heart suddenly swelled for him. He was such a good egg. The best friend she could have ever asked for.

"What's wrong, girlie?" he asked. "What's going on in that head of yours?"

"So many things. We'd be out here all night."

"Well, just give me the nutshell version then. And if we're out here all night, we'll hunker down under a log or something. It'll be great. Bestie-storm nature-immersion therapy."

She laughed. And she really needed to laugh. Her heartbeat had begun to get so heavy that it felt like it was affecting her lungs. Making it hard to breathe. Making her want to step outside her body and run away.

She forced another deep breath—a deepish breath—and closed her eyes for a few seconds. Focused on the feeling of the icy wind against her cheeks. Of the smell of the salt water, a scent that she'd grown up with, a scent that was so ingrained in her being that it was hard to untangle herself from it sometimes. From the ocean, and the sleepy town on the edges of it.

"Scootch," Thomas said, nudging her.

She scooted over, and he sat, too. His body was solid and comforting. His Thomas scent mingled with the salt in the air.

"Come on," he said. "Talk to me. What's going on? I have a feeling it's more than just being out here again."

She nodded. "It is. It's a lot of things."

"Like?"

"Like Hudson."

"I knew this guy was going to be a big deal for you. I knew it."

A gust of wind nearly blew Georgia's hat off her head. She reached up and pushed it back down over her ears, thinking of the night she'd spent out here. So scared and cold that she'd barely slept. Wondering if she'd end up another casualty of these rugged, south coast mountains. And then he'd found her. Bonnie had found her. Her guardian angels. Thomas was right—Hudson was a big deal for her. If only he knew how big a deal.

"I wasn't expecting this, you know?" she said, looking over at him. "I was at Mom's earlier, and admitting it out loud, how I feel about him… I just wasn't expecting it."

"It knocked you off your feet."

"That. Exactly that."

"What are you going to do about it?"

"Mom wants me to fight for him. For this, whatever it is. But what is it? I mean, he doesn't live here. He doesn't have a life here."

"True. All true. But it also sounds like he feels pretty strongly about you. If that kiss you told me about is any indication."

Georgia was having a hard time with that kiss. Mostly because all she could think about was more kisses. More everything. Which led right back here to this moment. With her heart pounding and her chest tight.

"He might," she said. "It feels like he does. But it's hard to say what I'd normally do with that. I met him right on the heels of losing Sophie, and I can't…" Her voice trailed off.

"You can't lose another person that you love."

She nodded. Knowing what she wanted to say before she could say it was Thomas's superpower.

He put an arm around her. "You know what I think?"

"What?"

"I think you're scared, and you have a really good reason to be scared. I also think—and don't get mad at me when I say this—that some of this might be a subconscious excuse."

"What do you mean?"

"I mean, you're making him feel really, really unattainable. If you're grieving, and he's grieving, and all these issues just seem insurmountable, then it's easier to let go of him. Not to fight for him, like your mama wants you to."

It made sense. And she'd probably known it deep down. But having Thomas say it so matter-of-factly was sobering.

"You might be right," she said.

"I usually am."

She gave him a small smile as the first stinging drops of rain hit her face. They both looked up at the same time. It was going to dump pretty soon.

"We're going to get soaked anyway," Thomas said, "whether we turn back now or not. What do you think about tackling the rest of this hike? As the first of the seemingly insurmountable things in your life?"

Thunder rumbled in the distance. It was only ten minutes to the lookout. She loved that lookout. And Thomas was right, as usual. They were going to get soaked either way.

Suddenly, tackling those insurmountable things seemed like exactly what she wanted to do.

"You're on," she said. "Let's go."

# *Chapter Eleven*

"We'd like to meet her, you know."

Grady took a long swig of beer and gave Hudson a look.

They'd been fishing most of the day and, despite the clouds, had both managed to get a nasty sunburn on their faces and the backs of their necks. Tad had slathered on the sunscreen, SPF one thousand, so he'd been busy gloating ever since getting in the Tahoe at the river. He was playing pool across the bar now with an attractive brunette and an even more attractive redhead.

"Will you look at that guy?" Hudson said. "He looks like hell, definitely smells like fish, and they're still lining up for him."

"Changing the subject," Grady muttered, but loud enough that Hudson heard over the jukebox.

He took a swallow of his own beer, then licked the tangy foam from his lips. Grady was right. He was changing the subject. Because thinking about Georgia was hard enough. Talking about her was proving almost impossible, without letting his true feelings show. And he really wasn't in the market for that, because then he'd be inviting everyone's thoughts and opinions on the matter.

No thanks. He could handle this on his own. Or not handle it, which was what he was busy doing now.

"What are ya'll talking about?" Tad asked, sidling up to the bar.

Hudson looked over at the pool table, where the brunette and the redhead were staring after him.

"What are you doing?" he asked his friend. "Are you *that* socially awkward?"

"Negative. If you must know, I'm buying them a drink. What'd you think? I just left them there?"

"Hell, I don't know. It looked like it to me."

"He's projecting," Grady said, taking a moody swallow of his beer.

"Excuse me?" Tad said.

"He's projecting what he's doing to Georgia onto you."

Hudson smiled and shook his head. "I thought you were an MD. Not a psychologist."

"You don't have to be a psychologist to see it."

"I'm lost," Tad said. "Who's doing what?"

"I told Hudson that we want to meet Georgia," Grady said.

"Oh. Yeah, we want to meet her, bro," Tad said, turning to Hudson incredulously. "Are you trying to keep this a secret? Because you know that's not gonna fly."

"I'm not trying to keep anything a secret. There's nothing to tell."

"Bullshit," Tad said.

"Yeah," Grady said. "Bull—"

"You're ridiculous. Both of you."

"Maybe," Grady said. "But we've got to look out for you."

Hudson knew what he meant. He had a tendency to curl into himself. Was that what was going to happen with Georgia? Was he just planning on sticking his head in the sand, then leaving here without ever looking back? Probably. Unless he listened to his friends for once.

"Why don't you invite her down for a drink?" Tad asked, laying down two crisp bills for the glasses of wine he'd ordered.

Hudson raised his brows. "Now?"

"Why not?"

"That's a good idea," Grady said.

Hudson cupped both hands around his mug of beer, rubbing his thumbs over the cool condensation on the glass. Then looked over at the dance floor, where no less than a dozen couples were two-stepping now to a Garth Brooks song that he'd always liked.

The truth was, he'd already thought about asking Georgia to meet him for a drink, but had dismissed it almost as soon as the idea formed in his brain. Because this was how he operated. This was how he'd always gotten along.

Regardless, he pictured dancing with her now—taking her hand in his, wrapping an arm around her waist and pulling her close. He knew what she'd feel like—soft and painfully supple. She'd smell good, her silky bangs skimming her eyelashes as she looked up at him in that way that made him feel like his walls might crumble around him. Leaving him exposed to whatever she might have in store.

The idea terrified him. And lit him up at the same time.

Tad clapped him on the back. "Life is short. Call her, dude."

Um, this feels significant.

Georgia smiled at the text from Thomas. Then swallowed hard and typed out a quick reply.

It was just a drink, right? Nothing to get all worked up about. But worked up she absolutely was as she sat in her car and looked over at the little honky-tonk on the side of the highway.

The dusky parking lot was bursting, and she could hear the music thumping from inside as a steady stream of people—couples, cowboys, people getting off work and looking forward to letting their hair down—made their way inside. There was a sign out front that said a live band was playing tonight, and according to Georgia's watch, they'd be taking the stage in about ten minutes. She was just in time.

Butterflies bumped against her rib cage. She didn't know why she was so nervous, except that, like Thomas had just said, this felt significant. Or, if not significant, at least *different.* And at this point, anything different with Hudson was reason to put on some lip gloss and a cute dress.

She looked into the rearview mirror and touched her hair. Her big silver hoops caught the headlights of the cars making their way through the parking lot, and her lips glistened pink. Understated, she hoped. But more glistening than they usually were. But when in Rome. Or, in a honky-tonk…

Taking a deep breath, she stepped out of her car and into the crisp fall evening. Her cute denim jacket wasn't exactly warm, but it held off most of the chill as she headed toward the door, her cowboy boots crunching in the gravel.

Her phone dinged from her purse. She pulled it out to see another text from Thomas.

Call me later. I'm dying here. Have fun. BUT CALL ME LATER.

She laughed. Then texted back, promising to call. Glad for the extra few seconds to gather herself before walking into the bar.

A group of women brushed past her, leaving a perfumed trail in their wake. And then, biting the inside of her cheek, Georgia followed them inside.

The place was dark. The only significant lights, aside from the neon beer signs behind the bar, were those on the stage and dance floor. The band had just come out, and the drumbeats reverberated inside Georgia's chest. It smelled like alcohol and cologne and hairspray, and the butterflies in her belly took flight.

Taking a deep breath, she looked around. The place was crowded, thumping, pulsing with energy. But when she locked eyes with Hudson across the bar, everything else seemed to fall away. There was a moment of warmth that settled over her, of tingling extremities, of a galloping heartbeat. For the first time since meeting him, since having his arms around her, she didn't feel scared. She felt in love.

He stood there watching her. His gaze slid down her body and back up again, and she knew that she'd worn the right dress for the occasion. A knee-length flowy fabric with a delicate flower pattern. Paired with her worn boots and denim jacket, she felt like she might look like a nineties' throwback, but Sophie had always said that everything comes back in style. And by the look on Hudson's face, he liked what he saw.

Her cheeks warmed as he walked up to her. And then

leaned down to kiss her on the cheek. He was so handsome, so sexy. She wasn't sure she'd ever met a man who'd affected her like this. Who took her to places emotionally that she'd only imagined before.

"I'm glad you came," he said into her ear. His lips brushed her earlobe, and his breath against her skin gave her goose bumps.

"Thanks for asking me."

"I want you to meet my friends." He turned to two men standing behind him who were looking at her expectantly. They were almost as tall as he was, but not quite. One of them was incredibly thick through the shoulders, imposing, but wearing a warm smile. The other wore black-framed glasses and had some gray threaded through his hair. They were both good-looking, but not in an unapproachable way. They immediately made her think of older brothers, and since she'd always wanted a brother, she liked them immediately.

"This is Tad," Hudson said. "Tad, this is Georgia."

Tad, the one with the broad shoulders, didn't hesitate. Just stepped forward to give her a big hug.

"Hi, Tad," she said when he pulled away again. "It's so nice to meet you."

"And this is Grady," Hudson said.

The other man pushed his glasses up and smiled down at her.

"It's nice to finally meet you, Georgia," he said.

She tried not to read too much into the *finally* part, but it sounded like Hudson had talked about her a little. Which was fair—she'd been talking about him practically nonstop.

The band was in full swing now, and they were good.

Really good. The electric guitar rang in her ears, making it hard to hear over it.

"What do you want to drink?" Hudson asked.

"A glass of white wine would be great. Thank you."

He motioned the bartender over. And then, surprising her, he took her hand. Holding it loosely while Tad and Grady headed to the pool tables, leaving them alone.

She gazed down at their fingers, casually entwined, looking pretty good together, if she did say so herself. Her pulse skipped in her wrists as he rubbed his thumb softly over her skin.

The bartender set her wineglass down, and Hudson let go of her hand to grab his wallet from his back pocket.

"Here you go," he said. "One glass of wine for the lady."

"Thank you."

He watched her as she took a sip, the alcohol warming her throat on the way down.

"You're beautiful," he said.

She smiled, feeling a little dizzy. A little unsteady on her feet.

"Dance with me?"

The band had changed tempo and were now playing something slow and soulful. Couples were headed to the dance floor to take advantage of the opportunity to hold each other close.

"I'd love to," she said. "But what about my wine?"

"We'll have Tad and Grady watch it." He took her hand again, and they weaved their way through the crowd of people to the pool tables. To his friends who were more than happy to oblige.

And then they were on the dance floor, the lights moving over them like a caress, the music thumping like a heartbeat.

Hudson wrapped an arm around her waist and pulled her close. His belt buckle bit into her hip, his thighs solid and muscular against her own. He held her hand in his and began to lead, then spun her twice, before pulling her close again.

She laughed, and then turned her cheek to lay it against his chest. She could feel his heart beating there. It kept time with her own as they made their way around the dance floor, the other couples falling away. The world falling away. Georgia was acutely aware that she was falling, too. She'd lost her heart to Hudson Cross, and now she was trying not to lose herself, too. But it was one of the hardest things she'd ever done, keeping herself grounded in his presence. In his arms.

He leaned down and kissed her temple. Then trailed his lips over her jawline and down to her neck. Chills rose along her arms, and she shivered against him.

"I've been thinking about what you said the other night," he said into her ear. His voice was smooth, even. But mostly it was soft. And that's what struck her so completely, because Hudson wasn't exactly a soft man.

The lights over the dance floor moved across his face, casting it in light and then shadow, and then light again. His eyes were dark, his jaw muscles moving methodically underneath his stubbly skin.

"What did I say?" she asked.

"You said you thought this was what healing might feel like. I'm starting to think you could be right."

She loved how that sounded coming from his lips. Because, like her, he was no stranger to pain. He knew suffering, like she knew it.

He gazed down at her, and his expression changed then. Grew more serious. She could almost see herself reflected in his eyes, and it did something to her. Made her feel like their connection had just deepened in the last few minutes.

"I've also been thinking about what it's going to be like when I leave," he said, splaying his hand over her lower back.

*When I leave...* She'd been thinking about it, too. In fact, it was all she'd been able to think about, and that annoyed her because she wanted to enjoy this time with him. She wanted to live in the moment. If Sophie had taught her anything, it was that.

He held her close as they danced. They were surrounded by people, but it felt like they were the only ones in the room. She gazed up at him, so many things teetering on her lips. So many questions. She bit her bottom lip to keep herself from saying anything at all. She worried if she did, she might do something ridiculous and ask him to stay.

"I'm not crazy about walking away from you, Georgia," he said.

"I'm not, either."

"What are we going to do about that?"

She hadn't been aware that there was a choice. Time felt like it was standing still, but she was vaguely aware that the song they were dancing to was getting ready to end. That life was going to be presenting itself again, along with all its problems and imperfections. The music would change, and the people in the room would reappear like unwelcome ghosts, and that question would linger. *What are we going to do about that?*

"Hudson," she began. "I—"

And then the song ended like she'd known it would. Everyone stopped dancing and burst into applause, drowning out her voice. But she wasn't sure what she'd been about to say anyway. Anything at all, other than telling him that she wanted to end this here and now, felt like putting everything on the line, and she wasn't sure how she'd manage if it went south. She thought about what Thomas had said. Was this insurmountable? Or did she just feel like it was?

He didn't press. Maybe he realized what this meant, too. That he'd opened the door a crack.

They walked back over to the pool table where Tad and Grady were and got Georgia's wine.

All of a sudden, her cheeks felt hot, her chest flushed. She fanned herself with her hand.

"Warm?" he asked.

She nodded.

"Want to go outside for a few minutes?"

"I'd love that." The thought of standing in the cool evening breeze, underneath the blanket of stars, suddenly sounded heavenly.

He took her hand and they walked toward the door with a wave to his friends. When they stepped outside, it felt just as good as Georgia imagined it might, with the air refreshing against her clammy skin. The parking lot was peppered with people, and they made their way toward a grove of evergreens on the outskirts where Hudson's SUV was parked.

He turned around and leaned against it, watching her in

the light from the bar and the few headlights that flashed through the darkness.

He smiled.

"What?" she asked.

"It's been a long time since I've fallen asleep with a woman's perfume on my skin. After I'm with you, I smell like you. I like it."

She laughed. "Uh-oh. Maybe that means I wear too much."

"No, it's the perfect amount."

"Nobody's ever told me I wear the perfect amount of perfume before."

"Maybe you haven't been with the right guy," he said. "Brutally honest, and a little random."

"I like random. I'm afraid of brutally honest."

"You've got nothing to worry about."

"I don't know. I feel like we're in scary territory."

At that, he crossed his arms over his broad chest. He was wearing a long-sleeve T-shirt that stretched over his shoulders and arms just right. His biceps bulged in a way that made it hard not to stare.

"You've got me there," he said, his voice husky. "I'm actually kind of terrified right now."

Despite how good the chilly air had felt a minute ago, Georgia shivered. She had to work to keep her teeth from clicking together. The way he was looking at her shot bolts of electricity straight through her. White-hot currents that sent goose bumps marching up her arms.

"And that brings me back to my original question," he said.

She raised her brows.

"What are we going to do about this?"

"Are you asking me what I want?" she said slowly. "Or what's possible?"

"Both."

She licked her lips, which suddenly felt dry. The hypothetical question of whether or not she was going to put everything on the line had just been laid out right in front of her. She felt the weight of his gaze, heavy on her shoulders. Felt it in her chest and stomach.

"If you're asking if I'd like more of you," she said, "the answer is yes. I do."

And there it was. The truth. The entirety of it. It was such a simple thing to say, such a simple thing to admit, but to Georgia, it felt like the very last of her barriers crumbling down around her.

"But you're leaving, Hudson," she continued. "Which is a lot more complicated than the question of what I want."

"You're right. And if someone were to have asked me if I saw this coming, I would've told them they were nuts. But you kind of hit me like a truck. Not something I can really ignore. Or forget when I leave."

She chewed the inside of her cheek. She could relate to that sentiment.

"I'm gonna be honest," he went on. "What I told you before is true. My scar tissue is deep. And talking about this is making me want to run in the opposite direction."

But he wasn't running. He wasn't turning away from her. He was standing there wearing an expression that she'd never seen before. It was like a layer of the roughness had been peeled back and she was seeing a softer man underneath.

After a minute, he held out his hand.

She took it and stepped close. She loved how he smelled, loved the feeling of her hand in his. She loved that he'd asked her here tonight, and that they'd danced in a crowded bar, and it had felt like their own private island. She was beginning to love everything about this.

He wrapped his arms around her, just like when they'd danced. Only this felt different. Like the beginning of something, and she just prayed that she wasn't wrong. Prayed that she could take it as it came, as precarious as it was, and wouldn't worry too much about the rest.

They stood there for a long moment. Until she lost track of time.

And then, he suddenly stiffened against her.

"What's wrong?"

"Over there," he said. "That guy across the parking lot. Is that Lucy's uncle?"

She turned and narrowed her eyes at the people walking through the parking lot. But it only took a second to recognize Brian Thorton through the shadowy light. He was leaning against the wall next to the bar's back door and had a cigarette between his lips. The collar of his worn denim jacket was turned up against the breeze.

Her heartbeat slowed. "That's him."

"I don't like it," Hudson said. "There's something about him that's off."

She watched as he flicked his cigarette ashes into the gravel and then leaned over to put the butt out against the sole of his boot.

When he stood up, he turned in their direction.

Georgia felt herself go rigid, her stomach tightening into a knot.

"I think he probably recognizes my truck," Hudson said.

The other man didn't move. Didn't acknowledge the people walking past him and into the bar. Just stared coldly through the night, making Georgia wish they'd never come outside in the first place.

The night was dark, but there was enough light in the parking lot to see the expression on his face. His lips were set in a hard line, his eyebrows a dark ridge over his eyes.

And then he smiled. It was maybe the most sinister smile she'd ever seen.

Georgia squeezed Hudson's hand.

"Let's get out of here," she said.

# *Chapter Twelve*

Hudson sat in the small waiting room of the doctor's office and looked around. It wasn't a modern-looking clinic, but rather a historic, Victorian house. There was one receptionist up front, a nurse and one whole doctor. Clarence Hill, MD, the plaque read on the front door. The entire place felt like a movie set.

Grady shifted in the chair next to him. No flimsy plastic waiting room chairs for Dr. Hill. These babies were upholstered in pink fabric and matched—rather nicely, Hudson thought—the flowery wallpaper behind them.

"We could still go to the hospital," Hudson whispered.

"I don't want to wait around in the emergency room for three hours. Google says this guy is great. And so did the lady at the market."

"Well, if the lady at the market says..."

His friend had taken a header on that afternoon's fishing adventure and wrenched his back, aggravating an old injury from boot camp. And now he was sitting funny, and looking very much in pain.

"I'm sorry, dude," Hudson said. "Are you gonna make it?"

"No."

"For a doctor, you sure are a crappy patient."

"Tell me something I don't know."

"You don't think anything's broken, do you?"

"Nah. I just need a couple of muscle relaxers and a good night's sleep."

Hudson picked up a *People* magazine that looked like it had been around the block a few times. And if the dog-eared pages weren't an indication, the cover story featuring a teenage Brittany Spears was.

He squinted at the date. Dr. Hill must have his magazines on a fairly healthy rotation. Or maybe he didn't like to throw anything out. Or both.

"Grady Wulff?"

Hudson looked up to see the nurse standing there, wearing a pair of purple scrubs, her gray hair pulled back into a neat bun. He guessed she was in her early sixties, and she didn't look like she was used to taking any guff.

Grady stood, grunting like a little old man. Then looked over at Hudson. "Want to come? You might get bored out here, and I'm not sure how long it's going to take."

Hudson put the magazine back on the elderly magazine pile. "Sure."

"I'm Florence," the nurse said. "You fell while fishing?"

"That's right," Grady said.

"That river looks calm, but it can be dangerous. You boys need to be careful."

Hudson's ears warmed. It was like being scolded by an aunt. If he had the choice, he'd rather be getting screamed at by a drill sergeant. The expression on this lady's face was much more stern, in his opinion.

"Right this way," she said.

She led them down the hallway to a stark white exam room to their left. Grady hobbled along with one hand on his back, looking fairly pathetic.

Nurse Florence got them seated, took some intake information, and when Hudson attempted a few jokes to see if he could get her to smile, he was rewarded with a slight tilt of her lips.

"The doctor will be right in," she said.

And then she was gone, leaving Hudson and Grady staring at each other.

"She scares me," Hudson said.

"That's the best kind of nurse," Grady said. "No nonsense, knows her job inside and out. Probably gives a shot that you can't even feel."

"I'll take your word for it."

"She seemed to like you just fine," Grady said. "You and your dumb dad jokes."

"I'm not above using whatever's in my arsenal. Also, Tad just texted. He's going to grab some takeout for dinner. What sounds good?"

"Ribs and beer sound amazing."

"Ribs and beer always sound amazing."

Wincing, Grady shifted on his chair. "This sucks. I feel like I'm a hundred years old."

"Good thing you don't look a day over ninety."

Grady flipped him the bird just as the doctor walked in.

"Gentleman," he said.

Hudson sat up straight.

"Uh," Grady said, sitting up straight, too. Or as straight as he could manage, which wasn't very straight at all. "Sorry about that."

Dr. Hill, a distinguished-looking man who appeared to be in his seventies, smiled. He had snow-white hair, rosy cheeks and a gentle demeanor, which Hudson immediately liked.

"No need to apologize," he said. "I'm the same way with my friends."

Hudson had a hard time believing that, but it was a nice thing to say anyway.

"You're Grady, I presume?" the doctor said, shaking Grady's hand.

"Yes, sir. And this is my buddy, Hudson."

He turned to shake Hudson's hand, too. "Florence said this was a fishing mishap?"

"Yes, sir."

"I hear the trout are biting up a storm over at Orion's Cove."

Hudson sat forward. This was interesting information. Inside information. He'd been in Christmas Bay long enough to know that all the good fishing holes around here were fiercely guarded secrets.

The doctor laughed. "Don't worry, I'll make sure you get directions before you leave. Everyone should experience that place at least once in their lifetime. You've never seen a prettier sunset in your life."

"I don't know," Grady said. "We've seen some spectacular ones over the cape."

"Where are you boys from?" the doctor asked, taking a seat on the rolling stool in front of Grady.

"Colorado," Hudson said.

"And what brings you to Christmas Bay?"

Hudson was used to these kinds of questions by now. It was a small town, and people were curious. They didn't think twice about asking all the things.

"We served in the army together," Grady said. "Hudson and I, and our other buddy, Tad. We lost a really good friend…" He paused for a few seconds and swallowed visibly. "We lost a good friend, and we decided to take a yearly trip to remember her."

Dr. Hill's expression grew somber. "I'm sorry to hear that. What a nice thing to do. We're proud to have you here. Thank you for your service."

They both nodded. They were used to this by now, too.

"I was in the army, too," the doctor said. "Where were you stationed?"

"The Middle East, mostly."

"I was a medic."

"I was, too." Grady seemed to forget about his back pain for a minute. He had a way of bonding with other doctors over their shared profession, but there was something special about other medics that always drew him in. Hudson also knew that he had a soft spot for older vets, because he'd never had much of a relationship with his own dad. He always seemed to gravitate toward father figures. Like he was still longing for that connection, even as a middle-aged man.

Hudson watched his friend, his chest tight. They'd all had issues with their families to varying degrees, and the look on Grady's face got him in the heart. Nobody else would probably recognize it, but Hudson did. He knew exactly how stoic his buddy usually was, and how in the last few minutes, he'd obviously let his guard down.

"A fellow doc," Dr. Hill said, slapping Grady on the shoulder. "Always a pleasure, son."

Grady smiled. "This is a nice practice. Can I ask how long you've been here?"

"Thirty years. Florence has been my nurse for twenty of those. We have a nice hospital in town, a few very good clinics, but I never wanted to be told how to treat my patients. At the risk of sounding a little cliché, they're like family to me. I'm proud that we don't turn people away here. Sometimes that doesn't make the best financial sense, but it's how I wanted to practice medicine. I guess that's more than you probably wanted to know, but there it is."

On the contrary, Grady seemed enchanted by this country doctor. By his charm and his rustic office—the whole package. It was a far cry from the army grind he was so used to, and Hudson recognized how much that probably appealed to someone who needed a fresh start.

"But, you know," Dr. Hill continued, adjusting the stethoscope around his neck, "I'm thinking about retiring soon. As much as I love what I do, I promised my wife that this time in our lives is for us. She's had to share me with work long enough. I'm taking her to Paris for our fiftieth, and I'd like to be wrapped up here by then."

Grady nodded. And Hudson saw the sudden spark in his eyes.

"Now," the doctor said. "Tell me exactly how this happened, and what's bothering you."

But Hudson's friend was somewhere else now. The pain taking a back seat to something bigger—

The need to put down some roots.

Georgia sat on an outcropping of rock at Agate Beach, the small, secluded cove where Sophie's ashes were scattered, and watched the sun sinking into the horizon. The sky was a mixture of colors—cosmic swirls of oranges and pinks, yellows and purples—and the wind was calm, leaving the mermaid-green water beyond the waves almost glassy looking.

Tilting her head back, she closed her eyes for a minute, basking in the rare warmth of the November sun on her cheeks. She breathed in the smell of the salt water and let it carry her back to her childhood. When her parents would bring her and Sophie here, so they could run and play, and splash in the waves. She could almost hear her dad yelling at them to stay close, and see her mother wearing her wide-brimmed hat and rubbing sunscreen on her shoulders.

She opened her eyes again and stared out at the ocean. For the first time in a long time, she felt some happiness, some contentment and peace. Time had something to do with that. And so did Hudson.

She smiled up at a seagull that dipped and bobbed on the evening breeze. She could see its speckled feathers underneath its outstretched wings, its little orange feet tucked neatly underneath its body.

"I miss you, Soph," she said quietly. "I have so much to tell you."

The seagull squawked in response, gliding toward the sparkling water.

A light breeze moved through Georgia's hair, and she chose to imagine it might be a sign that her sister was listening. That it might be a caress from the other side.

"I'm pretty sure you'd like this guy that I'm seeing. I think you'd tell me to grab on to him with both hands… Is that what you'd say, Sophie?"

She gazed out over the water, thinking about Hudson, and the fact that he'd never get to meet her sister. He would've loved her. It hurt to know that meeting would never happen. It would only happen in her mind, and on evenings like this when her imagination was at its most vivid, and her heart was open wide.

"I just want you to know that I love him. And I'm scared of that. But I know what you'd say..."

The waves crashed onto the beach, thunderous and adamant. It was the only answer she was going to get, but it was enough. The peace she'd felt earlier spread into the rest of her body—into her arms and legs, into her fingers and toes. It brought with it a tingly, soft warmth that eased the ache in her throat.

And then, from down the beach, she heard barking. Muffled in the breeze at first, but growing louder with each passing second.

She turned to see a small dog bounding toward her. Brown, nondescript. Floppy ears, big, blocky paws. A puppy, probably not more than a few months old.

"Fiona!" called a woman running after her. "Fiona, come!"

The dog did no such thing. Instead, she galloped straight for Georgia, her ears flying, her long pink tongue lolling out the side of her mouth.

Georgia had just enough time to brace herself before the puppy launched herself at her chest. Licking her face and hands, anything she could reach.

"Fiona, no!" the woman cried, clearly out of breath. She'd given up on running, and was now walking toward them, looking for the most part like she wanted to collapse. There was no telling how long she'd given chase.

Georgia grabbed on to the puppy's collar. Up close, she could see that Fiona the dog was probably a hound mix of some sort. Her ears were impossibly long, her tail skinny and whiplike, her paws looking like something straight out of a *Scooby-Doo* episode.

"Oh, my gosh, I'm *so* sorry," the woman said, walking up to where Georgia was still perched on the rock. Precariously now that Fiona was practically in her lap.

"It's okay, she's adorable."

"She's a little naughty," the woman said, giving the puppy a look before reaching out to scoop her up. She was immediately rewarded with dog kisses and frantic tail wags.

Georgia laughed. "But very sweet."

"You wouldn't be able to tell at the moment, but she's actually really smart. And she's a people pleaser."

"A very good girl," Georgia said. "And she loves her mom."

"Well, foster mom. I volunteer at the shelter." She deposited the wiggly puppy onto the sand and bent to click a leash onto her collar. "I have her and her brother with me for a few weeks. Trying to get some training in while they're little. Makes them much more adoptable."

"That's wonderful."

Georgia smiled down at the little dog, who was gazing back adoringly. Definitely hound something or other. She immediately thought of her sixth-grade teacher reading *Where the Red Fern Grows* to the class after lunch, and bawling her eyes out.

"I hope she didn't get paw prints on your jacket," the woman said, pushing her hair out of her eyes. "She follows her nose and gets carried away."

"No paw prints. And even if she had, it's okay. I love dogs. My boyfriend—" Georgia stopped herself short. She could hardly believe she'd just said that, but out it had come. She wondered what Hudson would think of this. And promptly pictured him running for the hills.

The woman raised her brows. "Your boyfriend?"

"Uh…he has a Lab. She's the best."

"Oh, Labs really are. Fiona here is half bloodhound. If you couldn't already tell by these ears." She bent down and gave one of the offending ears a scratch. "I think she'd make a wonderful search and rescue dog."

Georgia gazed at her, her heart beat slowing a fraction.

"Well," the woman continued, "have a lovely evening!"

And before Georgia could reply, she was trotting off with the puppy—the little dog's ears flapping in the breeze.

*Search and rescue.*

If Georgia didn't know better, she'd think it was a sign. Or maybe she'd known she'd get a sign all along.

Hudson looked at his watch. He was supposed to meet Georgia at the movies in an hour, but Grady had wanted to have pizza and a beer with him and Tad first. There was something he wanted to "run by them." Whatever that meant.

He looked over at his friend now and steepled his hands on the table. Mario's was the best pizza in town, even if the place was a little threadbare. There were worn spots in the carpet, which looked like it had been around since the eighties, and the windows were cloudy and single paned. But the view was spectacular, and the pepperoni was delicious. Hudson's stomach growled now, thinking about it. He just wanted to leave room for popcorn.

"What's this all about?" he asked. "You're making me very nervous."

"Me, too," Tad said, stuffing his face with a chicken wing. "Oh, mer God. These are ah-mazing."

Grady smiled and leaned forward in the booth. He

looked different today than he had a few days ago, but Hudson thought that might be because his back felt better. He had some healthy color in his face that was partly because of his fishing tan, but there was something else that Hudson couldn't quite put his finger on. He looked happier than he had in a while. But why?

"Okay, brother," Hudson said. "Out with it."

Grady cleared his throat. "Alright. First of all, I want you guys to know I'm in my right frame of mind. I have all my faculties. I didn't fall and hit my head or anything."

Tad slid Hudson a look.

"I've been doing some thinking," Grady said. "And what the hell do I have to go back to in Colorado?"

Hudson stared at him. "Your home?"

"What home? It's a barely furnished apartment with boxes in the corner of the living room that I haven't unpacked for months."

"Okay. But that's what we're all going back to."

"Exactly."

Tad shook his head. "What are you saying?"

"I'm saying—"

Their server walked up with their pizza and set it on the table with a friendly smile. Steam curled off the top, and warm cheese oozed from the sides. Hudson could almost taste the pepperoni just by breathing it in.

He narrowed his eyes at Grady. "You're saying?"

Grady thanked the server, then watched her walk away, her ponytail swinging.

When he looked back at them again, it was with an expression that Hudson had only seen a handful of times. He meant business.

"Losing Jesse was the worst thing that's ever happened

to me," he said quietly. "I'm not sure that I'll ever get over it."

Tad nodded. Looked at his hands in his lap. There was nothing to say to that—they could only offer a silent agreement. A silent understanding. They all felt the same way.

"But I'm hoping that I can get through it."

Hudson stiffened. It was the same thing that Georgia had said about losing her sister.

He sat there, breathing shallowly, trying not to see it as some kind of cosmic sign. Trying not to jump to conclusions about what Grady meant. But it was becoming clearer by the second.

"I'm going to see about buying Dr. Hill's practice," Grady finished evenly.

A deep hush fell over the table. It was deafening.

Finally, after a minute, Tad scrubbed his hand through his hair. "What?"

Setting his jaw, Grady sat back in the booth. He'd thought this through. Even without the country doctor's clinic in the picture, he'd probably been thinking about it long before they'd stepped foot inside Christmas Bay.

"I'm going to move," he said. "Here."

Hudson let that settle. Mostly because he couldn't think of an appropriate response. He immediately dismissed *Are you nuts?* But it was the only thing he could conjure up.

"I love you guys," Grady said. "You're my family. But we'll be family no matter where I am, and I need this. I need a new start. I can't explain it in a way that probably makes sense to you, but I know I'm not going to get that start in Denver. I feel nothing there. And I need to feel something again."

And there it was. Hudson took the deep breath he'd been craving for the last few minutes. Because a complete and whole understanding moved through him. It was as if he was the one who'd just spoken the words.

Grady watched them carefully. Obviously wanting their blessing, but something told Hudson that even if he didn't get it, it wouldn't matter. He'd made up his mind. This was a done deal.

Tad was the first to break the silence.

"I get it, man," he said. "Denver was always going to be a temporary stop for you. For all of us, I think. You're just the first one with the balls to move on."

Grady smiled. Then looked over at Hudson. Waiting for him to say something. Anything.

"Someone told me that once," Hudson finally managed, his voice husky.

"Told you what?"

"That you can't get over it, but you can get through it."

Grady's eyes were full of that ever-present pain they were all so familiar with. But they held something else, too. *Hope*. It made sense. A new start was all about hope. Jesse would have wanted this for him.

"I guess this means we'll be back here more often than we thought," Tad said.

Hudson thought it was more significant than that. How significant, only time would tell.

# *Chapter Thirteen*

Georgia walked down the sidewalk beside Hudson, his arm around her shoulder keeping her warm in the chilly November evening.

Thanksgiving was still a few weeks away, but Christmas Bay was already dressed up in her holiday finest. Living up to its name, Christmas came early to the little town that Georgia called home. Sparkling trees were already gracing the shop windows. Lit wreaths were already swinging from the old-fashioned light posts on Main Street. Some people got grumpy about welcoming Christmas before Thanksgiving, but Georgia had always loved it. If she had her way, she'd start celebrating in September, which had always driven Sophie crazy. Sophie had been team Thanksgiving all the way.

Georgia looked up at Hudson as they walked, as they passed tourists with their ever-present bags in their hands, and locals who were bundled up against the cold. He smiled down at her, making her heart skip behind her breastbone. She kept thinking about what she'd said to that woman on the beach the other night. *My boyfriend...* She thought about it now as they walked so comfortably beside each other. It was like they'd known each other for a long time. It was almost like this was meant to be.

"What are you thinking?" he asked.

"If this movie is going to be any good," she lied. "I've read mixed reviews."

"But Scarlett Johansson…"

She laughed.

"Okay," he continued quietly. "What are you really thinking?"

She was so torn, so scared of letting him in. But if they were going to make anything work, for any amount of time, she was going to have to be honest with him.

She sighed. "That I met a lady on the beach the other night. She was fostering the cutest puppy. And I was telling her about Bonnie, and I said you were my boyfriend. It just slipped out. I've been thinking about it ever since, wondering what you'd say about that."

He slowed, and she slowed with him. Her stomach curled into a knot. She could hardly believe she'd just told him that, but here she was.

"Boyfriend, huh?"

She nodded.

"I haven't been anyone's boyfriend in a long time."

"Well, it's fast. And I'm not sure why I said it, except that I feel so comfortable with you. And I'm starting to…"

She let her voice trail off. The boyfriend thing was one thing. Mentioning the *L* word was something else altogether.

"Miss Gallagher! Miss Gallagher!"

Georgia looked over to see two of her students running toward her, the pom-poms on their knit caps bouncing.

"Uh-oh," Hudson said. "They spotted their teacher in the wild. A sacred thing."

Georgia laughed. It was true. She'd never get used to

the look of wonder on her kids' faces when they saw her at the grocery store or on a walk in her neighborhood. To them, she belonged in the classroom, period. Any adventures beyond that were cause for jubilation. With a hefty side of confusion.

"Hi, there, girls."

"Hi!" they said, coming to a breathless stop in front of her and Hudson.

Georgia looked down the sidewalk to see a woman trying to catch up. She had her hands full of coffee and bags.

"Where's Bonnie?" one of the girls asked.

"My friends are babysitting," Hudson said. "Er, dog-sitting."

They giggled.

"What are you girls out doing this evening?" Georgia asked.

"My aunt took us shopping," the other little girl said. Her name was Bethany, but everyone called her Bethy, which Georgia thought was the cutest.

"And for hot chocolate," her friend Laila chimed in.

"Yum. I love hot chocolate."

"What are you doing, Miss Gallagher?" Bethany asked, her brown eyes wide. This was the I'm-seeing-my-teacher-outside-of-the-classroom look that Georgia was so used to getting.

"Mr. Hudson and I are going to see the new Marvel movie."

"*Ooohhh*," the girls said in unison.

Hudson winked down at them. And Georgia fell a little harder. Just like that.

"Mr. Hudson, are you going to come to our Christmas party?" Bethany asked. "It's going to be so fun, and Bonnie can come, too!" She lisped that entire sentence since she was currently missing one of her front teeth.

"Oh…" he said. "Well, I'm not sure I'm going to be here."

They both frowned dramatically, but Georgia looked up at him with the smallest bit of hope in her heart. He wasn't sure he was going to be here wasn't the same thing as he *wasn't* going to be here.

Despite trying not to, she kept wondering what it would have been like if she'd met Hudson at a different point in their lives. If he'd been more settled, or if she'd been more healed. What would that have looked like? It didn't make sense to think about those things, or ruminate on them, since this was their reality. But it was still hard not to go there sometimes.

"Bethany, Laila, we've got to go!"

Georgia waved to Bethany's aunt, and she waved back with her elbow—her hands full, and her expression frazzled.

"You'd better run, girls," she said. "Scoot. Enjoy your evening, okay?"

They both came in for a quick little girl hug, all pigtails and mittens. They hugged Hudson, too, before turning and running back down the sidewalk, toward the rest of whatever they had planned for the night.

"Wow," Hudson said. "They sure do love their teacher."

"I love them, too. But to be fair, most little kids love their teacher. At least at this age."

"Don't sell yourself short. You're amazing."

Her chest warmed. That meant a lot, since she thought he was amazing, too.

"You're invited, you know," she said.

He brushed her bangs out of her eyes. "Invited?"

"To our Christmas party. You and Bonnie. Just consider it a standing invitation. You know, to all the things."

"I take that honor very seriously."

"You should. We don't invite just anyone to our festivities."

"Well, then. I might have to come."

She swallowed hard as he reached out to take her hand.

"Hudson," she said.

"Mmm?"

There was a Salvation Army bell ringer on the corner, and the sound chimed through the cool evening. People continued passing them on the sidewalk, and Georgia was only half aware that if they stood out here much longer, they might miss their movie. But at the moment, she could only focus on Hudson and the way his lips were tilted just so. Not quite a smile, but not a frown, either. It was something else, something that made her take a small step closer to him.

"You said you *might* not be here," she said. "I thought you were going home before Thanksgiving."

He rubbed his thumb over her knuckles. "I know. And that's what I thought, too. But Grady said something today…"

The bell kept ringing, the people kept brushing past. It felt like they were at some kind of juncture, and Georgia had to work not to hold her breath.

"He's thinking about staying here," he finished evenly.

"What? Why?"

"I'm not sure. And then again, I know exactly why." He paused for a second, looking like he was searching for the right words. "When you've been stuck in a box most of your life, even if that box was where you wanted to be, the prospect of being free to live the way you suddenly want to…well. That's a very powerful thing."

She nodded slowly. "Do you feel like you've been stuck, too?"

"Not necessarily stuck. But there have been limitations, of course. Physical, emotional. All of it."

He paused again, and she sensed he was digging deep for things that might be eluding him.

"But now," he continued, "I'm thinking about doing things differently, I guess. I'm thinking about all the things I want, but never knew that I wanted. Does any of this make sense?"

She squeezed his hand. Felt the calluses on his fingers. The way the short, fine hairs on the side of his hand tickled her skin.

"It does," she said.

"I haven't even talked to the guys about this. But I knew you'd understand. If I can just get through this next part of my life without any more…"

He didn't finish, but he didn't have to. He meant without any more loss. Without any more trauma.

"But that's not how it works, is it?" he finished, his voice husky.

"No," she said. Understanding that, too. "It isn't."

They stood there, quiet, holding hands on the sidewalk. She guessed that anyone passing them right then would assume they were in a committed relationship. That they were in love, and probably had been for a while. But the truth was, they were still getting to know each other. Their connection was true and deep, but there were so many questions that they made Georgia's head spin.

"I hate to tell you this," he said, "but I think we're too late for the movie."

She smiled. She really didn't care if they went to a movie or not. She was just enjoying being with him.

He reached up and cupped her cheek in his hand.

"You're kind of sweeping me off my feet," she said. "So, what now?"

"We keep coming back to that, don't we?"

"That, we do," he said.

"If I said I was looking forward to you leaving, I'd be a big, fat liar."

"Well, then. That makes two of us."

"But there's a possibility that you might stay. Or you might come back…"

"I think there might be."

It felt like he meant it. That he was telling her what lay in his heart. She was starting to trust him, trust what little foundation they had, and that was a very new thing for her.

"Do you think you might keep volunteering for search and rescue here?" she asked. "You're so good at it. I know they'd be thrilled to have you."

"I'd like to. I mean, Bonnie is slowing down, but this has been good for her. It's been good for me, too. Helping people…it's important to me. After seeing so much carnage in the service, I feel like I'm doing some good here."

He held her gaze for a long moment. Her heart was a wild thing behind her breastbone, thundering like horses' hooves, reminding her every second how precarious this was.

He wrapped his arm around her waist and brought her closer.

"I don't know what this will look like, Georgia," he said, his mouth impossibly close to hers. But not touching it. Not quite yet.

"I don't care," she said. "As long as I don't have to say goodbye to you, I don't care what it looks like."

And then he kissed her. And all other thoughts were lost. Like a cry in the woods.

Hudson sat on the balcony of the Airbnb and looked out at the ocean—sparkling tonight underneath the moonlit sky.

He'd never been a huge drinker. Beer after fishing was about as wild as he ever got. His mother had been a drinker, and it had nearly killed her on several occasions, leaving him with a rigidity about alcohol that wasn't exactly normal.

But tonight was different. He'd woken up out of a dead sleep and had started pacing the floor. Something he hadn't done since he'd been in the service. He'd done it a lot after Jesse had been killed—walking back and forth, back and forth, until he thought he might wear a hole in the floor. But then he'd retired, and his mind had quieted some. Not a lot, but some. He'd learned how to still himself, working with Bonnie, being with his friends, doing things he felt were meaningful and that gave him purpose.

But tonight, he'd woken up from a vivid dream and had started pacing again. Not necessarily a nightmare, but somewhere on the outer edges of one. He couldn't even remember what it had been about now, but the feeling remained. The uneasiness. Georgia had been in it. And he'd lost her.

He sat on one of the weary balcony chairs now and

brought the small glass of whiskey to his lips. It burned going down, which was exactly what he wanted. He wanted to feel something other than the cold fog of the dream, and the unraveling of the peace he'd managed to build over the last six months. It wasn't the dream making him feel that way, of course. That was just the manifestation of thoughts and feelings that he was used to pushing down. Buried deep, where they couldn't mess with his head. Or so he thought.

He licked the whiskey off his lips and set the glass down beside him. No, he wasn't a big drinker, but something about the darkness of the night, so complete, even with the pretty moon hanging as if on a hinge in the sky, called for it at the moment.

"What's going on, brother?"

He turned to see Tad standing behind him, wearing a hoodie and a pair of blue checkered pajama bottoms. His hair was going in every different direction, and from here, Hudson could see the beginnings of a receding hairline on his forehead. Something he'd rib him about later.

"Couldn't sleep," he said.

"Me, neither. Heartburn. Want some company?"

Hudson nodded, and his friend pulled up a deck chair. It was chilly tonight, but not overly so. The salty breeze felt more refreshing than anything else. The perfect sweatshirt weather, something that Hudson was beginning to find was an actual thing on the Oregon coast. He was starting to love it here. He was starting to love the people here—one in particular.

Tad rubbed his chest. "Good God. Next time we have Thai, please remind me to not have it so damn spicy. My lungs are on fire."

"Copy that."

"I think I ate half a bottle of Tums. By the way, we need more Tums."

"Copy that."

Tad turned to him, his face bathed in moonlight. The scruff on his jaw was more salt than pepper. He looked like his dad, a lieutenant colonel whose reputation preceded him. Tad had been living under his shadow his entire life, his entire military career. Hudson wasn't sure he'd ever step out from under it.

His friend raised his brows. "Whiskey, huh?"

Hudson didn't answer that. Just looked past him to the water, to the waves that were hammering the beach with their ferocious tenacity. Over and over and over, they'd been smashing against those rocks, since the beginning of time. And they'd be smashing those rocks long after Hudson was gone. It was a humbling thought.

Tad put his hood up, stuck his hands in the front pocket of the sweatshirt and looked out at the water, too. "Want to talk about it?"

Hudson was much more comfortable stowing things, but he and Tad had been friends a long time, and he knew that if he didn't throw his buddy a bone, he wouldn't let up.

He pulled in a breath and let it out slowly. "I think I might've made a promise that I'm not sure I'll be able to keep."

"To Georgia?" Tad said this while still looking out at the water.

"Yeah."

"How?"

"I told her that I'll be back. And I will come back. It's not that I won't."

"For her?"

"Yeah. And for the town, for the people, for all of it. But mostly for her."

"Then what's the problem?"

"I told her the truth…but I didn't tell her the whole truth."

Tad sighed and leaned back in his chair. It creaked under his considerable weight. "Ahh, the whole truth. That can get sticky, as we all know."

Hudson didn't answer that. His stomach was turning.

This was exactly why he preferred keeping things to himself. When he spoke the words out loud, it forced him to look right at himself. What kind of man wouldn't want to be with a woman like Georgia? But he knew that wanting to be with her wasn't the problem. It was wanting to stay with her that was.

"What's the whole truth, bro?" Tad asked evenly.

"That I'm scared."

Tad laughed. "Aren't we all?"

Hudson took another sip of his whiskey despite his roiling stomach. Screw it. He might just have another glass.

"This is different," he said.

"Because she's different."

"Yes."

"So, what are you saying exactly?"

Hudson looked down at the drink in his hand. Swirling it so the amber liquid rolled like the ocean in the distance. A tiny sea of tranquility. At least until the morning and the inevitable headache followed.

"I don't want to disappoint her," he said.

"So don't."

"Don't you get it? I don't want to let her down. Like I let..."

"Oh, God. Like you let Jesse down?"

Hudson put his drink down and got up. He wanted to pace. He wanted to pace right out of his skin.

"You know that's messed up," Tad continued. "You feeling that way? It's the PTSD. It's lying to you, Hud."

"It's doing a pretty good job of it."

"Yeah. It does that. It's a master manipulator. It will ruin your life if you let it."

"It's not that easy. You've been where I am. You get it."

"Yeah," Tad said. "I do. And I regret it."

Hudson turned and looked down at his friend. "With who?"

"It doesn't matter. It was a long time ago. The point is, I wish I could go back and change some things in my life, but I can't, and those bridges are burned forever. You have a chance to have a meaningful relationship with someone, Hud. You could build something with her, if you gave it a chance."

"And when it doesn't work?"

"If it doesn't work, it's not the end of the world."

"I don't want to hurt her."

"Sorry to tell you this, bro," Tad said, "but she's going to be hurt either way."

Hudson shoved a hand through his hair.

"You care about her, right?"

"Yeah, I care about her. But it doesn't matter. I should've put the brakes on in the beginning."

"You're full of it, man."

"What's that supposed to mean?"

"You heard me," Tad said. "I know you're struggling, we all are. We all lost someone over there."

That was true. And they were all working through their trauma in their own way. Or, not working through it. It depended on the day, the hour, the minute. It depended on who came into their life at exactly what time and place.

"Right," Hudson said. "And I can't just snap my fingers and be okay with it."

"Everyone you care about could be wiped out tomorrow. Just like that," Tad said, his expression stormy. "There are no guarantees, you know that. So why are you using this as some kind of excuse not to get close to someone who cares about you?"

Hudson stared down at him. It wasn't like Tad to get this worked up. Of the three of them, he was the least likely to show emotion over much of anything. It wasn't that he didn't feel it, he felt it plenty. But having a father who was so buttoned up, it had always been expected that he be buttoned up, too.

But as his friend glared at the water in the distance, Hudson knew he didn't understand all that was going through his mind and heart at a given time. He wondered who this woman was that he had regrets with. He hadn't even known Tad had been serious about anyone over the years.

"I know your family life sucked," Tad continued. His voice was gravelly now. Strained like a wire about to break. "I know you didn't have anyone to write to, nobody to come home to. Neither did I. I had family, but that didn't mean we were close. Don't let those things define you, Hudson. You can break that cycle, but only if you want to."

Hudson stood there for a long minute, letting that sink in. The words made sense. Intellectually, it all did. It was the taking them to heart part of the equation that was going to be hard. Or damn near impossible. The question was, was he willing to try? He wasn't sure yet. But he was grateful for his friend who was telling it exactly how it was.

"I'm sorry," Hudson finally said.

"For?"

"Everything."

Tad looked at him again. He knew what Hudson meant by that. Everything meant everything. The things they could control, and the things they couldn't. The things that had happened in the service, and the people they'd lost, who had come into their lives like storms, and had gone out like the softest of exhaled breaths. Hudson was sorry for all of it. But mostly, he was sorry that there was a place inside his friend, like there was a place inside himself, that couldn't be touched. At least not without a hell of a lot of trying, and maybe not even then.

Tad nodded, the ocean breeze moving his hood about his face.

A deep understanding passed between them then. The kind that was built on years of friendship and trust.

Without another word, Hudson walked past his friend, patting him on the shoulder as he passed.

He'd left his phone inside by the couch, and it had dinged with a text a few minutes ago. Maybe it was nothing.

But at this time of night, his gut said it was something.

## *Chapter Fourteen*

Hudson sat underneath a sturdy pine tree, downing another cup of coffee. He'd had two while sobering up back at the house, and at this rate, he probably wouldn't sleep for a week. But that was fine because he needed to be sharp for this one. Awake and on point.

He looked around at the volunteers and their dogs, at the deputies talking among themselves in the dusky predawn hour. There was a sense of urgency in the air that was familiar—all searches felt urgent. But to Hudson, this one also felt different. To the point where his stomach, which had been turning a few hours ago, was now upside down. His palms were damp and his pulse was rapid. He was ready to go. Bonnie was ready. She wouldn't lie down, instead choosing to stand and watch him, waiting impatiently for the sign that they were heading out.

"Cross."

Hudson looked up to see Sheriff Hicks walking toward him. He wore a thick uniform jacket and a Stetson pulled low over his eyes. Heavy boots that would be impervious to the mud they'd encounter on the trails. He looked formidable. He looked like he'd done this once or twice before.

"Morning, Sheriff."

Bonnie wagged her tail as the big man bent to pet her.

"I was glad to see your name on the volunteer list," the sheriff said. "We need the best people on this one. The best dogs."

There were dark shadows underneath the other man's green eyes. Deep wrinkles between his brows. He looked like he hadn't slept at all last night, and Hudson felt a connection that went beyond their shared law enforcement background. This was a man who shouldered every lost person, every worried family member and more. The buck stopped with him.

"Good luck today," he said. And gave Bonnie one more pat before turning to walk away.

Hudson watched him go, swallowing hard and finding that his throat was dry and scratchy. The sheriff wasn't the only one on edge. The entire search party seemed to be humming with nerves. They were looking for a sixteen-year-old runaway who had a history of drug use. His mother had reason to believe that he'd gone into the woods, as that's where he spent most of his time, hunting and fishing with his dad, who'd been killed in a car accident last year.

It was a sad case, a very heavy case. This wasn't a hiker who'd left for an adventure and taken the wrong trail. This was a child who, intentionally or not, might come to harm if they didn't find him in time. They all felt the weight of it. It hung in the air, impossibly thick, impossibly sobering.

Bonnie nudged Hudson's hand with her cold, wet nose. She felt it, too.

Rubbing his jaw, he let his thoughts wander for a few precious seconds. Back to Tad, and the talk they'd had before he'd gotten the text from Search and Rescue. He couldn't stop thinking about what his friend had said. *If it doesn't work, it's not the end of the world...*

That was true. Hudson knew that, in theory.

So why did he feel like he was at the edge of a precipice, about to step off? What made committing to Georgia such a daunting prospect, when he'd done daunting his entire life?

He knew why. Despite what Tad had said, if he committed to Georgia and it didn't work, the world as he knew it would come crashing down around him.

And just as the search he was about to go on felt fundamentally different—so did she.

"Robin!" Hudson's voice was beginning to go. Straining over his vocal cords and sounding hoarse and weak to his own ears.

Bonnie bounded through the brush up ahead, not wanting to stop for water, or a breather, or anything else. The sun was low in the sky, beginning to sink toward the ocean in the distance, and it didn't seem like they were any closer to finding Robin Breck than they had been that morning. This was a kid who didn't want to be found, which made the search and rescue team's job about ten times harder.

"Rob—" Hudson tried calling again, but ended up having a coughing fit instead.

He was starting to notice more changes with his age lately, more fatigue, more aches and pains, which pissed him off. The drive was still there, the determination, and his work ethic was stronger than ever. But his body was undeniably different. He wasn't the same man he'd been at twenty-five, and as much as he tried to ignore that fact on the daily, it was hard when his job demanded peak everything.

Coming to a stop between two towering pines, he fished his water bottle out from his pack and took a long swallow. Despite the chilly weather, he'd been sweating all day, and if he wasn't careful, he'd end up dehydrated. And then he wouldn't be much use to anyone.

He thought briefly about making Bonnie stop, too, but she seemed to be on the trail, or on *a* trail, and he was reluctant to pull her back. He looked at his watch. Ten more minutes and he'd make her stop, on the trail or not.

Putting his water back in his pack, he looked up at the canopy of trees overhead. Some of them were hundreds of years old, but that was nothing compared to the redwoods a few hours south of Christmas Bay. Some of those had been around since Jesus walked the earth.

Hudson licked his lips and closed his eyes for a second. Listening to the sound of his dog crashing through the brush in the distance. Of the squirrels and birds rustling in the bushes all around him, of the insects buzzing in the air—sounds that would gradually fade away as night pulled her veil down. And then other sounds would rise—voices of midnight owls and coyotes. Snapping twigs that would leave the imagination roiling. Hudson knew that one night alone in the woods could easily feel like three. But Robin was outdoorsy, which was good. He was used to this. But there were so many other things to consider. Like his mental state for one. And his physical state for another.

Opening his eyes again, Hudson took a deep breath. Conjuring up images of the people he'd found while doing search and rescue. And then picturing his favorite of those images—Georgia, curled up next to a downed tree, with Bonnie licking her face and bringing her back into the world again. She'd looked up at Hudson like she'd been waiting for him all along. Not just for anyone—but for him. He hadn't realized it then, but he'd come to think of it as one of the best days of his life. Finding Robin would be different, of course, but he hoped it would be just as happy.

He began walking again, toward the sound of Bonnie making her way over the forest floor. His radio crackled at his hip, and every now and then a voice would come through, advising of a location, or giving a status update. Hudson stepped over a downed log, weaving in between prickly shrubs that snatched at his jacket and pants. He tried to clear his mind for the task at hand, but the thought of Georgia hovered anyway. Just beyond his subconscious. She was a general feeling that he carried with him lately. It was as if she'd worked herself into the fibers of his life and was part of his daily existence.

He stepped over another downed log, mossy and damp. And then Bonnie gave a succession of sharp barks.

He jerked his head up, all his senses coming together instantly. She sounded different. Almost shrill.

He broke into a run and put his hand up to shield his face, but the twigs tore at it anyway. One slashed his cheek, right below the eye. Blood, warm and wet, trickled down his face. But all he felt was a strange panicky sensation—no pain, no breathlessness, nothing other than a sense of dread as he crashed through the woods. Toward his dog, and an unknown outcome.

"Robin!" he managed.

Bonnie's barking became sharper, more erratic.

He was forced to slow some as he pushed his way through the bushes, having to kick at some of the thickest branches and break others with his hands. They snapped in two, the sound echoing sharply into the abyss of the darkening forest.

And then he broke through to a small clearing. A floor of smooth rock stretched out where the trees couldn't follow. And then a drop-off. A cliff, but it was impossible to tell how far down it was from where Hudson stood. Bonnie was at its edge, barking down at something, and his gut twisted.

"Bonnie," he said. "Come!"

It was obvious she didn't want to leave that spot, but she did as she was told. Hudson thought he knew why she didn't want to leave it. He just wasn't sure how dire this was yet. He hoped and prayed it wasn't as bad as he imagined it might be, but years and years of working with people and through all kinds of circumstances had given him something of a sixth sense.

He told Bonnie to stay and then walked carefully up to the edge. The sky was a swirling yellow and purple now. Softer colors, more pastel than the deep, rich strokes of summer. It was deceptive how lovely the sky was. In his heart, he knew it was masking something darker, something tragic.

Pulling in a steadying breath, he came to a stop where the rock stopped abruptly. Where it dropped dramatically off into space. Into those swirling colors, and into the oblivion.

He leaned over the edge. And there, on an outcropping of the cliff no more than ten feet across, was Robin

Breck, lying motionless in a white hoodie and jeans. Exactly what he'd been wearing when he'd gone missing.

Hudson's gut twisted. "Robin!"

Staring down at the limp body, he queued his radio and gave his location. Requesting medical with a voice that cracked, despite willing it not to.

Behind him, Bonnie barked. Once, as if to remind him that her job wasn't done yet. She was waiting to finish it. To find her person.

What she didn't understand yet was that she already had.

But this time, he might not be coming home.

Georgia sat on the edge of her couch, staring at the newscaster on her television through blurry eyes. The boy that Hudson and the sheriff's office had been looking for had been found dead. Fallen, most likely, from the top of the cliff where he'd been camping to an outcropping forty feet down.

She crossed her arms over her chest and rocked forward, the reality hitting her like a brick to the stomach. *Found deceased*, the anchorwoman had said. Her tone and demeanor in direct contrast to her cheerful floral blouse and sleek, blown-out hair. To her, it was another story, another sad case to report on, but there were lots of those, and she had to make room for the others that would inevitably come. But to Robin Breck's family, this was the worst day of their lives. The knowledge of that made it hard for Georgia to take a full breath. Because she understood what it was like to have an ordinary day suddenly become so dark that it was impossible to see into the future at all. Not to the next day, or the next hour, or even the next minute.

She understood now that she had PTSD. She understood that her physical reactions to things like this meant that she was wrestling with her own trauma, her own memories. And she knew that Hudson would be wrestling with them, too.

She licked her lips, tasting the tears she hadn't even been aware of. All of a sudden, she wanted to call him, to hear his voice and gentle reassurances that he was okay. Or at least as okay as he could be.

She reached for her cell on the arm of the couch and dialed his number. She wasn't sure if he was still out in the field, but probably not. He was most likely back at the house by now. Decompressing. Processing all of this.

Holding the phone with a trembling hand, she listened to it ring. Once, twice, three times. And then his voicemail picked up, and she took a deep breath.

"Hey," she said. "It's Georgia. I was just calling to see how you were. I'm thinking about you. Give me a call, okay?"

And then she hung up with a strange longing in her heart. Until she heard his voice, she could only guess at how much pain he was really in.

Hudson walked along the beach with Bonnie running up ahead, bounding into the foamy waves and back out again. She barked joyously, her jet-black coat glistening in the morning sun. The November air was cold, but not too cold for a Labrador that had just figured out she was on vacation.

Hudson smiled, but it didn't last long. He felt it go,

like sunlight being snuffed out by storm clouds. And he guessed that's exactly what this was. Another one of life's storms that he was going to have to weather. He'd done it countless times before. His life in the army had been one storm after another, but he'd thought that maybe when he finally got out and got on with civilian life, those storms would be fewer and farther between.

That had been naive. Especially when he was involved with something as precarious as search and rescue. Not everyone was going to be found healthy. Not everyone was going to be found alive. And that happy image of locating Georgia that morning was now like salt in a blistering wound. He couldn't stop thinking about it. He'd let his guard down. He'd thought he'd be able to leave some of his past behind, but he was starting to realize that nothing, not time or distance, or even love, would soften those scars.

Bonnie came running up to him, her ball stuffed in her mouth, and wagged her sopping wet tail.

"Drop it," he said.

She did as she was told. She was such a good dog. Such an innocent, hard-working soul. She hadn't understood why she'd gotten the scent of Robin Breck but hadn't been given the ultimate reward of licking his face.

Hudson's heart had already begun to crack by the time he'd loaded her up in the SUV to go home. But her soft whimpers on the drive back broke it completely.

He bent now and gave her a soggy pat. Then picked her ball up and threw it as hard as he could. *A country mile.* A favorite saying of one of his old sergeants. The things that came rushing back at any given moment were a mystery. He hadn't thought of that in years.

He watched his dog, older now, grayer in the muzzle, but still nimble when she had to be. She jumped up and caught it in her mouth. Then trotted back to him with a barely perceptible limp in her back leg. She was slowing down, a fact that, like the hardest memories of his time in the service, he was used to pushing away. He wouldn't think about it. It was as simple as that.

Which was crap, of course. There were a lot of things that Hudson had been forced to realize since coming to Christmas Bay. A lot of painful things that he knew he was going to have to eventually face—his relationship with his parents, his experiences on the battlefield, losing Jesse—because ignoring them wasn't going to keep them from surfacing.

Bonnie dropped her ball again, and he picked it up. But this time, he didn't throw it nearly as far. That limp bothered him. It bothered him a lot.

His phone dinged with a text, and he pulled it from his back pocket to see Georgia's name across the screen. She'd left a voicemail earlier, too. He frowned as a gust of wind buffeted his jacket, making the hood blow against the back of his neck.

Over the last few weeks, whenever he'd heard from Georgia, his chest would tighten in warm anticipation. It seemed like the more time he spent with her, the more time he wanted to spend with her. Until he'd begun to fall for her in earnest. Until he'd told her the other night that he'd be coming back to Christmas Bay. Hell, he'd even started to wonder if, like Grady, he might end up staying here. He hadn't let himself get past that particular thought, but it had stayed with him anyway. Even nibbling away at his defenses when he'd talked to Tad last night. A conversation that already felt like a lifetime away.

The truth was, Hudson had been at war with himself ever since Georgia had come into his life. Stay or go? Love or leave? He'd had doubts about his ability to commit all along, but there had been a small part of himself that had entertained the idea anyway. But now, since finding Robin Breck, his lifeless body hovering on the edge of the cliff, even that small part was starting to disappear.

He knew that without Georgia, his life would go back to that steady, low, lonely hum. He knew how to dance to that music. He'd been doing it for a long time.

He held the phone in his hand, his grip much tighter than it needed to be, as Bonnie came back and dropped the ball at his feet. He was only half aware of his dog now, as he read the text from her. So sweet. Checking on him, making sure he was okay. Wanting him to call when he could.

So, she'd seen the news. She'd be wondering why he hadn't told her himself. But she had no way of knowing that this was what he did. This was his modus operandi. He shut down, he ran away. As tough as everyone believed he was, as tough as he'd tried to be in his army career, he was just scared.

He tucked his phone back into his pocket as Bonnie sat there looking up at him. Staring a hole right through his soul with her deep brown eyes. She wanted her ball, nothing more, nothing less. But it felt like she was reading his mind. That she had a very sad opinion of the main man in her life.

"Don't look at me like that," he said.

She wagged her tail. It swept the sand like a broom.

"It wouldn't have worked anyway."

She cocked her head.

Kneeling down to one knee, he took her face gently in his hands. She licked his palms, trying to squirm away. Impatient with this conversation now. Trusting that whatever he was going to do with his life was the right thing.

He just wished he had that much faith in himself.

## *Chapter Fifteen*

Georgia drove down the two-lane road with her mother's Thanksgiving grocery list on the passenger seat next to her. She was supposed to be swinging by Cartwright's Market to pick up the turkey, since they were on sale today, but instead, she'd found herself driving toward Hudson's Airbnb. A split-second decision made at the stoplight two blocks from her house. Turn left, and get the turkey. Turn right, and chase down a man who might not want to be found.

Turning right it was.

She gripped the wheel with both hands as the dusky evening light enveloped the car. The lights on her dash glowed bright—warm and cheerful compared to the task at hand. Because she wasn't at all sure what the reception would be when she got there. Hudson had only answered one of her texts briefly—telling her that he was alright, and thanking her for checking. But other than that, the rest of her texts, and a voicemail or two, had gone unanswered.

Right now, she was trying to keep her mind from going to all those dark places. Those places where he was going to leave and break her heart, and she'd never see him again. Instead, she was forcing herself to think about what he'd said the other night. That he wanted to try to make something work, whatever that ended up looking like. Maybe a relationship with Hudson would look something like this. Maybe he was just used to retreating inside himself when he was triggered. It made sense. But what she'd have to find out for herself was when he'd come back out again. Or *if* he'd come back out again, at least as far as she was concerned.

She licked her lips, watching the narrow, winding road ahead. She was only a few minutes away now, and she wondered if he'd even be there. He and Tad and Grady might be fishing, or maybe they were grabbing a beer before coming home. She found herself almost hoping that he wasn't there, imagining him dropping his phone in the river, or being somewhere without reception. At least then there would be a good excuse for his radio silence.

But when she turned the corner to see the house up ahead, she also saw his black SUV in the driveway. And her heart, even though she'd tried to prepare it for this, sank. It was harder now, picturing her texts going through and him looking at them, just to set his phone aside. Maybe casually. Or maybe not. There was the chance he was conflicted about not answering her. Or then again, maybe she was just in over her head with this entire situation.

Biting the inside of her cheek, she pulled in behind Hudson's SUV. Then took a deep breath, put her car in Park and stepped out into the early evening air. Something told her that it was now or never with Hudson. Either he talked to her, or what kind of relationship could they ever have? Even a casual relationship required communication.

She walked up the steps to the little house that sat on a bluff overlooking the beach. She knocked on the door, then took a step back and waited with her heart in her throat.

When the door opened, she looked up into Tad's handsome face. He was wearing sweats and a hoodie and looked like he might've been napping when she'd knocked.

"Georgia," he said with a smile. "What are you doing here?"

"Hey, Tad. I haven't talked to Hudson lately, and I was out and about and thought I'd swing by. Is he home?"

His expression, that friendly, slightly goofy look he had, fell a little.

"Would you like to come in?" he asked.

"I don't want to impose. I know this is unannounced." What she really meant was that she was well aware that she was dropping by a bachelor's pad without any notice. Who knew what kind of shape the place would be in? Boxers on the floor, maybe. Food in the sink. But at the moment, she was too focused on Hudson to care.

"Don't be silly," he said, standing aside. "Come in. Want something to drink? Beer? Wine? I think we have some Diet Pepsi in the fridge."

She stepped inside and was immediately met with the smell of bacon. Breathing deeply, she looked around. The place was impeccable. And someone had been cooking in the kitchen. The food was still out on the counter and it looked delicious.

"We're eating in tonight," Tad said. "I'm making my famous BLT sandwiches and potato salad. Would you like to stay for dinner?"

The invitation was genuine and warm, and for a few seconds, she was tempted. She hadn't had lunch, and the bacon was making her stomach growl.

But then she thought about Hudson again, and any possibility of sitting down and joining them vanished immediately. She hadn't even laid eyes on him yet, and this wasn't exactly a carefree visit.

"That's so sweet," she said. "But I don't think I'd better. I haven't talked to Hudson for a couple of days, and I'm not sure..."

Tad frowned, his blue eyes darkening. "I know what you're getting at. Hudson is... Well. He takes these things to heart. Almost personally, if that makes sense."

"It does."

"He has a tendency to shut down. Not the best characteristic when he's involved with someone."

"I care about him," she said. "But at the same time, I don't know him that well. So I'm kind of in the dark right now. I'm not sure how much I should push. Or if I should push at all."

Tad motioned toward the couch. "Want to sit with me for a minute?"

She nodded, following him over.

He sat and leaned forward, resting his elbows in his knees.

"I like you, Georgia," he said, "so, I feel like you should know a few things about my friend. Things that might help you have a little perspective where he's concerned."

She nodded, wishing her stomach would settle.

"I've known Hudson a long time," Tad continued. "And I've never seen him this confused before."

She'd wondered about his feelings for her, and he'd definitely alluded to them. But hearing Tad say this was something else altogether. It made everything seem deeper and scarier.

"He doesn't open up," Tad said. "The fact that he's let you in this much says a lot. But I have to be honest with you when I say that his clock is ticking."

Her face felt hot. Her entire body felt like it was burning from the inside out. She shifted on the couch, having a hard time getting comfortable.

"I know what you're saying," she said. "I can feel him pulling away."

"It's going to take a strong woman to be with Hudson. He's got a lot of stuff to work through, but he's not damaged goods. He's a good man. He's loyal and loving, even if he's only an okay fisherman."

She smiled.

"But he's not going to be easy to love," Tad finished. "I just wanted you to know that before you see him tonight. Before you make your mind up about anything. I think you needed to hear it from someone else who cares about him."

Georgia's throat began to ache. He hadn't said anything that she hadn't already guessed at herself, but it was validating, nonetheless.

"Thank you, Tad," she said. "I appreciate that."

Surprising her, he leaned forward and gave her a hug. He was such a nice guy. They all were. Not at all the hardened army vets that she would've imagined before.

When he pulled away, she was embarrassed that she'd teared up. "Sorry," she said. "Just emotional. For a lot of reasons, I guess."

"Please. You don't have to apologize."

"Hudson might've already told you, but I lost my sister

a few months ago. I think we've bonded over that. Shared loss. He's helped me find some joy again. I hope that I've helped him find some, too."

"I know you have."

"So…is he around?"

"He's out walking Bonnie," Tad said. "He's been doing that a lot over the last few days. There's a path by the side of the house that goes down to the beach. When you get there, turn right toward the cape. That's where he goes."

"Thank you."

He nodded. But there was something in his expression that told her to be prepared for anything.

Hudson walked along the beach with Bonnie trotting up ahead. The first of the evening stars were just beginning to make their appearance, barely visible in the bluish-pink sky.

Putting his hands in his pockets, he hunched his shoulders against the wind and wondered why he couldn't seem to let himself be happy. The second that some of the weight started lifting from his shoulders, it was like he had to pull it right back down again. If it wasn't there to ground him, he'd go floating off somewhere. Losing the parts of himself that he'd identified with for so long. The warrior. The grieving friend. But what else was he? He'd spent so much time with those parts, he was afraid to look too hard at anything else. What if there wasn't anything else?

It was a sobering thought. And now that he was out of the army, he was being forced to look, to find more meaning inside himself. It was like looking for a needle in a haystack.

"Hudson!"

He stopped. Then glanced around for whoever had called his name in the distance. When he saw the figure walking toward him on the beach, nothing but a shadow in the dusk, his heart beat heavily in his chest. He felt a small smile play across his lips. Things that he found he couldn't control when he saw Georgia. Things that she simply did to him.

It was too dark to see her face, but her short hair blew in the wind. He thought it looked a little longer than when he'd first met her. Maybe she was letting it grow. He hoped she'd keep it short, and he wondered if he'd ever told her that. How much he liked it like this. It was possible that the memory of cutting her hair was so painful that she didn't want the reminder anymore, and he realized how little he really knew about her.

He watched her approach, her hands buried in her jacket pockets, her jeans hugging her curves just right. Every instinct he had was to walk to meet her. To take her in his arms, and kiss her long and slow. To slide his hand up the back of that jacket and feel the warmth of her skin against his palm. He wanted her more than he'd ever wanted any woman in his life. Which was exactly why he couldn't do any of those things. Which was exactly why he needed to leave town while his heart was still somewhat intact. Otherwise, he was in danger of coming apart with Georgia, and he didn't trust himself to be able to pick up the pieces again. To be able to function as a fractured person.

"I'm so glad I found you," she said as she got close.

He could see the pale outline of her face then, her delicate features—her full lips and high cheekbones. Her small nose that turned up a little at the end. Her dark brows that were perfectly arched. And then there was her smile, something that lit him up from the inside. *Georgia...* His Georgia.

He'd formed the words in his head before he could help it. They shot like an arrow through his heart. What the hell was he doing? He'd made a career out of self-control. Out of doing the hardest things, and then mastering them. But the second he'd met her, he'd had to start accepting the fact that he wasn't as much of a badass as he'd always thought he was. In fact, he had a blind spot when it came to this woman. How had he not seen her coming?

He knew the answer to that. Because love was blind.

She walked up to him, and he thought he could smell her faint perfume. But that was probably impossible because of the wind. It didn't matter. Her scent, her touch, everything about her was tattooed onto his brain by now. The memory of her lingered long after she'd left the room. She was someone he was going to have to get over.

She slowed and then stopped a few feet away. The water churned in the distance, the waves farther out to sea thundering against themselves.

She smiled, but it was hesitant. Like she knew what he might be thinking.

"I was running errands," she said, "and I found myself driving over here. I haven't been able to stop thinking about you."

"I'm okay," he lied. It was the only thing he could say. He'd said it so many times before, it was automatic by now. People would ask, and then they wouldn't anymore, and life would go on. And his wounds would heal, only to be ripped open again down the road. It was a vicious cycle. It was his cycle.

Her dark eyes looked troubled. “I don’t believe you.”

“Well… I don’t know what to tell you.”

“You can start by being honest with me,” she said. “I’m here. I want to help.”

He laughed softly, but it sounded bitter. He hated that it was all coming to this. This ridiculous need to push her away, when all he wanted was to hold on to her. “You want to help?”

She nodded.

“There’s nothing you can do, Georgia. We failed him, and now I need to process that.”

She flinched as if the words had caused her physical pain. But then, she raised her chin. She wasn’t going to make this easy for him. Not by any stretch.

“You didn’t fail him,” she said. “You did everything you could. And I understand that you need to process. That’s all I can really understand about what you’ve been through, but I want to try.”

“I know. But you can’t.”

“You can tell me.”

“Why? What good would that do? So you can feel as bad as I do?”

“No. So you have some support. So you have someone to love you through this.”

“I have Tad and Grady.”

He was being an ass. He was pulling out everything in his arsenal, and it was working. She blinked up at him incredulously.

“You have me, too, Hudson,” she said.

“Do I?”

"I thought that was where this was going. You said the other night—"

"I know what I said. But I let my feelings for you cloud my judgment. I'm not what you need. I've known that from the beginning, and I don't want to hurt you."

Now she looked angry. Her dark brows knitted together. "You mean you're not going to try. Just call this what it is. You're afraid of trying."

He wasn't used to people calling him on his BS. Usually they just left him alone. Georgia was not going to walk away that easily, despite how much he wanted her to.

"Okay," he said. "So what if I am. I'm human."

"Now we're getting somewhere. If you'd just *talk* to me."

"I am talking to you."

"No, you're pushing me away."

"I'm trying to—"

"Save me from you?" she asked bluntly, cutting him off.

He didn't have anything to say to that, since it was fairly obvious that was what he was trying to do.

"Don't bother," she continued. "The damage is done."

He watched her. The words cut like a dull razor blade.

"I'm just trying to reach you," she said, softer this time. "You say you don't want to hurt me, but you're doing that by not letting me in, Hudson."

Bonnie trotted over and leaned against Georgia's legs, clearly upset by the tone of their voices.

She reached down and gave her a pat. "It's okay. It's alright."

"She's sensitive," he said.

"She's just in tune to her master."

He put his hands in his pockets, watching Georgia with his dog. Bonnie loved everyone, but it was obvious that she had a special place in her heart for Georgia. It was like she knew how Hudson felt about her and figured she was just part of the family.

At that thought, he swallowed uncomfortably. *Family...* Was he ever going to let himself go there? Was he ever going to open up, like Georgia was practically begging him to? She'd said he was afraid to try, and she was absolutely right. He was afraid of all of this.

She gave Bonnie one more scratch and then stood up straight, looking up at him with a no-nonsense expression. He'd been to her classroom enough by now to know that this was the look she gave when she was tired of getting the runaround. When she was done with the BS.

"I love you, Hudson," she said evenly. With some steel in her voice that went side by side with the softness. She was an anomaly. "I'll walk into the darkness with you, if that's what it takes. But you have to let me in to do that. If you'll let me in, there's nothing I wouldn't do for us."

Knowing he wouldn't be able to answer that without naked emotion showing in his expression, he turned away. Looked out at the ocean, sparkling now underneath the half-moon. He wondered how much of this conversation he'd be able to take before one of two things happened—he walked away and didn't look back. Or he took her in his arms and never let go.

She stepped forward and touched his arm. "Sophie used to tell me that when I met the right guy, I'd know." Her voice, which had sounded so strong a second ago, broke. "And she was right. But I have to know you're going to meet me halfway."

He looked down at her hand. The gentle weight of it, saying so much. Saying everything that words couldn't.

Without thinking about it, he covered it with his own. Because that's what he wanted. He wanted to touch her and be close to her, and to hear her say she loved him again. But at the same time, he didn't know how to give her what she wanted. And despite everything, despite her opening up to him like this, he wasn't willing to let her be the sacrificial lamb here. He just couldn't do it. Not until he could kick this uncertainty aside, and who knew how long that would take?

He turned then, facing her like he hadn't been able to before.

He was stunned by the trust in her eyes. Even though she had to know the chances weren't great at this point, he could see that she had faith in him. She had faith that he would take her in his arms, and kiss her, and tell her he loved her, too.

How he wanted those things. He ached from wanting them.

But then he thought of Jesse. Of her unborn baby. He thought about how precarious life was. Robin Breck had reminded him of that recently. Nothing was promised, nothing was guaranteed, and that was what Hudson wrestled with now, like a monster underneath the bed.

No, he'd been right all along. Walking out of Georgia's life as quickly as he'd walked into it was going to be the best thing for both of them. Even if she ended up hating him in the end, he was willing to live with that. Just so long as he didn't have to see that look of trust turn into cold, hard disappointment when she discovered that him trying didn't necessarily mean him succeeding.

"I can't do this," he said. "I'm sorry, Georgia."

She stood there for a moment. Maybe stunned into silence. He'd misjudged how strong that trust in him was. And with a few simple words, he'd shattered it beyond recognition.

"So, you're just going to leave," she said.

"Yes."

She looked down then. The wind continued whipping through her short, silky hair. The night was properly dark now, but he could see the color had drained from her face. It was a pale moon in the beachy shadows.

Bonnie wagged her tail and nudged Georgia's hand, which had dropped to her side.

"Okay," she said. "If that's what you want."

He opened his mouth to say something, but then froze. Probably because he didn't trust himself to utter a single word. He just kept reminding himself that this was the best thing in the long run. It would save them both a lot of heartache in the end.

Without another look, she squared her shoulders and turned away. Her hood immediately whipped against her slender neck. She stuck her hands in her pockets and began walking away for good.

Georgia reached into the pile of paper turkeys on her desk, the ones that her students had made the other day, and that she was decorating the wall with.

She grabbed one with a torn beak and six crooked toes on its right foot and smiled. But she felt listless. Lifeless. Which was how she'd felt ever since leaving Hudson on the beach the other night. And now she was having to face a holiday that she'd been hoping he'd show up to.

She tore a piece of tape off and hung the sad little turkey up. This was her own fault. She'd known very well how it might end with Hudson, and she'd jumped right into loving him anyway. Although, she wasn't quite sure how she could've prevented loving him at this point.

She shook her head, trying to clear it for what seemed like the hundredth time that afternoon. It didn't matter anymore. Hudson had put a stop to any kind of future they might've had, and that was probably for the best. She'd been living in a fairyland, thinking that it could work between them. It was too fast. And they were both too broken to have any kind of a healthy relationship anyway.

She sighed, sticking another little turkey to the wall. That's what her brain told her. Her heart kept telling her she should've tried harder. That broken didn't necessarily mean beyond repair.

"Hey, girl."

She turned to see Thomas walk in wearing one of his signature fall-themed sweaters. This one had orange and yellow leaves all over it. Yesterday's had had a giant embroidered pumpkin on the front. He'd told her once that his grandmother had made all his clothes when he was little. Apparently, it was a hard habit to break.

"I like that one," she said.

He touched his chest. "Oh, I know. She outdid herself, right?"

"She absolutely did."

"She digs the holidays. Bless her."

"She likes what she likes."

"Yes. She also likes me looking like a four-year-old."

"I can't blame her," Georgia said. "You look pretty cute, and the kids love it."

"No argument there."

He watched her for a long minute. "How are you doing, kiddo?"

"I'm fine."

"This is me you're talking to."

"I know." Georgia picked up another turkey and taped it to the wall next to the others. It was turning out to be quite the display.

"So, you don't have to act like everything is okay if it isn't," Thomas said.

He had her there. There was no point in pretending with Thomas. He had some kind of emotion radar that she'd never been able to dodge.

Crossing her arms over her chest, she turned to him. Then felt the backs of her eyes begin to burn. "Alright. I guess I'm not fine."

The look of sympathy on Thomas's face was almost more than she could bear.

"You're going to make me cry," she said.

"I'm sorry. I know, I can't help it, though. I've never seen you like this. I know how much you liked this guy."

"Like. Present tense."

"Right."

"Or…more like love."

"Seriously?"

She nodded. "Yeah."

"No wonder you're having such a hard time."

"It doesn't matter. He's leaving, and I'll probably never see him again. I'll get over this. It's just…"

Thomas sat down in one of her students' tiny chairs and looked up at her. It was comical—his bottom was spilling over both sides, but he didn't seem to notice.

He was very invested in her personal life, and she loved him for it.

"It's just, what?" he asked.

She shrugged, looking down at the carpet. At her white Keds. Her teacher shoes that went with anything. She remembered buying them on a shopping outing with Sophie. They'd had so much fun that day.

"It's just that I really thought he might want to try and make something work. I thought he felt the same way about me."

"I'm sure he does, Georgia. How could he not?"

"You're sweet. But I'm not sure. Even if he does, it wasn't enough. That's the hardest part. That you can be in love with someone, and it's just not enough."

Thomas leaned forward and put his chin in his hand, looking contemplative.

The janitor walked by in the hallway and waved. Georgia waved back. It was strange how the outside world kept spinning, even when hers was so upside down.

"I guess my hope for you," Thomas said quietly, "is that you remember how wonderful you are, Georgia. And even though this didn't work out, it doesn't mean you're not going to be happy again. You will be happy. You will heal. Losing Sophie will always be a part of who you are, but you're going to be okay."

That did it. Georgia's eyes filled with tears. She looked at the little paper turkey in her hand and saw Lucy's name written haphazardly across the front. Sweet Lucy. She'd been so wrapped up in her heartache over Hudson that she'd almost let herself push thoughts of her student to the side for a bit. She made a mental note to call Grace Thorton when she got home. Make sure she and Lucy were doing okay. Or as okay as they could be under the circumstances.

"Oh, honey," Thomas said. "Don't cry."

She laughed. "I'm okay, I promise. All this is just hitting at once. But it is what it is, right?"

Thomas stood up and gave her a hug. "It is what it is, honey."

"What would I do without you?"

"Oh, I know. You'd be a mess. An absolute mess." He winked. "You'd be just fine."

She turned her head and laid her cheek against his fall leaf sweater. Breathed in his comforting scent. And was grateful for his presence in her life. She was lucky. It was a moment of much needed perspective, and she was grateful for that, too.

There would always be a part of her heart that belonged to Hudson Cross. But now was the time to try to move forward the best way she knew how.

# Chapter Sixteen

"So, you're just gonna punk out, huh?"

Hudson looked over at Tad, who was reeling in his line, his baseball cap pulled low over his eyes to shield them from the bright afternoon sunlight.

Tad didn't look back. Just kept his gaze on the tip of his pole and the emerald green currents of the river.

"Did you just say, *punk out*?" Hudson asked.

"You heard me."

"I just was just checking. Because you're not thirteen."

"Shut up."

Hudson looked back at the river, too. He reeled his line in slowly, trying to ignore the sick feeling in his stomach. He knew he'd made the right decision with Georgia. He knew that, so why was he feeling like he'd made the biggest mistake of his life?

Tad shook his head. "I thought you were smarter than this, man. I thought you'd listen to your buddies for once. I mean, I know you haven't exactly made a habit of that in the past, but you know."

"Say what you really feel."

Tad shot him a look. "I'm trying to snap you out of this."

"Out of what? I know what I'm doing."

"I actually don't think you do. I actually think you're making a huge mistake, here."

Hudson had just been thinking the same thing himself. He was heartsick as hell.

Taking his pole out of the water, he reached down to open the small bait pack at his hip. He was a horrible fly fisherman. He'd decided to use a regular rod this morning and good old-fashioned spinners, but the fish weren't cooperating.

"I'm just going to say this once," Tad said. "Grady would give anything to go back and have the chance you've got now, Hud."

"That's a crap thing to say."

"Why?" Tad bit out. "Because it's true? You know it is. And you know he'd say the same thing to your face."

"It's none of your business."

Tad looked over, his face contorted in anger. "Don't you dare say that to me."

Hudson had said it without thinking. Because he knew it wasn't true. It was Tad and Grady's business, because they were his best friends, his brothers. They loved him, and they'd all made a pact to be there for each other, no matter what. The army had brought them together, but Jesse had bonded them in a way that nothing else could've.

He set down his pole in the gravel and then clasped his hands behind his neck. He looked up at the sky, at the puffy silver clouds that were such a rarity on the coast. Normally the clouds were low and full of moisture. But today was sunny and unseasonably warm, making him think of a spring day, instead of the fact that it was almost Thanksgiving.

He squeezed his eyes shut for a few seconds. *Thanksgiving.* Another holiday that would come and go. Another holiday spent without close relatives, without a solid place to call home.

"I'm sorry," he said. "I didn't mean that."

After a long minute, Tad walked over, his boots crunching in the gravel. He stopped in front of Hudson and then slapped him on the shoulder.

"I know you didn't. That's what I'm talking about. You're not thinking clearly right now. And I know why."

Hudson watched him.

"You're in love. Maybe for the first time in your life."

*In love.* That's exactly what he was. And now he was in over his head. Too in love to be able to leave Georgia without feeling like he was leaving a part of himself behind. He still wasn't sure how he'd let this happen. He'd always been so in control of his feelings, of his entire damn life.

"Maybe," he said. It was the best he could do under the circumstances. And it wasn't that great.

*"Maybe?"* Tad laughed. "Come on, man."

"Okay. You're right. I love her. But that doesn't change anything."

"Doesn't it?"

Hudson shook his head. "It's not as simple as you'd like it to be."

"I'm not saying it is. I get how you feel. I've been there. It's anything but simple. But I know how much you're going to regret it if you leave here without at least talking to her again. Without telling her how you feel."

"I've done that."

"No, you haven't."

Hudson scrubbed his hands through his hair. There was no use trying to hide anything from Tad and Grady.

He looked out over the river, at the swiftly flowing water, sparkling underneath the golden shafts of sunlight shining through the pines overhead. The jagged mountains in the distance were purple as amethysts, piercing the robin's egg sky. He brought the crisp mountain air into his lungs, reveling in the salty scent.

He stood there for a long minute, listening to the rushing river and the cry of a circling hawk above. He loved this place. Just like he'd come to love Georgia. And he knew that Tad was right—he'd regret it if he left without telling her everything.

But that meant opening old wounds and letting them bleed.

Georgia pulled her softest blanket up over her stomach and stretched her legs out in front of her. A light rain had begun to patter against the living room windows—a marked change from the mild, sunny weather earlier in the day. She went to college with a friend who'd grown up in Oklahoma and they had a saying there—if you don't like the weather in the Midwest, wait five minutes. She guessed that could be true about the Oregon coast, as well.

She blinked at the Lifetime Christmas movie that was playing on TV, the sound turned down low so she could hear the rain. She was having a hard time concentrating on the storyline. She was having a hard time concentrating on anything, really. Anything other than Hudson.

Her phone dinged with a text, and she picked it up half-heartedly, wiggling her toes in her fuzzy socks. Feeling sad. Feeling like she needed to cry. Feeling all the things, and just wanting to crawl underneath a rock and sleep for a week. But she had a job, she had a mother who needed her, students who needed her, and she had a life to live.

Just checking to see if you're watching this drivel??

She smiled. Thomas was her Christmas movie touchstone. They both had the same taste—the cheesier, the better.

I'm watching, she texted back with a heart eye emoji.

And the Oscar for the worst southern accent goes to...

She laughed. He could always make her laugh.

Be nice, she texted back. He's gorgeous.

He's alright. But what's going on with his facial hair?

Her heart squeezed. The leading man had the beginnings of a beard. Not as amazing as Hudson's scruff, but it reminded her of him anyway. Everything reminded her of him.

I like it. She swallowed hard, telling herself that she was going to enjoy this movie, even if she had to force herself to do it.

Of course you like it. Because of you know who...

She didn't answer that. Just sat looking at her phone for a few seconds, lost in the memories from the last few weeks.

Which reminds me, Thomas texted. How are you doing?

Should she be honest? Or give him a reply that wouldn't

make him worry? Otherwise, he'd probably show up on her doorstep with a pint of Ben & Jerry's, and he had his own stuff going on. His own love life to attend to.

I'm okay, she pecked out on her phone. This movie is just what the doctor ordered! Lol. But thanks for checking.

Okay. Let me know if you want to talk. Love you!

Love you, too.

She sent a series of smiley face emojis, and then put her phone down, feeling like she'd thrown him off pretty well. In person he could pretty much read her mind, but texting was a little trickier.

Leaning back against the couch, she turned to the TV again and repositioned her blanket. Yes, this leading man was handsome. But he didn't hold a candle to Hudson.

She watched the couple on screen kiss. But could only think of Hudson's kisses, of how he'd held her close. Of how he'd made her feel so safe when the world felt like it was opening up at her feet.

And then her phone rang.

She looked down at it, immediately thinking it was Thomas. Maybe he'd been able to read her mind after all. But when she saw Grace Thorton's name on the screen, she reached for it with a feeling of dread in her stomach.

"Grace?" she answered. "What's wrong?"

"He's got Lucy. Brian just took her."

Hudson sat on the balcony of his Airbnb and leaned back in his chair. Grady sat beside him nursing a beer.

They'd been quiet, pensive, staring out at the ocean. At the evening clouds that were misty over the water. They were bringing rain, a lot of it, but for right now, it was calm and peaceful. But none of that mirrored the feeling in his heart, which was making him more uneasy by the second. He'd been asking himself the same question for hours now. *What the hell did you do?*

He shifted in his seat, and Grady turned to him with a frown.

"What is it?"

"Nothing," Hudson said.

"You can go back and tell her how you feel, you know. It's not too late."

"You sound like Tad."

"I sound like Tad because we both feel the same way. We know what's best for you."

Hudson smiled, reaching up to rub the back of his neck. "Right."

"I'm serious."

"I know you are."

"So. What are you going to do?"

"I don't know," Hudson said. "Grovel? Lie, and say I was wrong? I don't know if I *was* wrong. I mean, at the end of the day, I still believe everything I said to her."

"Good God, Hudson. You're just scared. That's it in a nutshell. Any therapist would tell you that in about three minutes flat."

"Thanks."

"You need to hear it."

"I did. From Tad. Multiple times."

"Okay, then. You're hearing it from me, too. Whatever it takes."

"For what it's worth," Hudson said, "I get it. I know this about myself. It sucks to admit it, though, when you're not supposed to let things like this interfere with your life."

Grady stared over at him. Then turned his chair so he was facing Hudson head-on. "Says *who*?"

"Says the army, for one."

"That's a bunch of crap," Grady said. "You know that as well as I do. Just because you're feeling something, just because you've let someone into your life, doesn't mean you're weak, or a failure for letting your guard down. It might mean that you've turned a corner, Hud. A corner that really needed to be turned."

Hudson ran his hand over his stubble. Grady was right. He guessed he was simply in denial. About a lot of things. And when he'd met Georgia, those things had worked their way into his consciousness again, and he was being forced to look them dead in the eye. Could he blame the army, or his experiences in the army? Sure. But he thought it might be time to finally stop doing that. To take some accountability for his own actions.

He'd said goodbye to Georgia. He'd broken her heart, he was fairly sure of that. And there was nobody to blame but himself.

Looking back out over the beach, he saw a couple walking hand in hand. They were older; he could tell by their slightly hunched shapes, by their halting gates. A little white dog zigzagged at their feet, running up ahead and then turning with its tongue lolling to make sure they were still coming.

Hudson looked down at Bonnie, who was napping at his feet. His best friend. She'd never let him down. She'd saved his bacon more times than he'd care to admit, not to mention saved countless of his fellow soldiers' lives. She loved without complication and was loyal to a fault. But he still felt lonelier than he'd ever been. Knowing that he didn't have the one thing he'd always longed for, but had never had the courage to admit until just now.

Someone like Georgia to share his life with.

Georgia buckled her seat belt with shaking hands. She could barely think straight, but she'd managed to remember her phone and purse when she was running out the door. She now knew that Brian Thorton had taken Lucy into the woods on foot. Drunk and mad as a hornet, he'd scooped her up while she'd been playing outside and Grace had been cooking dinner. And now she was missing. Taken by a man whose only twisted loyalty was to his brother. In the end, Eddie just wasn't going to allow his family to leave.

Georgia started her car and forced a deep breath. Getting into an accident on the way to Grace's house wasn't going to help anyone. An Amber Alert had been issued, which was terrifying in and of itself, but it was going to be the best chance of getting Lucy back safely. According to the police, she was missing and endangered, so they were going to be doing all they possibly could to get her back as quickly as possible.

Still, there was one person who might not know yet. One person who Georgia felt was Lucy's best chance yet.

She picked up her phone and dialed Hudson's number.

# Chapter Seventeen

Hudson pulled into Grace Thorton's gravel driveway, kicking up mud behind him. It had started to drizzle now that the sun had set, the coastal weather providing an appropriately grim backdrop to this particular story.

He pulled over behind a long line of sheriff's department SUVs. Red-and-blue lights were flashing through the damp evening, uniformed men and women were walking around the house, dogs were being held close to their handlers.

Stepping out of his SUV, he slapped his thigh for Bonnie to follow. She jumped down beside him, on full alert. She'd been here before, after all. She remembered.

Hudson looked around. He didn't see the sheriff among his deputies, but they'd talked on the phone on the way to Grace's house. He'd graciously welcomed Hudson and Bonnie's help and had said he'd touch base later that evening. Tad and Grady were on their way-they were picking up coffee for the volunteers, knowing the hours ahead might be long and cold.

Hudson clipped Bonnie's leash on and then straightened, his chest tight. He'd worked many, many nights with his dog. Nights where people's lives had been on the line. But he could safely say he'd never felt such a strong sense of dread as he did right then. It was always going to be different when he was personally invested. And he was personally invested tonight. With Lucy. With her mother. With this town, and most of all, with Georgia. How stupid he'd been to think he could've left here with a simple snap of his fingers. Christmas Bay had already worked its way into his consciousness. Into his heart.

Just like Georgia had.

Wrapping the leash around his hand, he began walking through the mist, feeling it cling to his hair and skin. It was cold tonight, and the temperature brought with it an added sense of foreboding. Who knew if Brian Thorton had thought this through? Even if he didn't have nefarious intentions with Lucy, Mother Nature didn't care either way. The elements were going to be a challenge. Cold and damp, with heavier rain and wind expected later on. Was he going to be able to keep her warm and dry? Was she hungry by now, or even hurt?

He stopped himself from letting the next thought take hold. He was going to operate on the assumption that Lucy was still alive. And he and Bonnie would find her safe.

Looking up toward the porch, a familiar shape came into soft focus. Georgia stood there, her pretty face as white as a ghost. Her gaze locked with his, and his heart dropped. He could live another thousand years and never feel as empty as he did right then. How could he have let her go? How could he have reconciled himself to be alone, when she'd been ready to settle in right beside him?

He took the steps two by two. Uniforms were everywhere. A temporary command center was set up in the garage, with bright lights blazing through the night. He had to squint to be able to see anything in that direction at all.

He stopped a few feet from Georgia and let Bonnie's leash go slack. Her lips broke into a smile as she leaned down and took the dog's face in her hands.

"Hi, baby," she said. "Are you here to save the day?"

Bonnie responded by wagging her entire body.

Laughing, Georgia let her lick her face. And then straightened to look at Hudson again.

He frowned. Wanting to say the right thing, and not wanting to be clumsy with a moment that deserved the utmost care and tenderness.

"Georgia—"

She shook her head. "Don't."

"I want to tell you that—"

"You don't have to say anything, Hudson," she said. "You're here for Lucy, which is exactly why you should be here. Let's just concentrate on that. On getting her home to Grace."

The words settled coldly over them both. Yes, that's what needed to be done. First and foremost, they needed to get Lucy home. But there might be other things that needed saying, too. There would be a time and place for that, though. And maybe by then, he'd find the right words.

"You said you'd need something of Lucy's," Georgia said, holding out a small pink sweatshirt.

Hudson reached for it and brushed her fingers in the process. His chest felt like it might crack wide open and spill his heart onto the deck. The sweatshirt was soft and worn, and he could smell the little girl in its fibers. Shampoo, probably. Left over from a bath from days ago. The knowledge knocked the wind right out of him.

"We'll find her," he said, his voice low.

He knew that was true. But would they find her safe? That was a question for the ages.

Hudson made his way across the forest floor, his headlamp shining through the rain and darkness. Through the ominous shadows cast by the giant evergreens overhead. He could hear the search party through the woods—voices calling for Lucy and Brian. The sheriff's department believed that Brian Thorton was still on foot, as he'd grown up in this area, spent days on end in this forest and knew it like the back of his hand. But that was the extent of what they knew, and the general mood among the police and volunteers was one of trepidation and dread. How would this night end? Would they see the sun breaking through the morning clouds without Lucy home safe?

Hudson was trying hard to stay focused—going to that place where he functioned more like a robot than a man. Putting one foot in front of the other for hours on end, and keeping his emotions at the farthest corners of his mind and heart. But it wasn't easy. He knew this little girl. He'd been to her house, had seen her room and toys. Had given her a hug and watched as she and Bonnie sat quietly together on her carpet, looking adoringly at each other. He was definitely invested in this one.

The dog made her way through the thick vegetation now. Her midnight coat blended into the darkness, and the only thing Hudson could see were the reflectors on her search and rescue harness.

He looked at his watch. Two in the morning. With every hour that passed, Hudson's stomach grew heavier. Sicker at the thought of Lucy out here with a man who might want to do her harm.

Scrubbing a hand through his wet hair, he plowed ahead after Bonnie. Walking deeper and deeper into the woods, and farther and farther away from Lucy's mother and her house and everything that was safe and familiar to her.

He walked like that for another hour. And then another, stopping only to make Bonnie drink some water and have a short rest. She didn't want either of those things. Whenever he called her back, she'd hesitate, and he understood that. She wanted to do her job. She wanted to find this little girl. She was invested, too.

Hudson kept going, feeling his pulse tap steadily in his neck. Listening to the sound of the raindrops slapping against the carpet of slick leaves and pine needles he was making his way over. Hearing small animals rustle in the bushes, and an owl question everything through the darkness.

And then, the sound he'd been waiting for. The one that made the hairs on the back of his neck stand on end. Bonnie gave one shrill bark. Then another. She wasn't far away, maybe a hundred feet, but he couldn't see the reflectors on her harness anymore. The darkness had swallowed her whole.

He broke into a run, crashing through the brush—through the rain and wind and damp.

"Bonnie!"

He needed her to bark again. To signal where she was, what she'd found. But in his bones he already knew. She'd found Lucy. But had she found her safe?

"Bonnie!"

He stopped and looked around, his headlight illuminating the black, dripping woods. Shining a harsh light onto its overnight secrets.

"Bonnie?"

She barked again. She was farther away now, more to his right. He turned and ran in that direction. The branches clawed at his face and clothes like they had so many times before. But this time was different. This time it felt like his own daughter was out there, which didn't make any sense at all. But he knew from somewhere deep down that it didn't need to make any sense. He felt the way he felt.

"Bonnie!"

Her barks were the only thing giving him any sense of direction. He was turned around, upside down, and like the countless hikers they'd looked for over the last year, he'd be lost without them. There was no trail to run over, no moonlight leading the way. Only darkness. Only forest. Only fear of what he might find.

"Bonnie!"

She barked again. But this time, they weren't the barks she was trained to give when she'd located someone. They were frantic, one after another. He could tell that she wasn't working anymore, she was operating on instinct.

"Keep it up, baby," Hudson mumbled under his breath, turning toward the sound and pushing his way through the brush and inky darkness.

He wasn't thinking anymore. That part of his brain, the part that was in charge of planning and worry, had shut off a minute ago. Like his dog, he was going on instinct.

"Lucy!" Hudson yelled, his voice echoing through the woods. "Can you hear me?"

If she could, she wasn't able to yell back.

Bonnie barked again. And then let out a yelp.

"Bonnie!"

Silence. The only sound the thumping of his boots on the wet leaves. The needle-like rain hit him in the face, feeling like stings from angry bees. His eyes were blurry, trying to focus but doing a miserable job of it.

Forcing himself to slow down, and then to stop, he stood there for a few seconds trying to get reoriented to his surroundings. His army life flashed behind his eyes then—moments of terror, uncertainty, grief.

He took a deep breath through the sudden tremors. Closing his eyes to ground himself.

And that's when he heard it. Soft whimpers. So soft he could've mistaken them for something else if he hadn't known his dog so well. His heart hammered in his chest. She sounded like a puppy. Like she had in those first few days when she'd cried for her mother and littermates. It was then that she and Hudson had bonded so completely. He'd held her close until she'd stopped crying and had finally fallen asleep in his arms. Her slight weight and soft warmth giving him comfort that he hadn't known he'd needed.

"Bonnie?"

More whimpers. And the thumping of something that sounded a lot like a tail against wet leaves.

He turned and began backtracking his way through the night. Slowly, so he wouldn't miss her. He was close. He could feel it.

And then his boot hit something soft and pliant. Something heavy and wet.

He looked down and saw his dog lying in the darkness, blending almost perfectly into it.

"Baby…" He bent to one knee but looked around, his scalp tingling with unease. Brian was close. He could feel it, just like he'd been able to feel Bonnie's presence.

Putting a hand on her head, he let his headlamp shine on her. Trying to see how hurt she was.

She was lying down, partly on her side, and holding her back leg funny. It was trembling.

"Okay," he whispered. "Alright. It's going to be alright."

Whatever she'd done to it, or whatever had been done to her, it wasn't life-threatening, thank God. He had to find Lucy. He had to deal with Brian, and that was going to take all his wits and both his hands.

"Be good," he said. "I'm not leaving you. I'll be right back, okay?"

She thumped her tail. Whimpered softly.

He stood slowly and turned around, his headlamp shining like a beacon through the night. Half expecting to see Brian Thorton standing right behind him.

But there was nothing. Only the forest, which was refusing to give him an inch.

He cupped his hands over his mouth. "Lucy!"

He paused and listened, straining to hear anything that would signal she was close. He could feel his heart beating in his neck, his pulse skipping in his wrists. It kept time with the raindrops on the forest floor.

Taking another breath, he cupped his hands over his mouth again. But before he could call out, there was a piercing scream to his left.

He whipped around. "Lucy?"

Bonnie growled, low and rumbling.

Hudson plucked his radio off his belt. "It's Cross,"

he said into it. "My dog is injured, but she's picked up a scent. I'm about a quarter mile to the north of Old Military Road and—"

"Put that down. And don't move a muscle."

He stiffened. The voice behind him was cold and measured. Not at all how he would've expected Brian Thorton to sound tonight. If the other man wasn't drunk, he was going to be much more calculating, and maybe even more dangerous. Not someone Hudson would want his back turned to on a good day.

He cocked his head so he could see Brian in his peripheral vision. He remembered him being a big guy. Barrel-chested, with big, meaty hands.

"Where's Lucy?" he asked, trying to keep the fury from his voice. The army had taught him how to negotiate. And he wouldn't get anywhere if he didn't use that particular skill now.

"Shut up," the other man said. His voice had an edge to it that sent chills up the back of Hudson's neck.

"Why don't you let her go home, and we can talk for a while? Figure this out."

"Toss the radio over here."

Hudson did as he was told. He had his phone in his pocket, which also had his location turned on, so it didn't really matter if he had the radio. He hoped this wouldn't occur to Brian. He obviously wasn't in his right frame of mind, sober or not.

"Is she okay?" he asked. "At least give me that much."

"I don't have to give you shit."

Bonnie growled again and tried to get up, then yelped and collapsed back down.

Hudson looked down at her helplessly, his mind racing. Tumbling over thought after thought. He had to do something before this guy did it first. There really was no telling what he was capable of.

Somewhere in the distance, through the woods and darkness, someone called his name. Their voice echoed eerily in the rain.

He heard Brian Thorton shift toward the sound. And knew it was probably the only chance he was going to get.

He pivoted to face him. Saw that he had Lucy pinned to his side, a hand clamped over her mouth.

And then Hudson lunged. Operating on that same primal instinct that had led Bonnie straight to this spot.

Brian startled, but it was too late. Hudson knocked him off his feet with all his strength and body weight.

The other man grunted and lost his grip on Lucy. He tumbled backward, falling to the ground where his head hit a rock with a sickening thud.

Lucy began screaming. Shrill, trauma-filled screams that the search party would hear far into the woods.

Hudson scooped her up, and she immediately wrapped her thin arms around his neck.

"It's okay, honey," he said into her wet hair. "It's alright, you're safe."

"I want my mama."

"I know you do. We're going to get you home."

Hudson stepped away from the big man lying still on the forest floor. Blood had begun seeping from the back of his head as the voices in the distance grew louder. As the lights from the search party began cutting through the gritty predawn light.

He set the little girl down and took her shoulders in his hands. "Are you hurt?"

Tears were streaming down her face. But she shook her head.

He looked her over quickly, making sure there was no blood or obvious injury. She was shaking so hard, she could barely stand.

"Is Bonnie okay?" she asked, her sopping hair hanging in her eyes.

Hudson's chest felt like it was going to crack wide open. As traumatized as she was, she was thinking about his dog. If only adults had room in their hearts for this kind of love.

"Hudson!" someone shouted.

"Over here!"

All of a sudden, there were lights everywhere. Voices calling through the woods. Men and women descending. The calvary had arrived.

Hudson turned to see deputies wearing reflective vests come up on either side of him. He motioned toward Brian, who was still knocked out, lying sprawled in the mud and pine needles. It could've been worse. Much, much worse.

They bent to check him out, taking over and leaving Hudson with a rushing sense of relief. It was over.

Sheriff Hicks walked up to him and shook his hand. Then bent down to Lucy. "Your mama is on her way," he said. "But for now, can you go with Deputy Lopez? She's going to check you over and make sure you're not hurt. And she has a nice, warm blanket for you. Does that sound good?"

Lucy nodded.

"And I bet we can rustle up some hot chocolate, too. How about that?"

He was rewarded with the slightest hint of a smile. The

same one she'd given Hudson that first day in Georgia's classroom. That seemed like so long ago now. So many things had happened since then. He'd come to Christmas Bay thinking it was going to be a getaway. A place to remember Jesse, and heal with Tad and Grady. But it had turned into so much more. It had turned into a place where he wanted to stay.

He stood there, watching Sheriff Hicks lead Lucy toward the female deputy with the warm smile, knowing there were still a lot of things he needed to sort through. Things that would take a long time to come to terms with. But he now knew without a doubt that he wasn't leaving this place, he wasn't leaving Georgia. Unless, of course, she'd changed her mind about wanting to be with him. And if that was the case, he'd just cross that bridge when he came to it. Pick up the pieces and move forward the best he could. What else could he do?

He turned to his sweet dog, his very best friend, who was still lying on her side a few yards away. His stomach sank.

"Bonnie girl," he said softly.

She wagged her tail over the wet pine needles.

He bent to gather her in his arms, careful not to jostle her or move her hind leg any more than he had to. But she whimpered anyway, and he grit his teeth. Then stood with a grunt.

"It's alright, honey," he said. "Good girl."

He turned to see Sheriff Hicks watching him closely, his hands resting on his duty belt. "We've got four-wheelers over there. It might be a little bumpy, but a hell of a lot better than walking."

"Thanks, Sheriff."

"Any idea how she found them?" the sheriff asked. "What happened?"

Hudson shook his head. The rain had turned into a light mist, and the sky was turning a grayish-blue in the east. It would be morning soon.

"I'm not sure," he said. "I don't know if she hurt herself chasing after him, or if he did something to her. Lucy will be able to tell us later."

A stormy look crossed the other man's face. "If he touched that dog, we'll just add that to his list of charges. He'd better get comfortable in jail, because he's headed there for a long time. Right beside his brother."

Hudson nodded. It was the right place for him. He was dangerous, and they were lucky that they'd found Lucy before anything else had happened to her. As it was, she'd have to deal with this trauma for the rest of her life.

He repositioned Bonnie in his arms, cradling her seventy pounds against his chest. Then began following the sheriff through the pine trees and the waiting four-wheelers.

He was exhausted and his knees ached from old injuries in the service. There was a headache throbbing at his temples. He was soaked and cold and hungry, and would give anything for a hot cup of coffee right then. Really, he should've been miserable. But he wasn't. Like the sun that would soon light up the morning, the shafts shining through the towering trees, all he felt inside was warmth. Gratitude for what he had, not pain at what he'd lost.

And this was new.

He simply wanted two things—to get Bonnie to a vet. And to see Georgia again.

# *Chapter Eighteen*

Georgia stood in front of her classroom and held a finger to her lips—their sign to quiet down. It wouldn't be easy. They'd just come in from recess, and they were excited. Today was the last day before Thanksgiving break, and they were having their party this afternoon. Apparently almost half an hour of running around in the coastal fog wasn't going to be enough to get all their wiggles out. But that was okay. Georgia happened to like their wiggles.

"Okay, everyone," she said with a smile. It was hard not to smile. She was looking forward to this party, too. It had been a long autumn, and so much had happened this last year. She was planning on spending her break snuggled in with a good book, and some good movies. And some new fuzzy socks that she'd just ordered on Amazon. "Quiet down," she said. "Quiet down."

Little by little, they began to grow still at their desks. Their voices turned to whispers, and then they stopped talking altogether as they looked up at their teacher. Trying their best to follow her directions. She knew how hard this was today. The fact that they were sitting at all was a win in her book.

Lucy Thorton's hand shot up from the front row. Georgia gazed down at her. This wasn't just a Thanksgiving party, it was also a goodbye party. Lucy and her mom were moving to Astoria and were about to start a brand-new adventure in a brand-new town. They were ready to leave their recent trauma behind and were excited about this next phase of their lives without Eddie in the picture. He was still in jail and wasn't getting out anytime soon. The police had slapped him with more charges since he and Brian had hatched the plan to take Lucy while he was still sitting behind bars. Now they were both in there together.

"Yes, Lucy," Georgia said.

"How is Bonnie going to get here if she can't walk right?"

At the mention of the sweet black Lab that had worked her way into Georgia's heart so completely over the last several weeks, she warmed.

"Mr. Hudson is going to help her."

The class gave a collective "Aww!"

Lucy raised her hand again.

"Yes?"

"Will we be able to give her hugs?"

All the kids sat up straighter at the possibility of giving dog hugs.

"I think she'd be disappointed if you didn't," Georgia said. "But you'll have to be very, very gentle with her."

More hands shot up around the room.

"Tristan?"

"What did she do to her leg?"

"She tore her ACL," Georgia said. "That's her knee."

Another collective "Aww."

Georgia clasped her hands in front of her belly. She was so looking forward to this Thanksgiving break. To spending some quality time with her mom, and with Thomas. Even though it was the first Thanksgiving without Sophie, in a lot of ways it felt like she would be right there with them. And that's how it had felt for Georgia for several weeks now. Her grief was softening some. It was more of an ache that she knew she would have to learn to make room for. Missing Sophie would never go away. But the memories, the love, would sustain her.

Lucy raised her hand again. Georgia was still getting used to this bolder little girl. The little girl who wasn't as afraid to speak, to ask questions, to laugh and smile. After what had happened to her, it really should've been the other way around. Everyone had been expecting her to shut down, but that hadn't happened. Instead, she seemed to understand that she was safe with her dad and her uncle in jail. But Georgia suspected that what had made the most difference was the change in her mother. Grace was lighter, happier. It was like a dark shadow had moved on, and the sun was now shining on her shoulders.

Georgia smiled again. This was bittersweet. She was so pleased for Lucy and her mom. But she was going to miss them like crazy.

"Yes, honey," she said.

"Is Mr. Hudson your boyfriend?"

The class erupted into giggles. Lucy's cherubic cheeks turned bright pink. And Georgia's cheeks warmed, too.

She held a finger to her lips again until they settled down. She was well aware of the rumor going around her classroom that she and Hudson were an item. Actually, she was well aware of that same rumor going around all of Christmas Bay. And she couldn't blame anyone for that. After all, they'd been very close to being an item. They'd kissed and held each other in public, and had fallen very much in love. But at the end of the day, it just hadn't been in the cards for them.

Georgia had done a lot of soul-searching in the last few weeks, especially in the hours after Lucy's abduction. She'd talked to Hudson briefly that morning—they'd hugged and she'd cried against his chest. And like how she felt about Lucy moving away, those tears had been bittersweet. She loved him, and she'd always love him. He was her hero. She knew they'd be forever friends, she'd make sure of that.

"No," she said. "But we care about each other very much. Not that it's any of your business."

She winked at them, and they giggled again.

There was a soft knock on the open door, and Georgia looked over to see Hudson standing there smiling in at her. Ruggedly handsome in a gray sheriff's department hoodie that said SAR across the chest, and a pair of faded jeans. *Speak of the devil.* She wondered how long he'd been standing there. And then decided it didn't matter. She'd have said it directly to him, and probably would someday. She'd tell him how much he meant to her, how much she'd always cherish his presence in her life. But for now, she'd just have to smile back, and hope that he could see that love in her eyes.

"Mr. Hudson!" half the kids shouted.

"Is this a bad time?"

"Not at all," Georgia said, so happy to see him that she wondered how she was ever going to get back to normal again. It was going to take a very long time. "We've been waiting for you."

He stepped inside, pulling a fire-engine red wagon

behind him. Inside it was Bonnie—sitting and wagging her tail, and looking very much like a princess with her back leg in a pink brace.

The kids just about lost their ever-loving minds.

"Boys and girls," Georgia said. "Eyes up front. Quiet down."

After a few seconds, she had their attention again. Or, at least, most of their attention. Bonnie and her wagon were still commanding a good part of it from across the room.

"Remember, Bonnie's still recovering. We don't want to cause her any more stress, so we need to be calm around her, okay? That means keeping our voices down."

She caught Hudson's eye, and her heart squeezed. The expression on his face made her think of the first night that he'd kissed her. When his eyes were so warm, and his touch had coaxed such emotion out of her.

They stood there for a long moment. And it really did seem like there was still something between them. But she knew whatever she was reading in that gaze was just wishful thinking. It had to be.

"We're so happy you could make it today," she said. "Class, can you say hello to Mr. Hudson?"

"Hello, Mr. Hudson!" they said in unison.

"Hey, kids," he said. "Bonnie, can you say hi?"

Bonnie pawed the air, and the kids nearly fell out of their chairs. Georgia had a feeling this was a brand-new trick meant to surprise them. She felt like she was falling in love all over again, and it was all she could do to get a handle on that before she spoke again.

"The class has some questions for you before we have

the cake that Lucy's mom made. And then we'll play a game? Will you be able to stay for a bit?"

"There's nowhere else I'd rather be," he said, walking up to the front of the room. He parked Bonnie in front of the whiteboard, and she sat there looking out at the students like she was holding court.

Then Hudson looked at Georgia and smiled. She smiled back, waiting for him to turn back to her students to start the question and answer session that they were so looking forward to. It was just like the Halloween party after she'd first met him. And here he was again—another holiday, another party, but this would be the last one. A goodbye that felt like they were trying to force a round peg into a square hole. No matter how much she tried to talk herself into it, it just didn't fit.

She cleared her throat. "Well…are you ready for some questions?"

Putting his hands in his pockets, he rocked back on his boots. "I am. But I have a question to start with. Is that okay?"

"Of course. Class, Mr. Hudson has a question for you."

"No," he said. "Not for them. For you."

Georgia raised her brows. Watched him curiously. "Okay…"

He stepped forward and took her hand in his. The kids shifted in their chairs, their bodies humming with excitement. They sensed that this was different. Georgia sensed it, too. It felt like the world had slowed, like time was standing still. Like this little classroom on the coast was the only place that mattered right then. Because it was where her heart was.

"I'm sorry it took me so long to figure things out,"

Hudson said. His voice was low, meaningful. And even though there was an audience of kids in front of them, she knew he was speaking only to her.

"I like it here, and I wasn't expecting that," he continued. "And I wasn't expecting you..."

Georgia gazed up at him, her chin beginning to tremble. He'd said the same thing on the beach the night they'd had the bonfire. He held her hand so gently now, and she could feel the calluses on his fingers and palms. The smallest imperfections that she didn't think were imperfections at all. His scars and calluses made him who he was.

"What are you saying?" she asked.

"I'm saying that I'd like to stick around and see where this takes us. And I'm asking if you'd like to be my girlfriend."

Her students went bananas. There was so much commotion that a few teachers stopped in the hallway, watching with interest. Georgia couldn't blame them. She'd be interested, too. It wasn't every day that you got to see a happily-ever-after in person.

She gazed up at him. Was that what this was? She knew what Sophie would say. *Enjoy the ride, sis.*

Hudson leaned close, smiling that sexy, irresistible smile.

"I'm putting you on the spot," he whispered. "You don't have to answer now if you don't want to. Take some time to—"

She reached up and put a finger to his lips. She'd been waiting a long time for this. Maybe even her whole life.

"How would you like to have some cake first?" she asked. "And a bonfire on the beach tonight?"

After a few long seconds, he nodded. "Okay. I could go for some cake. And a bonfire."

She smiled up at him. At the moment, nothing sounded better. What was it he'd said a few weeks ago? They'd simply take it slow.

He looked over at the class then and gave them a wink. They responded by clapping, by cheering in the most adorable way. There was a small crowd in the hallway now, watching it all unfold.

Hudson produced a Pee-Chee folder out of nowhere and held it up in front of their faces. So they were hidden from the class, so they had a small moment of semi-privacy.

Georgia laughed. He laughed, too. Bonnie barked from her little wagon, sensing the joy in the air. The excitement. Could she know this was a new beginning? Somehow, Georgia thought she might.

Standing on her tiptoes, she wrapped her arms around Hudson's neck and kissed him. Breathed in his scent and reveled in his touch. She'd been lost before. And he had found her again. He'd brought her back to life. She wished she could tell Sophie about this.

But somehow, she thought she already knew.

# *Epilogue*

Hudson stood by the Christmas tree, the one that he and Georgia had cut down themselves, and looked down at the leggy brown puppy with the impossibly floppy ears.

"Sit," he said, trying his hardest to be stern with her. But not doing a very good job of it. She was too damn cute.

She gazed up at him with her liquid brown eyes and cocked her pointy hound head.

"I said sit, Fiona," he said again.

She pawed the air with one of her huge paws.

Leaning down, he took it gently and set it back down on the floor. "No, that's shake. I said *sit*."

She barked. Once. Twice. Then cocked her head again.

"No, that's speak."

Georgia walked in wearing a cherry red dress that flared out from her waist. She looked beautiful, as always. "Mom says dinner will be ready in about twenty minutes," she said, giving him a kiss on the cheek. "How's it going in here?"

"Not well."

She laughed, and he put his arm around her. Holding her close against his side where she fit so well. They'd turned into one of those couples that he used to roll his eyes at. The kind that couldn't be in the same room without touching each other. He couldn't help it. He was in love.

"Maybe she just needs to see her big sister model it for her?" she said.

Hudson looked over at Bonnie, who was snoozing by the fire in her plush new bed. The one that Georgia's mom had bought her for an early Christmas present. *I have to spoil my granddog!* she'd said over pizza one night. Hudson had laughed. It was still very much early days with Georgia, but he'd be lying if he said he hadn't thought of the possibility of marriage, of kids in the future. There was nobody else he'd rather have a family with than Georgia. Early days or not, this was a first for him. He was learning that life was all about those firsts.

"I tried that," he said. "Since she's a full-time therapy dog now, she's decided that she'd rather nap over doing anything for treats. And I blame your mom for that. She gives her treats for doing absolutely nothing, so there goes my leverage."

"Sorry, babe. She and Mom are kind of a thing."

"Oh, I know. What's this I hear about her sleeping under the covers?"

"It was only that one time when we went to the Blazers game."

"She's going to get used to it. And then I'm gonna have to get black sheets so the dog hair will blend."

Georgia laughed. "Now you know what I got you for Christmas." She stood on her tiptoes and nuzzled behind his ear. "Have I told you lately how much I love you?"

"Yes. But I don't mind hearing it again."

"I love you."

"I love you, too."

He looked at his watch as the puppy bounded over to jump on Bonnie. She grunted but was as sweet as ever, licking Fiona all over her saggy face. Hudson thought she probably thought of herself as the puppy's mother. Which suited Fiona just fine. It was a match made in heaven.

"Tad and Grady should be here any minute," he said. "With pie. Grady's grandmother's recipe."

"He's putting that new kitchen to good use."

Hudson nodded and kissed her temple. His friend was renting a small cottage on the beach, and was in the very beginning stages of taking over Clarence Hill's practice. It had all happened so fast, he'd barely had time to fly home, move his things out of his apartment and ship them out to Oregon.

Tad and Hudson had gone home to Colorado, but only temporarily. They'd both decided to come back to Christmas Bay to stay. Tad had a condo right down the road from Hudson, who'd found a small ranch house on the river. He was renting for now, but had a lease with an option to buy. He thought he might do just that. He was getting used to waking up and having his morning coffee on the deck, watching the herons and osprey fly overhead.

He was now an official volunteer for the sheriff department's search and rescue division, but Sheriff Hicks was trying to get him to come on board with a full-time, paid position. He wasn't sure he was ready yet. For now, he was just enjoying training his new rescue puppy, taking Bonnie to schools and retirement homes, and most of all, being with Georgia. Life was simple. Life was good. And he thought that living it this way was the best way to honor Jesse, and all of the friends he'd lost over the years. They hadn't been able to come home. He was coming home for all of them.

Holding Georgia close, he looked out the window to the little neighborhood street that was all decked out in Christmas lights. There was a thick fog rolling in from the ocean, but the lights were bright and cheerful, giving the whole scene a surreal quality. Like something out of a painting.

He'd never felt like he belonged like this before, even in the army where his belonging was complete, but conditional. Here, he knew he was on the cusp of building something special. He was going to build a life here.

Georgia turned to look up at him, the fire snapping and hissing in the fireplace. "Penny for your thoughts?"

He brought his arm tighter around her waist. She smelled so good, like peppermint and vanilla. She smelled like Christmas itself.

"I was just thinking how lucky I am," he said. His voice sounded thick to his own ears. It was the emotion rising to the surface. The same feelings that he'd been so used to pushing down were now making themselves more familiar to him. He was learning to get his arms around them, to appreciate the lows with the highs. And there were so many highs.

"We're both lucky," Georgia said. "Merry Christmas, baby."

He leaned down to kiss her again. And was grateful.

* * * * *

*Look for Grady's story, the next installment in*
*Kaylie Newell's new miniseries*
*Veterans of Christmas Bay*
*Coming soon to Harlequin Special Edition!*